Reid Hudson did

She had known it in his office, and she knew it now. But he also held her in contempt, and she feared he hated that part of himself that was drawn to Diana Rowe.

She must never let him know that for four years, she had seen his face in her dreams, mocking her, taunting her, making her feel hot—as if lit by some unseen fire. His was a dark flame, she told herself bitterly. Once caught, she would be destroyed by his fierce burning.

In his office, she had been defiant and angry and proud. She felt none of those things now. Now she felt only very, very frightened....

Dear Reader,

Happy February! Happy St. Valentine's Day! May this year bring you love and joy. And to put you in the mood for hearts and roses, Silhouette **Special Edition** is proud to bring you six wonderful, warm novels—stories written with you in mind—tales of love and life that you can identify with—romance with that little "something special" added in.

This month, don't miss stories from Patricia Coughlin, Tracy Sinclair, Barbara Catlin and Elizabeth Krueger. February marks the publication of *Ride the Tiger,* by Lindsay McKenna—the exciting first book in the wonderful series MOMENTS OF GLORY. Next month brings you *One Man's War,* and *Off Limits* follows in April. February is also the month for *A Good Man Walks In* by Ginna Gray—a tender tale featuring characters you've met before in earlier books by Ginna.

In each Silhouette **Special Edition** novel, we're dedicated to bringing you the romances that you dream about—stories that delight as well as bring a tear to the eye. And that's what Silhouette **Special Edition** is all about—special books by special authors for special readers!

I hope you enjoy this book and all of the stories to come.

Sincerely,

Tara Gavin
Senior Editor

ELIZABETH KRUEGER
For the Children

Silhouette Special Edition

Published by Silhouette Books New York

America's Publisher of Contemporary Romance

Our birth is but a sleep and a forgetting:
The Soul that rises with us, our life's Star,
Hath had elsewhere its setting,
And cometh from afar;
Not in entire forgetfulness,
And not in utter nakedness,
But trailing clouds of glory do we come
From God, who is our home....

—William Wordsworth
"Ode: Intimations of Immortality"
from *Recollections of Early Childhood*

SILHOUETTE BOOKS
300 East 42nd St., New York, N.Y. 10017

ISBN: 0-373-09723-9

First Silhouette Books printing February 1992

Printed in the U.S.A.

Books by Elizabeth Krueger

Silhouette Special Edition

For the Children #723

Silhouette Romance

A Saving Grace #774
And the Walls Came Tumbling Down #798

ELIZABETH KRUEGER

left her home in Chicago to marry a widower with nine children and live on a small farm in northwestern Michigan. Twelve years and four more children later, Elizabeth has successfully pursued a new career—writing. Perhaps her creativity has been inspired by the many lives she has guided and loved, or maybe her writing was her one escape from a household that at times must be impossibly chaotic. All we can be sure of is that we, her readers, are her true beneficiaries.

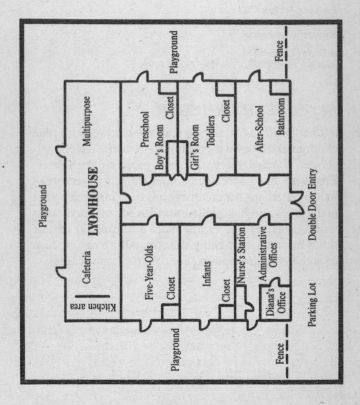

Chapter One

Diana Rowe sat calmly on the forest-green sofa, her eyes surveying the elegantly subdued and luxuriously appointed lobby. The administrative offices of Heritage House Furniture doubled as a not-so-subtle reminder of the high-end wood furniture produced at the manufacturing facility, located a half mile to the west. Several exquisitely crafted pieces—a hutch, an entertainment center, a free-standing bookcase, along with four highly polished mahogany occasional tables—stood in sophisticated groupings with quietly tasteful sofas, love seats and easy chairs.

The doors to the lobby swung open, and Tilly Martel entered, her clear gray eyes sweeping the room before fastening upon Diana.

"Diana dear, you look absolutely *marvelous!*" Tilly exclaimed warmly. Diana rose, smiling at the approach of her old friend.

"Hello, Tilly."

But a simple hello was never enough for the whirlwind energy that was Tilly Martel. Striding forward quickly, the diminutive woman placed a well-manicured hand on Diana's shoulder and gave her a quick hug. "Are you ready, my dear?" Tilly asked, then laughed lightly. "But what a silly question! Of course you're prepared, and excellently, as usual. I'll just go tell the receptionist we're here."

Diana had long ago grown used to the aura of almost breathless enthusiasm that constantly radiated from her fifty-two-year-old friend. She smiled inwardly as she watched Tilly move at her usual near-running pace to the receptionist's desk. Dressed as Tilly was in a conservative rose suit with a white blouse, an ebony-and-silver pin neat against her collar, no one meeting her for the first time would guess that her favorite clothing included wildly patterned caftans and multiple pieces of huge, chunky jewelry. Tilly's attractively styled gray hair coupled with her careful choice of clothing proclaimed her to be a person of maturity and good taste. For Tilly was wise in the ways of the world, especially the business world, and she had dressed today to conform to an image. Diana knew that it was not all illusion. Tilly could be comfortable anywhere.

Diana had also dressed carefully, in a simple gray silk shirtwaist dress. A single long strand of pearls circled her collar and draped down her chest. A thin cloth belt made of the same material as her dress cinched her waist snugly. She had pulled her hair back in a smooth chignon, and her makeup was intentionally light. The resulting effect was plain, almost severe, but the dress was quality, and she knew her appearance was just right to give her the added maturity to deal with a group of people all decades older than herself.

But then, she had known how to dress to please since she was ten years old. It was one of the few lessons her mother had thought important enough to emphasize.

Always remember, Diana, men will like you when you look beautiful.

Shaking off the suddenly intrusive thought, Diana took one last look around the lobby. Heritage House had been owned by the same family for three generations. Yet just last week the company had been acquired by a New-York-based organization. The resulting merger had caused a panic among the employees here, despite reassurances that Heritage House would continue as it was—producing the fine furniture for which it was famous.

But the important thing to Tilly and herself was that Thomas Lyon, the former owner and chief executive officer of Heritage House, had negotiated his own private project into the final purchase agreement.

Lyonhouse. An on-site day-care center to be located on the grounds of Heritage House's main manufacturing facility. Lyonhouse was scheduled to open its doors to children four weeks from today.

"Come along, Diana," Tilly called lightly, and Diana turned to cross the floor with the older woman. They entered an elevator, which quickly carried them to the fourth and highest floor of the building.

A pretty young woman with brown hair and designer glasses met them when the elevator door opened. "Miss Martel? Miss Rowe? Will you follow me, please?"

As soon as they had entered a room at the end of the hall, the door was shut quietly behind them. Four people were already in place around a small conference table.

Three of the four were men; they stood immediately. The one on the right, portly and balding, left his chair and walked toward Tilly and Diana. "Good morning," he said, extending his hand first to Tilly. As his hand then clasped Diana's, he continued, "I'm David Stone, senior vice president here at Heritage House. May I present Stella Waters, the personnel director at Heritage, Holland Cartier, who serves on the board of directors of our new parent company, Knotingsly, Inc., and of course Mark Lyon, Tom Lyon's son and president of the Heritage House Division as it has been reorganized.''

Diana looked at Mark Lyon curiously. Of medium height and compact build, he had his father's fair skin and the blond hair that went with it. A handsome man, Mark was likely to present the greatest difficulty in today's meeting. Tilly had told her Mark was often impatient with what he termed ''the old man's ideas,'' and Diana thought it unlikely that he was pleased with having Lyonhouse one of the first orders of business under the new regime.

''May I get you some coffee, ladies?'' David Stone queried as they took their places at the table—Diana with her back to the door, Tilly at her immediate right. When they shook their heads, he seated himself. ''The floor is yours, then,'' he said. ''I think all of us are interested in hearing about this most unusual proposal.''

Diana heard the unmistakable coolness in his tone, and glanced around quickly. Stella Waters, looking poised and professional in a beige suit, seemed to be carefully studying some notes that were laid on the table in front of her. David Stone was sitting back from the table, one leg crossed over the other. Holland Cartier was looking at Tilly, but there was no friendliness in his eyes. And Mark Lyon's plastic smile was only a shade away from a downright smirk.

Thomas Lyon may have thought he had covered all the bases, but the mood in this room proved otherwise.

Diana's eyes met Tilly's, and held. *Plan Two.* At Tilly's barely perceptible nod, Diana stood.

''Before we actually get started,'' she said, ''I wanted to tell you about the remarkable person who is sitting next to me, and give you some information of which you may or may not be aware.'' She saw Mark Lyon shoot her a startled glance; she, in turn, gave him her most dazzling smile.

This one's for Tom, she told him silently. *Did you think we would let you beat us, after all?*

"When you hear Tilly Martel speak," Diana continued, "I'm sure it will not take you long to understand why this woman is held in the highest esteem by people all over the state of Michigan.

"But just in case you are unaware of Tilly's background, I thought I might mention that a year ago, the governor of Michigan appointed Tilly to coordinate a task force, named the Michigan Child Care Coalition. The purpose of the task force was to study the child care situation in the state. The coalition was comprised of twenty-five leaders of business, labor and government throughout Michigan. These executives in turn designated persons from their companies or organizations to serve on a working group exploring child care issues. Only Thomas Lyon of Heritage House did not designate anyone. He attended every meeting himself.

"Out of his experience with the coalition, and also, I might add, out of the experiences of his own life, Mr. Lyon began a very personal dream, which he has entrusted to Tilly and myself. Lyonhouse is the fruition of that dream. Miss Waters, gentlemen, I am proud to be here today with Tilly Martel, to share with you Tom Lyon's vision."

Diana delivered her speech softly, with a smile of persuasion on her lips. That it had been at least partially effective was apparent by the slight softening of the atmosphere in the room, which told her clearly that at least three of the four decision-makers present had not known about Tilly, or the Coalition. With all the negotiations regarding the sale of the business, Thomas Lyon had relied on his son to give these key players all the information they needed. But Mark had little loyalty to his father, and none at all to Lyonhouse.

Well, she had delivered some of that information now. And Tilly had their attention. The older woman stood, holding her five-foot frame as tall as possible, allowing her gaze to travel slowly around the room, giving each participant a very personal smile. Her gray eyes were sparkling with enthusiasm, reminding Diana that, even when silent, Tilly Martel had the poised charisma of a star.

"As you are aware," Tilly spoke with gracious confidence, "the plans for an on-site day care facility at Heritage House Furniture have been given the stamp of approval by both Thomas Lyon, and the negotiators at Knotingsly. In fact, the building that will serve as Lyonhouse is already completed, except for the painting of the interior, which is beginning today.

"However, as Diana knows but was perhaps too tactful to say, we are afraid you may have the perception that this project has been thrust down your throats, perhaps a little like some detested food is urged down the throat of a child. I am truly sorry for this state of affairs, and can only say in peace offering that Thomas Lyon really did sponsor this project. However, the normal business courtesies regarding its inception must have been lost in the greater business of negotiating the 'friendly' acquisition that has just occurred."

David Stone gave a slight chuckle, earning him a knowing wink from Tilly. Even the most friendly of takeovers could not help but cause a high level of anxiety among the existing personnel at Heritage.

"Our objective today," Tilly continued, "is that by the end of this presentation you will be just as enthusiastic about the center as we are. And we hope that you will take this enthusiasm back to your various associates and departments."

Diana noticed with satisfaction that Mark Lyon had lost his look of patient condescension. Tilly Martel could handle a hundred Mark Lyons, she thought, as her friend explained further, "The Lyonhouse Center will be a model day care facility. In one way or another, it will incorporate all fifteen recommendations made by the Michigan Child Care Coalition to the governor of this state. As a model center, its doors will be open to the press by appointment. Four times a year, a formal open house will be held, with invitations issued to reporters from various media throughout Michigan.

"Also, Lyonhouse will be open to others who are dealing with the problem of day care, including other businesses who are interested in setting up a similar program, people in social services who are responsible for licensing such day care programs, and others, such as members of the Child Care Council and the Association of Child Development, who work with day-care providers throughout the state. This is a big and important project, and even the governor is well aware of the planned proposal for this particular center...."

Diana sat back and allowed herself to relax slightly. Stella Waters was scribbling notes as Tilly talked. David Stone had uncrossed his legs and leaned his elbows on his knees; Holland Cartier's hands were folded in front of him on the table. Mark Lyon's face wore a careful expression of bland interest.

So far, so good, Diana thought as she listened to Tilly with only a part of her brain, simultaneously reviewing her own section of the presentation with the other.

When the door opened behind her, it took her a moment to realize that Tilly had fallen silent, and that the expressions on the faces of the other participants in the room had all changed to a kind of surprised expectancy.

Mark Lyon stood. "Reid," he said, his voice low and respectful. "We weren't sure whether to expect you. I'm afraid we've already begun."

Then a silken male voice said from behind and above her right ear, "No problem. I wasn't sure until this morning that I could make it."

Later Diana would wonder why she had felt no warning of danger, no prickling to give her advance notice of the shock that raced through her, numbing her so that her reactions became slow and unfocused. For that voice was one she recognized all too well, even though she had not heard it in over four years. *Reid?* she asked herself in sudden frantic disbelief. *Reid Hudson?*

In her panicked confusion, it seemed that the pounding of her heart was the loudest sound in the room, until a sharp crack had her looking around with eyes that had become abruptly shadowed, only to see that everyone else was looking at her. Glancing down, she saw the broken pieces of a pencil in her hand.

Get a hold of yourself, she commanded herself desperately as Reid Hudson came forward into the room. She forced herself to relax, to lean back in her chair easily. She looked up casually, as he took the only remaining chair, directly across from Tilly and to Diana's immediate left.

She had remembered great height, yet while tall, Reid Hudson was not abnormally so. He was dark, though—she had got that right. With his brilliant white shirt covered by the regimental blue pin-striped suit, a fine silk wine-red tie decorating his front, he looked like some twentieth-century transplant from gypsy forebears. Even though his thick, black hair was cut conservatively short, its styled precision still managed to emphasize his dark potency.

His glance flicked over Diana lightly, just once. Yet it was enough to tell her two things: his eyes were just as piercingly blue as she remembered, and he was totally unsurprised to find her there. His night-dark depths held no startled recognition, neither was there any surprised lifting of his heavily defined brows.

It was a very bad sign.

Then, as if he were reading her thoughts, he inclined his head very, very slightly.

Mark Lyon was still standing. "Reid, you know Stella, David, Holland and myself. May I present Tilly Martel and Diana Rowe? Ladies, Reid is president and chief operating officer of Knotingsly, Inc., which, as David Stone mentioned earlier, now owns Heritage House."

"Tilly and I go way back," Reid said, flashing an easy smile that was meant to disarm, and did. "She knew me when I was in short pants." His smile faded. "And Diana and I are also... acquainted."

Diana closed her eyes briefly. Reid Hudson was president of Knotingsly? Tilly knew Reid? This was the first Diana had heard of that. She wondered at the restraint that had kept her from telling Tilly about her last stormy meeting with Reid, or from mentioning his little sister, Lucy.

Although Tilly knew what came after, well enough.

"How are you, David?" Reid was asking with calm geniality. "And how is Martha?"

"I'm fine, and she's great," David Stone answered readily. "She has her first one-woman show next week, and the excitement around our house is electric." David stopped and looked sheepishly at the others. "My wife has discovered she's something of an artist, now that our children have grown," he said.

Reid Hudson's greeting to Holland Cartier was just as warm. "Holland," he said, inclining his head. "I heard you were going to be here."

"Hullo, Reid," Cartier replied.

"And... Stella." Reid treated the personnel director to a slow, glamourous smile, and Diana saw Stella Waters almost visibly melt beneath the warmth of Reid's charm.

He's in his element, and he's master of it, she had to admit. A few words, a deliberate smile, and he's made everyone feel noticed, important. He's energized the entire room, just by being here.

But to Diana he said nothing at all. She was the only one who felt the shadow.

For Reid's benefit, Tilly briefly reviewed what she had covered so far. Diana was grateful, for watching Tilly perform gave her something to do with her eyes. Reid stretched his hands out on the table, clasping them and leaning forward in an attitude of rapt attention. Diana had been sitting in much the same posture—she had to pull her own hands back to give him room.

But she had heard everything in this presentation before, and she found it impossible to concentrate on what her friend was saying.

A chain of events, once set in motion, cannot be stopped by man or God....

Tilly had taught her that, in a long-ago classroom. And now Reid Hudson was here, sitting next to Diana, so close she could feel his body heat. Making her recollect things with unwelcome clarity. Reminding her with cruel honesty that no matter what she had achieved in the last four years, her past was still there, waiting to be accounted for.

But not now. Please not now. Lyonhouse means too much. I want it too much. Why did Reid Hudson have to show up now?

Sitting there, listening to Tilly's confident voice, surrounded by people successful in their occupations, so close to Reid that if she moved her hand three inches to the left she could touch him, Diana began to experience a terrible sense of unreality. Memories crowded her, making the present seem distant and far away.

Only the past seemed real . . .

It was New York, four years before. The huge living room was much too dark, the music far too loud. Someone had set a strobe light on a corner table, and its pulsating beam flashed in odd syncopation to the pounding rhythm pouring from an unseen speaker. Young men and women—many still in their teens—gathered in the shadowed corners and dimly lit spaces. Several couples were sitting on sofas or chairs, involved in intimate caressing, while others danced with overt sensuality in the area that had been cleared for exactly that purpose. The cloyingly sweet smells of stale beer and old wine combined with a heavy layer of smoke to drug the unsuspecting senses. Other odors—perfumes and aftershaves, human perspiration, and something else that tickled the nose and spoke of illegal pleasures—burdened the air with their bitter savors.

Diana was in a far corner, reigning over the activity in her parents' New York home with a brittle carelessness.

The door to the penthouse opened, and a man entered. Against the pulsing white light, he appeared taller than he actually was, larger than life, and everything about him was dark: his skin, his hair, his eyes. Even his black trench coat added to the illusion of dark power.

Diana recognized him immediately. He was Reid Hudson, searching—no doubt—for his little sister, Lucy. And Diana was neither stoned nor drunk enough to be unaware of the fear that crept down her spine. For Lucy was here, and Reid would be as furious as the devil himself.

She watched as he reached out to the wall behind him. With a single movement against the switch he lit the room. In the soft glow of the hidden, expensive lamps, his eyes swept the startled faces, until he found the one he was looking for.

"Where is Lucy?" he asked Diana, his voice a whipcord of arrogance that lashed at her unmercifully.

She stood, forcing her body to remain steady under his regard. "Lucy's asleep," Diana said. "You don't have to worry about her. I wouldn't let her take...anything. No one has bothered her...or anything."

"Where?"

Diana knew she was not going to be able to stand much longer. "She's down the hall," she replied unsteadily. "Second door...second door to the left."

Reid neither nodded nor spoke, but instead started forward into the room, and where he walked, silence fell, until the entire room seemed filled with an electrically charged soundlessness. An unseen hand turned off the music, and the swaying motion of the dancers was abruptly stopped. Every eye in that darkened room was upon the man who passed through them as if he were a fierce avenging angel.

A few minutes later, Lucy's slight feminine form held sleepily to his side, Reid faced Diana once more. "Once I thought you were beautiful," he said, ignoring his attentive audience. "Once I thought you were special, Diana. But no more. Now I only want one thing from you—leave my sister alone. Absolutely alone."

Diana didn't remember much more of that night. She knew that she chased everyone out. "The party's over," she told them flatly. She knew that she sat for a long time in the darkened room, hearing again and again Reid saying: *Once I thought you were beautiful. Once I thought you were special, Diana. But no more.*

And, much later, she knew that she had cried.

Now, halfway across the country and four years later, Tilly finished her part of the presentation, took a sip of water, and said, "Diana will continue from here...."

Diana stood, hoping her face was as expressionless as she willed it to be. Yet it was useless to berate herself over not knowing the name of the president of Knotingsly. Thomas Lyon had been understandably reticent about the take-over—negotiations could have been broken off at any time.

The deal had only been consummated last week, and Reid's name had not been mentioned in any of the reports she had read. Only a Bill Tyrell, spokesman for Knotingsly, Incorporated.

Diana forced herself to meet Reid's gaze directly, before smiling at the room at large. He was studying her with seemingly open candor, but she was no fool. She could read the faint derision in the blue-black depths, and it was that derision that made her stand just a little straighter, gave her voice the little extra edge of poised confidence, as she began, "Over a period of six months ending last February, at the request of Tom Lyon and Tilly Martel, I conducted a series of surveys of the work force at Heritage House. These studies also included anyone who had quit working within the last year. This was done with the full knowledge and cooperation of Miss Waters and those under her supervision, although for reasons of his own, Mr. Lyon did not divulge the real motivation behind having them done."

"*You* conducted these surveys?" Reid asked, almost lazily.

"Yes, Reid."

"Then you must know Tom's reasons for refusing to take any corporate officers into his confidence." One of Reid's arms was crooked behind his chair; the other was still stretched out in front of him, where he was making little circles on a legal pad. His eyes were on his doodling.

"Yes, I do," Diana replied to his slightly bent head.

"Well?" Reid's voice was soft, deceptively undemanding, and he was still not looking at her. But Diana knew her testing had begun.

"I hardly think it appropriate that I speak for Tom Lyon—"

Reid's eyes flashed into hers, hard and impatient. "Tell us the reasons, Diana."

The authority in his tone was unmistakable. Diana's eyes flew to Tilly.

"I don't think you need anyone's permission to speak except mine," Reid said.

Diana felt her cheeks begin to burn at the cool rebuke. It was one of the curses of her pale skin, and once begun, she knew there was nothing she could do about the betraying blush except wait it out. She straightened her shoulders and began to answer Reid's question.

"From his experience on the Child Care Coalition, Tom was aware that the idea of on-site day care centers was generally not well received in the business world. He felt that there might be people in his own organization who would feel the same way, and who might knowingly sabotage the survey results, making them less than objective."

"How could someone do that?"

Diana could only shrug. "I'm not sure that I know—"

Again Reid's eyes darkened, even though his posture was still relaxed, nonthreatening. "How could someone sabotage such a simple thing as a survey regarding day care issues, Diana?"

Diana felt her confidence begin to slip further. One day at a time, she reminded herself. One moment at a time.

Keeping her voice calm and trying to ignore the heat she still felt on her face, she said quietly, "I think Mr. Lyon felt that the results of our studies might be put into the hands of someone within the company who thought he or she had the authority to simply say, so what? If that person had no belief in the project at the outset, he or she could simply say that the surveys were done, the results in and the conclusions clear. And, sure it would be nice to do something about this need, but we don't really have the resources...or the inclination...to take any real action. After all, Heritage House has been a solid money-maker for years. In terms of the bottom line, there is no real financial need to offer this benefit."

Everyone was certainly listening now. Diana had put into words the doubts of the high-ranking people in the room. She saw Mark Lyon nod, and knew she had been manipulated into playing devil's advocate.

"So Tom Lyon wanted to present everyone with a fait accompli?" Reid continued, again in that slow, lazy tone of voice.

"Yes. After all, Tom was also working with his own private timetable. He was determined that Lyonhouse would exist. Even if his other concerns turned out to be groundless, and everyone in the existing corporation was in full agreement with the concept, timing was essential. Because he was also seeking a buyer for his company, he was afraid that by turning the Center over to someone else, the process of organizing Lyonhouse would lengthen past the sale of the corporation."

"Do you know why this . . . Lyonhouse . . . was so important to Thomas Lyon?"

Diana looked around. The eyes of everyone in the room were on her, and for a moment she damned Reid Hudson for forcing her so far off her prepared presentation.

"Yes," she answered shortly.

"Will you explain it to us, please?" Reid's eyes had grown grim and calculating. She met them evenly before replying, "No."

"Excuse me?"

"Reid," she said. "I've shared as much as I have with you because I want Lyonhouse to succeed. I believe everyone here had a right to know what I have related. But Mr. Lyon's personal motivations are just that—personal. I would be less than loyal if I divulged what he shared with Tilly and me in privacy and trust."

He inclined his head toward her in mock salute before saying, "I believe you were going to explain some other things to us, Diana, when we got off on this tangent?"

When *you* deliberately led this conversation, you mean, she thought, anger surfacing at last. Tilly's face was quite expressionless, and she wondered what her friend was thinking. She hoped Tilly wasn't disappointed in her responses. But no amount of coaching could have prepared her for Reid Hudson's presence, or his dismayingly controlled questions. She had simply done the best she could. At least the revealing warmth had left her face.

She realized that everyone in the room was waiting for her to continue. Forcing a smile, she made a conscious attempt to regain the control Reid had stolen from her. "More than half of all American households rely on others to watch their young children during part of the day," she said quietly. "At Heritage's manufacturing facility here in Lansing, about two hundred of your four hundred female employees fall into this category...."

She felt that she was speaking too quickly, and forced herself to slow down. When her words began to sound stiff and memorized, she tried for a softer, more relaxed tone. But it was not until she referred to statistics found in the folders given to each of the people present that she allowed herself to again glance at Reid Hudson. He had shrugged out of his suit coat, and was sitting with his chair pulled slightly away from the table, his arms crossed over his chest. "If you would like to use my folder, Reid, Tilly will pass it to you," she commented briefly.

"Please," Reid responded, stretching out one long arm to accept the proffered folder. His expression had remained unchanged since she had begun speaking.

"Lyonhouse will be licensed for one hundred twenty-five children. The money for the actual building has been donated by your former chief executive, Thomas Lyon. However, the first year's budget for this center will run about five hundred thousand dollars, as you can see on the bottom of page four. One fifth of that amount will be subsidized by the company.

"Of course, your employees who choose to use the center will pay for its services, just as they would in private day care..."

Diana knew her presentation by heart, and could have given it in her sleep. Which was a good thing, as her awareness of Reid Hudson's hooded concentration grew. Even though she was directing her comments to everyone in the room, she was aware when Reid reached up to loosen his tie with his right hand, when he later began to drum the pads of his fingers in silent rhythm against the conference table. Most of all she was aware of the sardonic challenge that sparked from his gaze every time his eyes met hers, that the effort of holding her cool confidence in the face of that challenge grew weightier with every second, that the palms of her hands were perspiring heavily.

But she would not give him the satisfaction of knowing how badly he rattled her, and she spoke with smooth precision as she reached her concluding statements. "Based on studies of ten other somewhat similar centers now in existence, you can be assured that employee morale will rise, turnover among your trained work force will decrease dramatically, absenteeism and tardiness will also decrease and productivity will actually expand.

"In addition, Lyonhouse will provide a valuable recruitment tool that will give you an edge over others who are competing with you in the hiring arena.

"Last, but certainly not least, Miss Waters, Mr. Lyon, Mr. Stone, Mr. Cartier, and—" here Diana met Reid Hudson's eyes directly "—Mr. Hudson, I am personally enthusiastic about working with you on this visionary project."

Diana sat down, and calmly accepted a glass of water. But when she tried to drink it, she found her hand was shaking uncontrollably. Carefully placing the glass on the table, she folded her hands into the fabric of her skirt. After a brief pause, Tilly spoke without standing. "Are there any questions?"

David Stone was the first to speak. "What assurance do we have that the program will be fiscally accountable? I can envision us dumping megabucks into this project based on these figures, which may or may not prove to be accurate. Our stockholders would surely have the right to demand satisfaction if their profits were suddenly being poured into an operation like this."

Holland Cartier added caustically, "This program may well be a fait accompli, but I'll be damned if I give it my stamp of approval without making sure there are some pretty strong safeguards against waste. Hell, this simply isn't Tom Lyon's company any longer."

"In its favor, I do believe such a center will be an effective recruitment tool, and I'm most interested in the information to that effect, as evidenced by the success of the ten centers studied," Stella Waters commented.

"Do you have any difficulty filling positions as they open up?" Reid asked.

"Actually, no," Stella admitted. "Because of our generous pay scale and current benefit package, we usually have many more applicants than we need to fill existing vacancies."

Mark Lyon smiled. "Really," he said. "I know that this was my dad's pet project, but I just can't see its ultimate benefit. Frankly I have been against it from the start. The risks of it being a money pit are just too high."

Judas, Diana thought.

"I understood Lyonhouse was a go no matter what," Tilly Martel said in her precise, well-modulated voice. "After all, the building is already in place."

Mark Lyon gave an exaggerated shrug. "It would make a perfect showroom."

The expression of disgust that flitted across Reid Hudson's features was so brief as to be practically unnoticeable. Except that Diana seemed to have a special frequency tuned in just to him, and she knew she had not imagined Reid's reaction to Mark's comment. For the first time since she had finished speaking, she began to feel hopeful.

"Wait a minute," Holland Cartier said. "We've all said we have doubts, not that we want to back out of this project completely. After all, Thomas Lyon felt he had an agreement."

"Is Lyonhouse actually written into the purchase contracts?" Mark asked knowingly.

David Stone replied to that one, his tone holding mild reproof. "Tom was always one who did business on a handshake and the honor of the consenting parties. You know that as well as any of us, Mark. I must say he is one of a dying breed, as far as trust in the business community goes."

"I, too, believe in honor." Reid's voice was soft, almost gentle. But his meaning was clear enough.

Mark looked at Reid sharply, before saying, "Of course. So do we all, I'm sure. It's just that—"

"Knotingsly made a commitment to Thomas Lyon. We will keep that commitment to your father, Mark."

Diana watched as Mark Lyon fell silent, his face turning a dull red. He might be president of the new Heritage House Division, she thought, but Reid Hudson was his superior. Yet she knew true irritation at the way Reid had played cat and mouse with them all, during the entire presentation. He had known before this meeting ever started that Lyonhouse was not in danger. Once again, she felt her temper begin to rise.

"I also know why Tom was so determined that Lyonhouse would open," Reid continued. "I had dinner with him just last night, and he entrusted me with the same information he gave to Tilly... and to Diana. With his permission, I will tell you what Diana would not. As you know, Tom's wife of forty years died last year. It appears he made a promise to her that he would use some of the money they had earned in this business to benefit the children of the people who worked for them. Lyonhouse is his way of keeping that promise."

Stella smiled. "That sounds just like Tom Lyon. He would rather die than break his word."

Reid nodded. "So. Lyonhouse opens exactly four weeks from today, as planned. But we do have a responsibility that it will not become a 'money pit,' as Mark so succinctly put it. To that end, Tilly, I have a few more questions that need to be asked."

"Surely, Reid." Tilly looked absolutely smug in her triumph.

"Your budget is how much?"

"Five hundred thousand dollars."

"How many employees did you say would be needed to work at Lyonhouse?"

"Thirty-five. Some of these will be part-time, however."

"Who will be responsible for hiring these people?"

"That would be the director's responsibility."

"And who will be responsible for hiring the director of the Center?"

Tilly looked at Reid, faint surprise showing in her gray eyes. "I thought it was understood, Reid. Diana has already agreed to be the Lyonhouse director."

Reid steepled his hands together. "Stella, did you agree with this decision?"

Diana's hands, still buried in the folds of her dress, tightened involuntarily.

"I wasn't asked, Mr. Hudson," Stella replied evenly. "Diana is part of Tom Lyon's...fait accompli, I think."

"And I think not," Reid murmured. "He left the final decision regarding Diana up to me."

Great. Just great. They had all sat there for an hour and a half just so Reid Hudson could deliver this little coup de grace. But Reid gave Diana no time to ponder her options before he spoke again.

"According to this presentation, Diana, you will have the responsibility for hiring and managing thirty-four employees. I think Stella would agree it takes an experienced and mature manager to handle a department that large. However, not only will you be required by this position to manage all those people, you will also be responsible for the safety, welfare and happiness of more than a hundred children, including infants. In addition, you will carry the ultimate responsibility for a budget of half a million dollars." Reid paused, letting his words hang in the room, until Diana was sure everyone had absorbed not only their impact, but Reid's opinion as well.

"How old did you say you were, Diana?"

Tilly spoke before Diana could answer. "Age is not the issue here, Reid. Ability is. Diana's qualifications are impeccable. I myself have known her for a period of years, and I have the utmost confidence in her ability to handle this project. She comes on my personal recommendation. Also, Tom must have told you what he thinks of Diana, and it was also his express desire that she head this center."

"Of course," Reid murmured, his voice so low that the others in the room were forced into absolute quiet in order to hear it. "Nevertheless, it is no longer Tom's name on the line here. Since you have so clearly pointed out the publicity this center is going to receive, and its importance to so many people, I think all of us need to feel confident in the capabilities of its managing director."

Tilly was too professional to argue further. Reid was looking at one of the pages in the folder when he asked again, "How old did you say you were, Diana?"

Diana knew she could probably raise the issue of age discrimination, but to do so would doom from the start any cooperation she might receive from the people sitting at this table. The best she could do was match Reid's tone in its low pitch and careless confidence.

"My age is no secret, Reid. I'm twenty-four."

She was unsurprised to see the triumph in his eyes. "Can you tell me what experience you have in the working world that would qualify you for this position?"

She refused to be cowed, even though she was quite sure everyone had heard the slightly cynical emphasis he had placed on the word *working*.

"My history is on the last page of your report," she offered, sounding infinitely more composed than she felt.

For a moment the only sound was that of pages turning, as the five executives all found the correct page. Diana took her hands out of her lap and put them on the table.

She wondered if Reid would have the grace to apologize, for she knew what he and the others in this room were reading. It had been a long four years since she had last seen Reid Hudson. They had been hard years, and she had learned the meaning of independence, self-reliance and pride of achievement. From her early graduation with highest honors from Michigan State University, with a degree in Early Childhood Education, to her appointment as the youngest member to serve on the Michigan Child Care Coalition, from her work in odd hours and summer vacations with children with special needs, to the nine months she had spent researching Tilly's latest book about childhood, she knew, as Tilly had said, that her credentials were impeccable. She would not shame herself by demeaning her own accomplishments now.

She met Reid's gaze squarely when he lifted his head. *Surprised you, didn't I* she taunted him silently.

And she read his own clear, silent answer. *I'm not sold yet.*

"I confess I'm slightly surprised to find that such a—" Reid paused infinitesimally, his blue-black eyes sweeping over her face and down her dress "—young woman like yourself has found time for such idealistic pursuits."

She said nothing, refusing to dignify his comment with a response. Out of the corner of her eye she saw that Stella Waters had put down her pen and was watching the interchange between Reid and herself with some puzzlement. David Stone was sipping a cup of coffee, also watching them. And Mark Lyon's eyes had narrowed, as if he were trying to decide what was really going on here.

"Which of these jobs gave you managerial experience, Diana?" Reid asked, his smooth voice revealing nothing.

All her life Diana had been managing and organizing people. It was a gift that had come to her almost as easily as breathing or talking. But that was hardly something you could put on your résumé.

Diana fought the urge to stand. "I'm sorry, Reid. I came here today on the presumption that I had been hired for a position, not that I was being interviewed for one."

"I guess in the final analysis it's up to me whether you're hired or fired, isn't it?" Reid asked, his eyes fixed relentlessly on her face, his low voice commanding her acknowledgement.

"Of course," she replied, her tone stiff with the effort of hiding the dismay and anger she felt. "But if this is an interview, I would like to request a private audience."

Reid smiled, that same slow smile he had bestowed on Stella Waters earlier, only this time there was no matching friendliness in his dark eyes. "Fine," he said, putting both hands on the table as he rose. "I think we all agree Lyonhouse will open in four weeks." He shrugged his shoulders back into his suit coat. "It was good to see everyone again." He tightened his tie, then glanced at the plain black-banded watch on his left wrist. "I have a couple of calls to make, Diana. I'll see you in my office in twenty minutes."

"Your office?" Diana queried blankly.

Once again his gaze met hers, as he eyed Diana measuringly. "Didn't Tom tell you?" he asked, his voice ominously quiet. "I'll be based here at Heritage House for at least six months. Like Tom Lyon, I also have a very personal interest in Lyonhouse. For as long as I'm here, my son, Jamie, will be enrolled at the Center."

And there, thought Diana with bitter understanding, goes my last chance at keeping this job.

Then he was gone, leaving them all slightly breathless, unsettled, as if his removal from the room had robbed them of some essential vitality.

"Diana?" Tilly queried gently as they left the conference room. "What was that all about?"

Diana shrugged helplessly. "I'm afraid he knew me in New York, Tilly. He's seen me only at my worst."

Silence. Then, "I see."

They rode together down the elevator. Diana walked with Tilly to the outside door, then said, "I think I'll go for a short walk, since I have a little time."

Tilly nodded, her gray eyes troubled. "Reid Hudson is a fair man, you know. He'll give you a chance."

Diana laughed lightly. "In any event, I'll tell him you said so."

"Diana..."

"Yes, Tilly?"

But the older woman shook her head, as if she had changed her mind about what she was going to say. "You're a fighter," she commented now. "You can handle this position. Don't let anyone tell you otherwise."

"I won't."

"I would stay with you if I could, but I have an appointment in thirty minutes on the other side of town."

"Don't worry, Tilly. I'm a big girl. I'll be fine."

"Shall I call you tonight, then?"

"Sure." Diana placed a kiss on Tilly's cheek. "I'll talk to you later."

Then Tilly Martel was gone, and Diana strode out into the sunshine alone, waiting for the minutes to pass until her meeting with Reid Hudson.

Chapter Two

Precisely twenty minutes later, Diana was shown back into the conference room by the same bespectacled young woman who had met Tilly and herself already this morning. "Mr. Hudson is still on the telephone," she was told. "If you would care to wait here, he will be right with you."

"Thank you," Diana said, testing her voice, finding it calm and steady. She did not sit down, but instead walked to a drapery-covered wall at the far end of the room. Hesitating only momentarily, she moved to the side and worked the drapery pull, until the entire expanse of window was revealed, and with it the parklike setting beyond.

The small labor afforded her tensely strung body some slight relief. She stood at the window, gazing sightlessly outward, her arms crossed in front of her at her waist as she tried desperately to control her thoughts. But seeing Reid Hudson again had brought compellingly vivid memories to the surface. Once begun, they would not be denied.

At eighteen Diana had graduated, as valedictorian, from an exclusive eastern private girl's school.

That same year Diana's favorite teacher, Tilly Martel, decided to resign from that same school, where she had taught English literature for many years. Tilly was going to return to her home state of Michigan in order, she said, to write the books she was convinced needed to be written.

And it was during Diana's eighteenth year that Diana's brother, Phillip, died. He had been killed in a freak accident in a national horse show—thrown from his high-spirited thoroughbred in front of five thousand horrified spectators.

After Phillip's funeral, Diana's parents had returned to the Far East, where they remained at the time of Diana's high-school graduation. Gregory and Alicia Rowe sent her a huge check—because she was first in her class, the keys to a new Corvette—because she was graduating, and a corsage—because they knew she would look beautiful. And they were so sorry they couldn't make it—but they were tied up with important business, and couldn't get away.

It was Tilly Martel who supplied the hugs and tears. "Come see me anytime," she had offered. "Here's my new address and telephone number." Then she had said something truly extraordinary: "I love you, Diana Rowe."

After graduation, Diana could not bear the thought of returning to her parents' Maryland estate, now that Phillip would not be there. So she had gone instead to New York, to the huge empty penthouse and the easy nightlife and the fast living. From there she had flown to Cannes, gambled in Monte Carlo, bought clothes in Paris. She had walked barefoot in the moonlight in the Bermudas, had danced until dawn in Mexico City. Always there were parties, and people, and emptiness. And every day that passed, Diana grew just a little more frightened, a little more desperate, until a wild carelessness appeared in her eyes, and a reckless, bored superiority colored her speech.

Then, back in New York, Diana had met Reid's little sister, Lucy.

Diana was at an exclusive night club, surrounded by her usual admirers, when she turned her head in time to see a man named Charles Wickstrom enter, a young girl clinging to his arm. Something in the girl's eyes—a burgeoning defiance, coupled with an oddly familiar expression of someone who had lost her way—had Diana standing and waving the couple to her table.

It had been the first truly spontaneous thing she could remember doing in a very long time. But she knew Charles Wickstrom only too well—he was a snake of the first order. And the girl at his side looked as if she had been newly hatched.

"Lucy Hudson," Wickstrom introduced the girl with one vague wave of his arm, before seating himself at Diana's side with an air of possessive propriety. It was immediately obvious that Wickstrom was less than sober.

Lucy stood there, looking as if she wanted to cry.

"How old are you?" Diana asked her bluntly, ignoring the man who leaned toward her so boorishly.

"Eighteen," the girl managed, although it was painfully clear she was unaccustomed to lying. Lucy's chin was wobbling noticeably, and her cheeks were rosy with her intense effort at self-control.

"Would you like me to find a taxi to take you home?" Diana said more quietly. "The present company doesn't suit you at all."

Lucy stared at Diana, her eyes wide with sudden hope. "Would you?" she asked. "Would you do that for me?"

Diana stood. "Of course. Come with me."

Outside, the night was as clear and warm as October nights get in the city. As the taxi pulled up to the curb and

Diana handed Lucy inside, she said, "My name is Diana Rowe. I'm in the phone book. Give me a call, if you like."

Two days later, Lucy did.

At first Lucy was no more than a novelty to Diana—it was amusing to be with someone as innocent and fresh as the sixteen-year-old girl. But later, as Diana got to know Lucy better, she became absolutely protective toward the youngster.

Lucy's parents had been killed in a private plane crash in the Adirondacks when she was just ten years old. Guardianship had been awarded to her older brother Reid, then twenty-two, who had taken over the family business as well. He had been a strict, if affectionate, caretaker.

Then Reid had married, and had somewhat naturally left the charge of his now teenaged sister to his new wife. He failed to see that his wife despised her young sister-in-law— so that it wasn't long before Lucy grew tense, miserable and rebellious. Such was the state of affairs when Diana first rescued Lucy from Charles Wickstrom.

But underneath her hurt and anger, Lucy was the kindest, truest person Diana had ever met. "Why do you go out with so many different men?" Lucy asked Diana once. "You're so beautiful, you could have anyone you wanted."

And another time: "You drink too much, Diana. And you use too many... other things. Don't you think you're a little bit out of control?"

Yet another comment: "You sure are smart. Why didn't you go on to college somewhere? You could really be somebody, Diana."

Diana would pass off the questions with a shrug of her shoulders, and a tired, worldly smile. But she made sure Lucy never went with her to the wilder parties, and she wouldn't let the girl drink or use anything at all. "Not for you," she would say gently. "One of us has got to grow up straight. It's too late for me. You've got to do it for both of us, Lucy.''

It was only natural that Diana would eventually meet Reid. At first Lucy's older brother had been supportive of Diana's friendship, especially after his sister had rattled off Diana's schoolgirl achievements. But it didn't take him long to realize the kind of company Diana now kept, and his support quickly turned to controlled hostility.

In the meantime, Lucy's relationship with her sister-in-law, Cynthia, worsened. Reid began to spend more time away from home on business, and during his absences Cynthia's taunts grew more and more cruel. Until during one such absence Lucy finally fled—straight to Diana.

Which was where Reid had found her that April night four years ago. And had told Diana that she wasn't to see Lucy again, ever. And had called Diana's father to ensure that his wishes were enforced.

Diana's father had immediately flown to New York.

As far as her father had been concerned, Diana could race, unchaperoned, around two continents with impunity. But to incur the wrath of members of another society—old, established wealth with whom he never tired of currying favor—was something else. He could never forgive her for that.

And the Hudson family was nothing if not pedigreed. Their money was so old and clean you could bathe in it.

So, giving her no chance for explanation, Gregory Rowe had raged and stormed at her for blackening the family name among people whom it was so important to impress.

"I don't care!" she had cried, rising from her chair in order to better meet her father's anger. "I don't care about any of those people, Daddy!"

His plain, square face had grown red with fury. "Of course not, Diana. Why should you? What do you know of working for a living? You've never had to bow and scrape to people more powerful than you because they had the one thing you needed more than anything else in the world—money! I grew up in the slums, Diana. *In the slums!* But I don't live there anymore, and neither do you." He had pointed a stubby finger at her. "But do you appreciate it? Of course not! Do you know how much this dining-room table cost, Diana? I'll tell you how much it cost—more than some people make in an entire year. And you eat off of it every damn day of your life!" He had made a fist then, a fighter's fist, and brought it down with one powerful stroke upon the highly finished surface, rattling the glass candlesticks, shaking the cup of coffee Diana had provided until it splashed onto his saucer and then over to the table itself. "If only Phillip were alive," he said with harsh cruelty. "He was a man. He would have understood."

"Phillip was a boy, Daddy. And he didn't understand you at all!"

"He was a son!" Gregory Rowe roared.

She tried not to comprehend his words, tried not to hear the accusation in his voice: *Phillip is dead, and you are not.* "I understand you, Daddy. I know you. I know your background—your immigrant parents, your poverty, the violence of the streets. And you rose above it all, didn't you, Daddy? Your son is dead, but you have a daughter that can achieve things. I can do things, Daddy. I can make you proud of me."

He glared at her, his thick, bushy brows snapping together. "What have *you* ever achieved?" he asked with cutting sarcasm.

Then everything had gone very still and very cold. To this day Diana could remember the sensation: as if she were on an island, being slowly covered with a layer of numbing ice. Even the beating of her heart slowed, so that for a moment she thought it had stopped altogether.

"I was valedictorian, Daddy. At one of the finest private schools in the country. Or don't you remember?"

He stared at her blankly.

She heard a slightly hysterical laugh; only later would she realize she had made that pathetically frantic sound. "Oh, no, Daddy," she said. "You don't know, do you? But you sent me money, and a Corvette...and flowers. And your secretary sounded so sad that you couldn't come, although I wanted badly for you to hear me speak. I wanted you to be proud of me, Daddy."

She pulled in a ragged breath; it hurt to do so, as if the muscles around her lungs had suddenly atrophied. "*She* sent me those gifts, didn't she? Your damn secretary sent them. *Because she felt sorry for me!*"

Gregory Rowe, who had rarely known a moment of softness in his entire life, reacted with the only language he truly understood. He straightened his five-foot-eleven-inch frame, sucked in his stomach and pushed out his chest. His two hands made tight knots at his side. "Now don't you take that tone with me, young lady. Phillip had barely been dead six months, and your mother was still grieving—"

"If Mother was grieving, it was because somebody had already purchased a fur she wanted, or someone else had a more expensive diamond." How wonderful it was to speak the truth, to feel empowered by exposing the hidden lie.

"You have no call to speak that way—"

"Come off it, Daddy dear." Words were pouring from Diana's mouth—she could almost taste their hot fire. "Mother is an empty-headed, self-centered beauty show, and you know it. But she's served her purpose in your life— she has the right bloodlines and she's made a pretty decoration."

"Shut your mouth—"

"But I'm no decoration, Daddy." She had been shaking then, her year of weakness and indulgence taking its toll.

Still, stumbling on, she continued, "And if money is all you have to offer me, I don't want any part of it. I don't want this table that's worth more than a year's labor, and I don't want these chairs and the rugs on the floor and the paintings on the wall. You care more about these things than you do about me, Daddy." She had taken a step forward, her eyes bright with unshed tears. "I am worth more than a table! I am worth more than a set of chairs! I am, Daddy! I am!"

He had actually brought his fists up, as if her words were physical blows that could be beaten off with a pugilist's power. "You are worth nothing!" he had shouted. "You have achieved nothing! And you are dragging my name back down to the gutter, Diana! I lived there once, but never again, do you hear? Never again! You will not shame me again!"

If she had been a man, she was sure her father would have struck her. Instead, his well-muscled arm had swept the table, flinging the delicately made crystal candlesticks across the hard surface, where they shattered before falling into the thick carpeting, spilling his coffee onto that same carpeting; the brown of the liquid coloring the pale blue fabric the shade of a dirty city sidewalk.

Diana had not spoken to her father since.

"Miss Rowe? Mr. Hudson will see you now." The secretary's voice brought her back to the present.

Diana turned, smoothing the material of her dress with fingers that trembled slightly. She followed the secretary through an outer office before passing through the door that was Reid Hudson's private domain.

Upon her entrance, he rose from behind his desk. His suit coat was on, and his tie was in place, she noted acridly. There would be no informality between them. Reid had been too well educated in the conventions of power not to take advantage of them now.

But she had been trained in much the same school.

When Reid motioned for Diana to take a chair across from his desk, she did so gracefully, in her best boarding-school style, with her legs pressed together and her ankles crossed. She sat very straight, so that her shoulders barely touched the back of the Queen Anne side chair. She placed both her hands in her lap, one set of fingers resting lightly on the other.

Reid Hudson also seated himself, the weight of the large desk in front of him, his elbows on its flat surface, his hands again steepled, his chin resting on both index fingers. The posture caused him to tilt his head back slightly, so that the dark eyes watching her seemed hooded, hostile.

"Diana Rowe," he said at last, his low voice rolling tauntingly over her given name, vibrating against her skin, pricking the hairs at the back of her neck.

"Reid Hudson," she replied evenly, staring back at him, trying to match him tone for tone, look for look.

The silence lengthened uncomfortably between them, bringing with it an electrical, highly charged tension. Reid moved his hands, opened the green folder Diana recognized as the one she had given to him earlier. He made a pretense of reading through its pages, making her wait for him. Making sure, she thought bitterly, that she knew just who was in charge.

"Twenty-four thousand dollars," Reid said quietly, not looking up.

"What?" she asked, momentarily at a loss.

"The position of Lyonhouse director pays twenty-four thousand dollars a year." Even though his tone was soft, she heard the accusation there.

"Yes."

He leaned back into his chair, his arctic-blue eyes holding absolutely no expression.

"I've no doubt you've spent that much money in a month, Diana."

She felt her fingers begin to tighten up. "Yes." Her tone was studied politeness. "I probably have."

Again there was silence. His gaze had sharpened, focused, traveling over her face and down her body, noticing as if for the first time her proper position, her simple clothing, before bringing his own eyes up to meet hers.

He stared at her for a long time.

"One could almost believe you had changed, Diana."

Her eyes shifted to the window. His statement asked for a reply, but she found she had none to give.

After a minute he said, "You cannot possibly be serious about wanting to work here."

"I am very serious."

His eyes were fixed relentlessly on her face. "And I say you're still playing games, Diana. What can twenty-four thousand dollars possibly mean to you? Your father is worth millions, if not billions. You need this job like you need another pair of hundred-dollar shoes."

He was overpowering her. She felt it in the way her hands fought to clench themselves into fists, in the breath that became abruptly shorter, more gasping; in the writhing uneasiness that was stirring in her stomach.

She forced herself to wait, absolutely unmoving, until she had regained some control. "The money means the same to me as to anyone else," she managed, her voice low like his, emotionless like his. "It will be earned by my own labor, at something I've been trained to do."

The fingers of his right hand drummed against the desktop; she remembered the gesture from earlier this morning. "For how long?" he asked. "A month? Two, perhaps? I don't need to hire anyone who is merely playing at working."

She took a deep breath. "Reid," she said, hearing as he surely must the stilted formality in her voice, "I am neither stupid nor irresponsible. I know what kind of commitment I'm making here."

His hand stilled its drumming. His hard blue eyes pierced Diana, as he said with open skepticism, "Oh?"

She could feel the color starting to creep up under her skin. She willed it away, breathing slowly, refusing to turn her eyes away from his. "Four years is a long time," she said coolly. "A lot of water under the bridge, and all that. Besides, you never really knew me, even then."

"Four years," Reid murmured, his night-blue eyes mocking her careful poise. "Longer to you than to me, perhaps."

Again she refused to rise to his bait. Silence was her only response, until Reid sighed.

"Even if I had never met you, Diana, I would have serious doubts about your abilities to handle the work load of the Lyonhouse director. You're a neophyte, straight out of college. Yet you're expecting to walk into a position that will require you to handle more responsibilities than most people twice your age could manage. I would be a fool to hire you."

"You would be a fool not to," she snapped, realizing too late the unforgivable insolence of her words.

A dark eyebrow shot up. "What did you say?"

She stood. She hadn't meant to, but once the motion was started, it had to be completed. She hadn't meant to curl her hands into tight balls at her sides, either. Most of all, she hadn't meant to let her voice go hot and furious. "Lyonhouse is mine," she said tightly. "All the research, all the planning, all the surveys and studies and interviews, all were mine. Tilly trusts me. Thomas Lyon trusts me. I deserve better than this... inquisition, Reid Hudson."

"I don't care if the Queen of England trusts you, Diana. *She* doesn't have to hire you." He leaned forward, his elbows back on his desk, his dark eyes burning into hers. "I say you're a dilettante. I say it's absurd for someone with your background to be working with children, who are, above all else, still in a state of innocence. I say you don't need this job, or the money it offers." Reid stood, signaling that her private audience was about to come to an end.

"I haven't seen my father in four years," she blurted, her hands twisting together at her waist. She was vaguely aware that she had gone too far in this confrontation, yet she felt unable to withdraw. "I've . . . I've changed, Reid."

Reid had walked around to the front of his desk. "Oh?" he queried softly.

"I sold my Corvette to help finance my college education," she continued, knowing she sounded hopelessly arrogant in her humiliation. "The dress I'm wearing is four years old." She paused. She disliked Reid more at that minute than at any other time in their sporadic, tumultuous acquaintance. "I need the work as much as anyone else, Reid."

He leaned his body back until he was half-sitting against the edge of his desk, his arms folded across his chest. "Did your father cut you off?" He sounded detached and only mildly curious.

She thought bitterly that he would have liked for her to answer affirmatively. No doubt he considered such an action exactly what she deserved. Yet she was living on her own by choice, not compulsion. "Not that I know of," she told him with quiet dignity.

"Then you don't need the job." He shrugged. "And you don't have the experience to handle it." Deliberately he looked at his watch.

"Three months," she said.

He paused in the act of turning from her. "What?" he asked, incredulous at her continued insistence.

"Three months trial, from the day the Center opens. I can handle this job, Reid. I'll show you I can." She had taken a step forward, and unconsciously her hands had separated and moved forward supplicatingly.

Something flickered in the back of his eyes, impossible for her to interpret. But he said nothing.

"Three months," she asked again. Then, the hardest word of all: "Please."

"Why, Diana? Why day care? Why Lyonhouse? Why work at all? Even if you and your father have come to a parting of the ways, there are dozens of men who would literally jump at the chance to... take care of you."

She heard with despair the open derision in his voice, she saw the contempt blazing from his dark eyes, and she knew that she had lost. For a moment she stood straight and motionless, revealing nothing. Then, gathering her pride about her as a protective cloak, she reached for her purse. "All right, Mr. Hudson," she said as sweetly polite as she could manage. "I certainly get your point. I'll go put an ad out for a sugar daddy right away."

"Diana..." He took a step toward her, and she sensed abruptly that he was going to touch her. She drew into herself, her entire body feeling the white heat of pride and the burning of injustice. *No,* she thought. If you touch me now, I'm liable to tear your eyes out.

But he stopped, a short foot from where she was standing. His face was cold, arrogant—yet she had the distinct impression that there were feelings behind the mask.

"I'm sorry if I've misjudged you," he said stiffly. "I'm not usually so..." He let the sentence hang, as if uncertain how to continue.

She stared at him in open amazement, understanding with quick intuition that apologies came hard and rare to this cold man.

"Yes. Well, I understand. I think." Diana turned to leave his office, feeling suddenly, inexpressibly weary.

Her hand had just reached the cool brass doorknob when his quiet voice stopped her. "Diana."

She paused, head up, not turning around, determined not to shame herself further.

"All right." He spoke the words tightly, as if the taste of them was sour in his throat. "Three months, Diana Rowe."

Disbelief washed through her. For a moment she was uncertain she had heard him correctly. "Pardon?" she asked faintly, unable to conceal her shock.

"Three months, as you said. Take it or leave it, Diana."

There was something in her that would have liked to fling his bleak offer back in his face. She left her hand on the doorknob, as she sensed the black impatience in his waiting silence.

But she would not allow him to see how close to tears she had been, how badly humiliated she had felt. She stood very tall, before slowly turning to face Reid.

"I'll take it," she said, forcing a cool smile, using her final reserve of dignity to speak as if the outcome of the conversation had never been in doubt.

His face was unreadable as he extended a hand. "Shake on it, Diana?"

The last thing she wanted was to touch him now, when every nerve end was shaking with reaction, but his eyes were watching her unwaveringly, challenging her to refuse, and she walked forward and gave him her hand.

Impossible to hide from him her trembling now. Her eyes met his in sudden hot defiance, hating the amazed compassion that flickered across his sculpted features.

"So," he said, in one word forcing her to acknowledge her own vulnerability, as his thumb rubbed gently against the quivering softness of her palm. "You're not as cool as you pretend, Diana."

He was too close; she could not think. She was aware only of his overpowering proximity and of the antagonism that seemed to electrify the space between them. Her reactions became purely instinctive as she took refuge as she always had—in silence. She felt her face go empty in its old remembered habit of self-preservation, even as her body stretched and arched itself into a posture of confident indifference.

He was not indifferent. His thumb continued to massage her hand, even as a light—hungry and primitive—appeared in the back of his eyes. She found that she could not look away. Desperately she began to cast around in her scrambled thoughts for some distraction, some interruption to this flow of feeling between them. "Your son..." she began, then stopped abruptly, horrified at the husky, breathless quality of her own voice.

"Jamie?" She felt Reid stiffen imperceptibly.

She pushed on. "Your wife . . . your wife must work also, since he will be at the Center?"

Her hand was dropped suddenly as if it burned him. He took two steps backward, and his voice, when it came, was harsh and ugly in its sudden anger. "Cynthia died six months ago."

"Oh," she said, remembering what it was like when Phillip died, feeling sympathy well within her. "I'm so sorry."

But he said nothing, revealed nothing, his obsidian eyes closed against her, until the strange silence had her backing toward the door. "I'll go then," she said.

"Yes." Never once, she realized, had he raised his voice during this entire interview, yet she knew that he was carrying with him a helpless, burning fury, and wondered how she had missed it earlier. For his voice was too controlled, his expression too unrevealing. These characteristics were her own tools, after all—her own defenses.

She said the first thing that came into her head. "You should allow yourself to grieve, you know."

His eyes flashed at her then, full of rejection and scorn and ancient torment. "I do not grieve," he said flatly. "You know nothing about it, and neither is it your business."

"I am so sorry," she repeated softly.

He turned from her in an abrupt action of dismissal, and she quietly let herself out the door.

Chapter Three

If Diana's mother had ever seen her apartment, she would certainly have hated it. Alicia Rowe's tiny, regal nose would have sniffed ever so slightly at the spartan furnishings; her carefully combed eyebrows would have risen in distaste over the simple, inexpensive curtains; her perfectly painted mouth would form a little O of dismay at the futon mat that served as Diana's bed. And the century-old red brick building that housed Diana's third-floor walk-up would not seem quaint or picturesque to Alicia Rowe. To her, the lack of an elevator, the absence of door service, the outdoor parking would all be absolutely appalling.

But Diana's mother had never been in her apartment, so she had never seen how completely her daughter had rejected her own flamboyant, extravagant life-style. Alicia always said she would come, of course. After the New Year. After Friday's party. After the trip to Paris.

Diana had been home for over an hour. She was sitting in a folding rope chair, sipping an iced tea, wondering where thoughts of her mother had come from, trying not to listen as her brain played out dialogues with her parent in her head. She was listening to Gershwin's "Rhapsody in Blue," and she had her compact disc player turned way up, but even the sizzling saxophone solos seemed unable to drown out her older, harsher recordings.

She reached out and turned the volume up another notch.

The throbbing syncopations of the brass section filled the room. She leaned her head back, letting her hair trail loosely behind her chair, feeling the wooden top rail hard against her neck. She raised her right hand, and with her entire forearm began to beat the hard, driving rhythm.

She did not want to think about her mother. She did not want to think about either parent, as a matter of fact. Because if she spent time thinking about her mother and father, she would start remembering Phillip, and that hurt too much. Lithely handsome, caring, brilliant Phillip, who was all she had lived for until she was eighteen. Little brother Phillip, although he had towered over her since entering puberty. All too dead Phillip: her last memory of him painted in vivid memory—his body still warm upon the green ground.

He had been just sixteen, his life snuffed out before it had begun, all his glorious potential unrealized.

Alicia Rowe had been properly devastated, of course. If she had seemed a little vague when someone mentioned Phillip's high grades, his little kindnesses, his sparkling humor, it was put down to her grievous loss.

Diana knew better.

She turned the CD player up yet louder. The pianist was just coming to the climactic end of his pulsing crescendo when her telephone rang. Making sure her tea was stable on the short table next to her, she switched off the recording, leaving her apartment in sudden, startling silence.

"Hello," she practically barked into the phone.

There was a short pause before Tilly Martel drawled, "Hello yourself, my dear."

"Oh. Sorry, Tilly. Hello."

"How did it go?"

"I'm on three months probation from opening day."

"Great!" Tilly enthused. "By that time, he'll be completely captivated."

"No, Tilly. I don't think so. At that time, I'll be leaving. On to fields of yet higher learning, I suppose. But I'll get things started, for you and Tom. And I'll find my own replacement, to ensure that things go smoothly."

"Why do I get the feeling there was more between you and Reid four years ago than you've told me, Diana? Not that it's any of my business, of course."

"I'm afraid the story is long but the point—as they say— is too short. Reid Hudson doesn't just dislike me. He distrusts me, he despises the life I used to lead, and he doesn't think I'm capable of changing. He gave me the trial period over his own better judgment, and I venture to say he is regretting that decision, even as we speak."

"His mind can be changed, you know."

"I don't think so. Besides, it's not worth it. I'll send in my acceptance to graduate school and go on with my life."

She heard Tilly sigh on the other end of the line. "I'm sorry, dear. I know this position meant more to you than just a job."

"And now it doesn't. But tell me something, Tilly?"

"Anything."

"How did Reid's wife die?"

Another pause. "In a car accident."

"Oh."

"Have lunch with me Friday?"

"Sure, Tilly. I'd love to."

Diana spent the next hour going over Lyonhouse procedures. Enrollment forms would be distributed among Heritage House employees by the end of the week, along with a packet of information regarding the Center. She didn't expect everyone with children to immediately sign up, of course. After all, most working parents had their offspring already placed somewhere, and many would be reluctant to make any sudden changes. That was fine with Diana. It would give her time to smooth out any bumps along the way, before the Center had to operate at full capacity.

Advertisements for workers at the Center were going in tomorrow's paper. One of the specifications regarding Lyonhouse was that it would not infringe upon the responsibilities of any existing Heritage House personnel, so Diana would be taking all the calls. She would turn on her answering machine first thing tomorrow morning, and return the calls in the late afternoon.

The next four weeks were going to be incredibly busy. Everything that could be done ahead of time was already done, from the written statement on discipline that all parents were required to sign, to the computerized accounting system that was already in place, with a multitude of other details in between. Still, in the next month, over two dozen people would have to be hired, parents would need to be interviewed, and the voluminous record-keeping required by the state would need to be initiated. Next week the building would be inspected, shelves would be going up, toys would be put in place, colorful pictures hung on the walls. A thousand and one responsibilities filled Diana's mind, and it was with no little relief she realized that she would be too busy to worry about Reid Hudson and his feelings toward her. In fact, she doubted whether she would think of him at all. She would simply do her job, to the very best of her ability, and then move on with her life, just as she had told Tilly.

When the phone rang again, she picked it up almost absentmindedly.

"Diana?"

She smiled. "Hello, Harry," she said into the mouthpiece.

"Jenny is studying for bar exams this weekend and wants to be left alone, can you believe it? And here I've got two tickets to the opera in Chicago Saturday night. Want to come?"

"Harry..." she began.

"You're about to say no, aren't you? Jenny said you would. Look, let me put it to you this way—I know you're busy. I know you don't want to lead me on. I know you feel guilty when I lavish my hard-earned dollars on you. But I've got box seats to *La Boheme* at the Lyric, and I know you'll love it. Come anyway."

She found herself laughing. "You read me like a book," she said. "I'd love to, Harry."

"Fine, then."

"Harry?"

"What, sweets?"

"Tell Jenny thanks."

"Hey, what about me?"

"You, too, of course."

Reid Hudson was working late. It was a habit he had formed when his parents had died, and he had been forced into a position of authority years before he was ready. At twenty-two, he had faced the proving ground of his own future, and had been absolutely devastated by his own incompetence.

Now he realized that twenty-two was no age to be faced with the responsibilities of his sixty-three-year-old father.

With a decade of experience behind him, he understood that the burdens he voluntarily accepted would have bowed much older men than himself. But at the time, he knew only that his parents were dead, his sister was not yet a teenager, and he was the last of a long line of Hudsons—none of whom, as far as he knew, had ever disgraced themselves.

Indeed, the Hudson name had long been synonymous with such words as: Responsibility. Duty. Accountability. Noblesse oblige. Do the right thing.

Reid had been taught these concepts since he was old enough to understand language. He remembered the first time he had gone with his father to the office, twenty-eight years ago. He was only five years old, but he still had enough understanding to grasp the significance of the pictures on the hallway walls: Hudson patriarchs going back six generations. He was the seventh, his father had told him. Someday his picture would be up there with all the rest. His place in the world had seemed fixed, immutable.

A lot of water under the bridge.

The words came to him so clearly, he looked up from the papers he was studying, as if he expected her to still be sitting there, in the chair opposite his desk. In his mind's eye he could see Diana Rowe watching him with the cool directness that he had found so oddly disconcerting. He recalled the way she had stood, facing him defiantly, telling him that he had no right to take Lyonhouse away from her. And he heard again the way she had continued to fight, after it was obvious he had dismissed her.

She had won, after all. *Three months,* she had said, and like a fool—against his own will—he had found himself agreeing. Fool indeed, he thought bitterly. For no amount of smooth persuasion could convince him that Diana Rowe had changed. Women like her were incapable of that particular feat.

Yet he had wanted to touch her—with a strength that astounded him. It had been a long time since he had felt that rush of feeling for a woman, and he had put out his hand just to know the feel of her smaller one in his own. Her trembling had only increased the fever in his own blood.

She had known that, too, of course. She was the one who had broken the contact, reminding him of his dead wife and Jamie and all that was real in his world.

Jamie.

He tested the name in his head, sending out feelers for any emotional reactions, but there were none. The child was staying temporarily with Reid's godparents in New York. Before coming here to Lansing, Reid had made an effort to spend as much time as he could with the boy, but no bond had sprung between them. Which was to be expected, given the circumstances.

Reid sighed wearily. Cynthia had been the last—and undoubtedly the worst—of several big mistakes he had made in the years immediately following the death of his parents. Unable to sort the good advice from the bad, having no experience in major corporate decisions, Reid had practically driven the family furniture business into its grave before he had found his feet. But he *had* found his feet, and the business had been saved.

Which was more than he could say for his disastrous marriage. Almost from the beginning, Cynthia had been unfaithful to him. But he had been so infatuated, so unwilling to see the truth even when it was staring him in the face, that he had been left feeling foolish and stupid and murderously angry when Cynthia had, at last, been discovered.

It hadn't helped that she had confessed to him—lightly, carelessly—that she had married him under pressure from her own socially ambitious parents. It was with a real sense of betrayal Cynthia had realized, after the wedding vows had been said and the marriage had been consummated, that while Reid's family name was still intact, his unlimited wealth was a thing of the past.

She seemed to find Reid's own feelings of being dealt with treacherously mildly amusing.

At the time, Cynthia had not wanted a divorce, and Reid could hardly afford one. He had moved out of the conjugal bedroom. His only request of his estranged wife was that she be discreet, so that his sister, Lucy, who lived with them, would not be hurt by Cynthia's reputation. Even then he had been blind to the greater danger. For it was not Cynthia's reputation that damaged Lucy, as much as Cynthia herself—with her cattiness and pettiness and downright cruelty.

But Reid had simply been too busy and too numb with his own shock to notice much. Instead, he buried himself in a business that was slowly building again, waiting with hard patience for the financial solvency that would allow him to be free of Cynthia once and for all.

Jamie's birth, over a year later, had been the final straw. While acquaintances murmured at the coldness of the man who never even visited his wife and newborn child in the hospital, and Lucy became more and more withdrawn, Reid made quiet plans to institute divorce proceedings.

Unfortunately Cynthia's unstable affections had fixed on Reid once again. Reid's business was doing well, very well, in fact. He was being called the *Wunderkind* by national news magazines, and suddenly he was on everyone's guest list. After years of grim struggle and gross insecurity, he found the sudden recognition ironic, and the social invitations unwelcome.

Cynthia more than made up for his lack of enthusiasm. Now that the Hudson name was once again in favor among New York's elite, she had no desire to give up her marriage. Acting the long-suffering wife, she told anyone who would listen how much she loved and admired her husband, and she taught her illegitimate son to call Reid *Daddy*. In the meantime, she had her lawyers use every tactic available to stall the divorce, while she played the loving wife and did everything she could to seduce Reid back into her bed.

A year ago, against the advice of his legal counsel—who feared a charge of abandonment in divorce court—Reid had moved out. Lucy was a junior in college, and Reid wanted nothing so much as to be left alone. The divorce, now costing him a fortune, would have been final the week Cynthia had crashed.

He had come that close to being free.

Instead, Cynthia had died, leaving behind her a little four-year-old boy who looked at Reid, and saw his dad.

Responsibility. Duty. Do the right thing. The old words still had their time-honored power. Weary and scarred and wanting nothing so much as to simply rest, Reid could still not turn his back on a child who knew no other parent except himself. In the end, he supposed it made no difference that he and Jamie had no blood relationship. He had a responsibility to the child, who was young and defenseless and had been traumatized. If he could find no warmth in him toward Jamie, he could at least ensure the boy some modicum of stability.

Your son...

He heard again Diana's voice, low and musically husky. She had walked like a model, and talked like an aristocrat, yet her eyes had held something else—something soft and wounded and almost frightened. He closed his own eyes against the image, and saw in the darkness there her legs moving with the grace of a young colt, her head held just so, her shoulders high and proud so that the shape of her breasts had been outlined against that ridiculous gray silk dress. A fine human animal, he found himself musing in honest appreciation, before the darker thought found a place: a fine used human animal.

What was he doing, mooning over the image of a young woman whom he had not seen in four years? Surely he could not be so feeble-minded as to fall again for someone so totally inappropriate. No. He would not be fooled again, as Cynthia had fooled him. He knew the rules of the game now, and he chose not to play. He had no desire to entangle himself with someone like Diana Rowe. He would watch her like a hawk for the three months he had so foolishly promised her, and then she would be gone. That, after all, had been his original objective when he had decided to attend that meeting today: remove Diana Rowe from his business.

But he was finding it impossible to concentrate. Restlessly he began to pace his office, not wishing to return to his rented house, not having anywhere else to go.

He knew practically no one in Lansing. Still, he had wanted to come here, to oversee this first acquisition himself. After ten years of practically destroying his New York furniture business, and then painfully rebuilding it, this was his first real expansion. He wanted to make sure everything was going to go just right.

At least that was what he told everyone else, when he left Bill Tyrell in charge of his New York operations. With himself he was more honest. For the past decade his life had been a constant struggle. He wanted to leave it all behind him, just for a little while. He would come out here, to Michigan, with the son who was not his son, and try to start again, to see if something could yet be made of his life.

The sound of his office telephone was a welcome relief to his dark thoughts, and he picked it up on its first ring.

"Reid? Are you busy?"

"Not at all. How are you, Lucy?"

"Bored out of my skin. Finals are over, and I'm missing my big brother. Are you really going to be out in the nether regions for half a year?"

For the first time that day, Reid felt his face softening into a genuine smile. He dropped back into his chair and propped his feet on his desk. Gone were the days when Lucy rebelled against everything he said. And now that Cynthia was no longer an issue between them, their relationship had evened out pleasurably.

Answering Lucy's question, Reid said, "I'm afraid so." Then, "The time here will be good for Jamie, I think."

A pause. "Is he speaking yet?"

"No." The child had been silent ever since he had been pulled, alive but terrified, out of the car in which his mother lay dying.

"So when are you going to fetch him?"

Reid sighed. "Not for a couple of weeks yet. Pete and Mary will keep him until then."

"Yes. Well, I didn't mean to depress you."

"It's all right. I'm not depressed."

"That's good, because I feel like doing something really outrageous. What do you say to a Chicago weekend with your little sister? We could meet at O'Hare Friday night."

"You want to spend the weekend with me, your big brother? What happened to Sean what's his name?"

"Old history, I'm afraid. I desperately need consoling. And it's been ages since we've done anything fun together, Reid."

"If I go anywhere, I should probably fly to New York and visit Jamie," he said more quietly.

"Jamie is as well-off with Pete and Mary as with anyone, and you know it. They positively dote on the boy. Come on, Reid. Take a few hours off and live a little."

"With you, my dear?"

"Why not? Who else are you comfortable with in that three-piece-suit world? And you can't be having a very good time stuck way out there in the boonies with a bunch of strangers."

He hesitated only momentarily. Lucy, after all, was *family*. In spite of all that had come after, she belonged to that other, simpler time, before his parents had died and his world had fallen apart.

"All right, Lucy," he said, feeling his spirits grow lighter. "Tell me what you had in mind."

"Opera."

"Oh Lord," he groaned in mock disbelief. "You know I hate the stuff."

"But it's *La Boheme*, my favorite, and I want to see it with you."

"All right, dammit," he growled. "But I'll have you know I wouldn't do this for anyone but you."

"I know." He could hear Lucy laughing lightly.

A day or two with his sister *would* be good for him, he decided. She was right about Jamie, and the thought of having something to look forward to would get him through the week.

"Reid?"

"What, peanut brain?"

"I love you, big brother."

His hand wrapped itself around the telephone a little more tightly. "Lucy?"

"What?"

"Thanks for calling."

When he hung up the phone, he was still smiling. And for a time, he forgot all about Diana Rowe.

Harry Reichenbach called for Diana shortly after noon on Saturday. The actual drive to Chicago would take about five hours, and he had promised her dinner before the performance. After the opera, they would stay in a hotel, and Harry would spend Sunday chauffeuring Diana around to anything she wanted to see, before heading back to Lansing. And he would never ask for anything but friendship in return.

Indeed, Harry was the best friend Diana had ever had. They had literally bumped into each other the first day she had attended classes at the University of Michigan. He had stopped to help her recover the books and papers that had gone flying. Then he had invited her to coffee.

An orphan, Harry collected friends the way other people collected books. When Diana had told him so, he laughingly said he liked her story the best of all. For three years they were inseparable, and few of their acquaintances believed in the truly platonic relationship they insisted they had. So Harry would shrug, and Diana would smile, and off they would go... to the movies, to dinner, even to study together.

But Harry knew that Diana Rowe was the family he never had. For a long time their relationship was more important to him than any affair of the heart, for it brought to him a kind of stability, a feeling of permanence, of peace.

And for Diana, Harry helped fill the void Phillip had left.

Then, at the beginning of Harry's last year of law school, he had met a black-haired, sloe-eyed young Italian woman named Justina Sevilla. Jenny to her friends, she was studious, determined, and absolutely smitten with Harry Reichenbach. Deciding to take at face value what everyone else had laughed at for years, she accepted the truth of Harry and Diana's relationship.

Within four weeks of their first date, Harry Reichenbach and Jenny Sevilla were engaged, and no one was happier for the couple than Diana Rowe.

But now, to have Harry to herself for the entire weekend was a true delight. They laughed and talked and were silent together all the way to Chicago. Over dinner he said, "So, how's your Lyonhouse thing going?"

"Exciting things have happened, Harry," she said ironically. "Reid Hudson seems somehow to have bought Heritage House, and he came to our meeting last Monday."

"Ah. Let me see if I remember. Big brother to famous Lucy."

"The same."

"So what did he have to say?"

"He wanted me out, but I convinced him to give me three months."

"The bastard."

She shrugged. "It has been rather stressful, but I'm not letting any grass grow under my feet. I sent in my acceptance to the University of Chicago on Tuesday."

"So what happens if he asks you to stay after the three months?"

"I say no. Finish. End of relationship."

He stared at her. "Come on, Diana. This is your own personal proving ground, remember? You can't possibly mean it."

"So now I'm proving something else. Lyonhouse will survive without me, after all. I don't need to work for someone that dislikes me. The world is too big."

"Does Hudson know anything of what you've gone through since you left New York?"

"He's seen my résumé. I'm certainly not going to tell him any more. Anyway, I've mostly caused my own problems— I'm too old to play any blaming games. I probably deserve every deep, dark thing he thinks about me." She paused to take a bite of trout. "You know what? None of this would bother me nearly so much if I could just like the man. But he's . . . cold, unfeeling." She pushed aside the memory of his hand holding hers, and the way she had reacted to his touch. "It's as if he locked all his emotions up long ago, and threw away the key." But even as she said the words, she knew they were not true. Reid Hudson had feelings all right. He was like a time bomb, ready to explode with them. She just wanted to make sure she wasn't around when someone lit the fuse.

Diana and Harry arrived at the Lyric Opera House exactly thirty minutes early, and entered laughing. Diana had not felt so carefree in days, and she knew true gratitude for the present moment. Their box was lovely, with a perfect view of the stage, and she thought nothing in the world could be so idyllic. She and Harry took the first two seats, and waited in comfortable silence for the performance to begin.

It was just five minutes to performance time when she heard the door of their box open. She turned, prepared to give a friendly smile to whoever entered, curious as to who would be sharing their box for the evening.

But her smile faded and her eyes turned disbelieving as she saw the tall form of Reid Hudson bending down to say something to a young woman who could only be his sister, Lucy. In that moment, before he looked up and found her there, she was aware of a feeling of absolute astonishment, not only at the cruel coincidence that was once again throwing Reid and her together, but also at the stranger that she saw. This man, dressed in fine wool slacks and a black turtleneck sweater, was nothing like the cold, rejecting businessman she had met with last Monday. This man was smiling, relaxed, and genuinely enjoying himself. Until he saw her, of course.

He straightened immediately, the laughter fading from his face as he looked at her with harsh incredulity. His eyes had barely time to flick to Harry seated comfortably at her side, before Lucy came all the way into the box.

Diana stood, trying to hide the fact that her breath was coming short and fast, that her blood had begun to race wildly.

"Diana?" Lucy whispered. "Diana Rowe?" Diana heard shock there, and pain, and unbelievably, joy.

"Hello, Lucy," she said. Then, inanely, "You're all grown up." She smiled, before once again meeting those other, colder eyes. "Reid," she acknowledged, giving a small nod, trying desperately to disregard the horrified dismay that was flowing through her. "Small world, huh?"

"Diana," he replied tersely, and she could see from the expression in his eyes that he was having much the same thoughts. His gaze shifted to Harry, who had risen to stand by her side.

Of course there was no help for it. Introductions had to be made.

Diana did so, hardly knowing what she was doing. *If there is a God in heaven,* she thought, *right now he is laughing. Only I don't see the joke.*

Reid and Harry shook hands, and for a moment their eyes locked as they studied each other in the age-old communication of the male of the species. Harry's mouth tilted up slightly, as if he found something secretly amusing.

Lucy continued to stand stiffly, her face white, her arms rigid at her side. "Reid?" she asked with sudden uncertainty. "Have you seen Diana recently?" Then her voice hardened slightly. "And you didn't tell me?"

Since Reid did not reply, Diana commented, "I work for your big brother, Lucy. For the next three months or so, anyway." Then Lucy was not saying anything at all, and the box was suddenly thick with undercurrents of what was not being said. It was Harry who broke the strange silence, as he eyed Reid with curious speculation. "Diana is the director of the new day care center at Heritage House, Lucy."

Lucy's eyes widened in amazement. She looked first at her brother, then at Diana. "I see," she managed, although she obviously did not see anything at all.

Diana could feel Lucy's distress; it was greater than anything she would have imagined. "Lucy..." she began, not really knowing what she was going to say next.

"I tried to find you, you know." The younger woman's voice was brittle with the effort of speaking calmly. "I called all your telephone numbers, but no one knew where you were. I wrote letters, and they all came back unforwarded. I even talked to your father."

"You did?"

"Yes. He said he couldn't find you, either."

"I wasn't in hiding," Diana said flatly, forcing herself not to look at Reid, sure of the condemnation she would find there. "My father wasn't interested in finding me. That's all, Lucy. I'm sorry. Truly."

Suddenly the younger woman's eyes were swimming with grief, her hands twisting in upon themselves in front of her stomach. "I missed you," Lucy said. "How could you leave like that, without telling me where you'd gone?"

Diana's eyes flashed upward to clash with Reid's glacial gaze. She thought perhaps he expected her to denounce him. "I'm sorry..." she said, instead. "I didn't know..."

She *had* known, though. Lucy had been so lonely and isolated. Of course Diana's disappearance would have hurt the girl, reinforcing the sixteen-year-old's insecurity. Diana could have left a note, called, anything. But at the time she had been so angry at her father and Reid Hudson that she had simply not been thinking clearly. Now guilt at her own carelessness swamped her.

That old hurt was in Lucy's eyes, plain for all to see. "You should have known, Diana," she said, regaining some of her dignity. "I loved you like a sister."

"I believe it's time for us to be seated," Reid's low voice interrupted. "Lucy?"

Abruptly Harry was at Diana's side, his arm around her waist, guiding her to her chair. She felt Harry give her shoulder an uncharacteristic caress—the touch of a lover, not a friend—and she looked at him questioningly. He leaned over to her and whispered in her ear. "My, my," he said. "On top of everything else, he's jealous, my dear."

She would have laughed out loud if they had been anywhere else. Instead all she did was widen her eyes in disbelief. Harry shrugged, then reached over and deliberately took her hand.

Reid was sitting directly behind her.

The black dress she was wearing had been a Paris original when she had purchased it four years ago. An off-the-shoulder design, it hugged her figure tightly, until it ruffled out abruptly in a dramatically sloped hemline, above the knee to one side, midcalf on the other. Her hair hung loose to her shoulders. Her diamond necklace—a gift from a long-ago admirer—encircled her throat. With dismay, she knew she looked every bit the dilettante.

Harry ran his finger up her bare arm.

Stop that, she commanded him silently. He grinned wolfishly.

At intermission, Lucy was up and out the door of the box before Diana had time to look around. Reid quickly followed his sister.

When the Hudsons returned, Diana handed Lucy a note. It contained her address and telephone number. *I really am sorry,* she had written. *Please call me.* Let Reid make of that what he would. Lucy was an adult now, and could associate with whom she chose.

Finally, after the curtain was down and the last applause died away, when they all stood and were looking at each other in self-conscious silence, Lucy spoke in a low voice to Diana.

"Surely you're not heading back to Lansing tonight?"

"No," Diana said. "We have reservations in the city. We go back to Lansing tomorrow." Reid's eyes narrowed as Harry slipped his arm around her waist, pulling her against him. *I'll kill you for this, Harry Reichenbach,* she thought.

"Couldn't . . . Couldn't we all go out and get something to eat?" Lucy asked, bravely hopeful. She turned to her brother. "Reid, don't you think . . ." But the look on his face was grimly forbidding, and her words died away slowly.

"No. I don't," he said with heavy emphasis. Once again his eyes met Diana's, and for a moment all else faded as she stared into his dark orbs. She realized that his expression had undergone a subtle change, and she saw his gaze travel downward, once again taking in Harry's possessive arm around her waist. "Good evening, Harry. Diana." Then Reid and Lucy were gone.

Diana pulled away from Harry. "*That* was completely unnecessary, you know." It was an effort to keep her voice light, steady. "Besides, I can't imagine what made you think he was jealous. The man can't stand me."

"He couldn't keep his eyes off you, you mean." His eyes dancing, Harry looked up at the ceiling and whistled tunelessly. "The next three months should be interesting indeed." Then he looked at her, his gaze softening as he absorbed the apprehension written clearly on her face. "Cheer up, Diana," he said. "It's only three months. And he's lucky you agreed to stay."

How she loved Harry. He always had such a wonderful way of putting things in perspective. Only later, as she lay in her bed in the hotel suite, did she allow herself to remember Harry's other words: *He couldn't keep his eyes off you, you mean.*

Reid Hudson did find her attractive. She had known it in his office earlier in the week, and she knew it now. But Reid also held her in contempt, and she feared he hated that part of himself that was drawn to Diana Rowe.

She must never let him know that for four years she had seen his face in her dreams, mocking her, taunting her, making her feel hot—as if lit by some unseen fire. But his was a dark flame, she told herself bitterly. Once caught, she would be destroyed by his fierce burning.

Three months, she had told him, defiant and angry and proud. She felt none of those things now, however. Now she felt only very, very frightened.

Suddenly three months seemed very long indeed.

Chapter Four

The next weeks flew by as Diana hired her staff, organized their responsibilities, and interviewed parents and children. She and Reid never crossed paths during this time, but she thought about him more often than she cared to admit. She told herself over and over that his opinion of her character simply didn't matter, but that sentiment made it difficult to justify the intensity with which she wanted to prove him wrong.

She heard nothing more regarding Reid's son, Jamie. She knew Reid had received the necessary information regarding registration procedures at Lyonhouse, and she took his silence on the subject to mean he had changed his mind about enrolling Jamie there. She thought with bitter resignation that *she* was probably the reason Reid no longer wanted his son at Lyonhouse.

Her first press conference was scheduled on the Friday afternoon before Lyonhouse opened. Diana had the reporters gather in the foyer, then greeted them with professional friendliness. "Welcome to Lyonhouse," she said. There were four men and three women, cameras slung around their necks and over their shoulders. "I thought we would begin here," Diana continued, smiling, "with a question. How many of you have children?"

Only two of the group raised their hands. "Not a majority," Diana said. "On the other hand, how many of you have *been* children?" Chuckles and smiles were her answer. "Good," she said. "So have I. So we all have something in common. For the duration of this short tour, try to imagine yourself as a child coming to this building for the first time. Then, after a while, still seeing yourself as a child, think what it would be like six months from today. How would you feel? What would your expectations be? Keep that vision clear, and I think you will begin to understand the essence of Lyonhouse."

As Diana turned to lead the group into the first classroom, a small sedan raced into the parking lot. With brakes squealing, the driver ignored the neatly painted parking spaces, pulling to an abrupt stop immediately in front of Lyonhouse's main door. The car doors opened, and two men raced to join the group that was following Diana.

The first of the latecomers was short and stout, with a too-small red sports shirt pulled tight over his belly. The second man was of more average height, with thinning hair and a sad, creased face. He carried two cameras; already he was removing one from its case.

"Michael Aninger," the short man introduced himself to no one in particular, flashing an identification card in Diana's general direction as he barked out the name of the paper he was representing.

Immediately Diana was filled with dismay, although she did her best to hide her unhappy surprise. The national tabloid of which Aninger spoke had a lurid reputation for delivering titillating gossip and fact-starved articles. Certainly no press release regarding Lyonhouse had gone to the New York office of this sensation-seeking newspaper; nor had the publication received an invitation to this rather ordinary news conference.

"Mr. Aninger," she acknowledged tersely. "Are you sure you have the right place? I can't imagine there is anything here to interest your readers."

"They'll be interested," Aninger said shortly, shaking his head. "My editor flew me out special, soon as he heard, Miss Rowe."

Heard what? But Diana had no time for further thoughts, as the man with the saggy face aimed his camera at Diana and she was momentarily blinded by the resulting flash. "You're here to see Lyonhouse, not me," she said, feeling her cheeks begin to grow warm as her voice sharpened defensively.

Michael Aninger didn't respond. He was too busy taking a miniature tape recorder out of his chest pocket.

Diana began to feel a horrible panic; she was afraid her sudden frantic unease was beginning to show in her eyes. "This way please," she said, turning abruptly, trying with all her might to disbelieve the dreadful implications of Michael Aninger's presence. Another flash went off—this one caught the back of Diana's head.

Stolidly Diana ignored Aninger's flash-happy friend. "Remember," she said to the group behind her, "you are now about three feet tall, you're somewhere between three and four years old, and this is your first day here."

"Cute," Aninger said.

Diana didn't bat an eye. Instead, she drew herself up to her full height, composed her features, turned and gave Michael Aninger a look that would wither the dead.

Sag-face took another picture.

"Look," Diana said, with a firmness born of her growing desperation. "All picture-taking will be done when the tour of Lyonhouse is complete."

That caught the photographer's attention. His drooping eyes slid around to Michael Aninger questioningly.

"Now, Miss Rowe..." Aninger said, his voice a ridiculous mixture of appeasement and belligerence.

"Sorry," she said sharply, hoping that no one noticed her voice had risen slightly. "Those are the terms of this interview. Anyone who has a problem with that is invited to leave."

The other reporters, eyeing Aninger uneasily, nodded their assent. Michael Aninger's round, pudgy face fell into an ugly expression of resentment, and his eyes narrowed until they appeared like black beads in the folds of his skin. Diana forced herself to stare at him unblinkingly. "All right," he said at last. "Agreed."

"Your photographer might as well wait here, then."

"*All right,*" Aninger said, not bothering to hide his displeasure.

Diana smiled thinly. "Fine," she said. "If you will follow me please."

He knows who I am, she thought hopelessly. *This is not going to be pleasant.*

She took them first to the multipurpose room, which would double as a gym and auditorium. Large colorful plastic toys—slides, playhouses, balls and mats—were placed against the walls, which were a neutral yellow-toned white. A mural of full-sized, happily playing children was painted on the far side.

Diana loved it here. This, after all, was a building of beginnings, of youth and innocence and wide-eyed wonder. She wanted the reporters to understand that, but she would never be able to inspire anyone if she let a jerk of a sensationalist reporter take control of her interview.

Slowly she turned around, raising her chin as she did so. Her smile became more natural, and she took the time to meet the eyes of everyone in the room. The dynamics of the group underwent a subtle change, and she began to feel in control once again.

"This building," she began, her voice low and well-modulated, "is like an empty heart, waiting to be filled..."

The tour took thirty minutes, ending in what was formally called the After School Room, especially designed for the use of latchkey children. On the whole the reporters had been polite and interested, but Diana had been constantly aware of Michael Aninger's eyes watching her like a hawk who has found its prey.

"Are there any further questions?" Diana asked. Her smiling mouth felt stiff and her body oddly tired, and she knew her effort at maintaining her controlled demeanor in the face of Aninger's continued presence was taking its toll.

"Yeah," Aninger said with insulting casualness. "Can we have some pictures *now,* Miss Rowe?"

She met his gaze directly, unaware that her eyes had grown shadows in the last half hour, or that her expression was strangely haunted. "Of course," she said calmly. "Go ahead and shoot all the pictures you want, *of Lyonhouse.* Afterward, I'll be available in my office to answer any further questions you might have."

Michael Aninger's face grew hard—almost cruelly avaricious. She felt herself shiver in revulsion, and she turned away from the group of reporters, all of whom were eyeing her curiously. She walked toward the door, for the moment uncaring that her behavior must seem erratic and rude. She just wanted to get away before Aninger could say anything else.

But the door to the After School Room opened from the outside, and Reid Hudson was there, standing in the doorway. His unexpected appearance took her breath away, and she stopped suddenly. She experienced an involuntary rush of breathlessness, and her eyes flew to his and held. Something hot and bright flashed in his dark depths before his gaze traveled to the reporters grouped behind her.

Released from her initial surprise, she saw for the first time the small boy who was standing, with unusual stillness, at Reid's side.

He was the most exquisite child Diana had ever seen.

Jamie Hudson. Reid had brought his son, after all.

The boy's hair was a deep glowing red, streaked with gold. His skin was smooth and fair—almost as fair as Diana's own. His features were utterly perfect, almost unnaturally ideal: a small, straight nose; eyes spaced with flawless symmetry, lips shaped with precise evenness.

She felt, fleetingly, as if she had stumbled upon a treasure, a priceless jewel: surely this boy was the crowning achievement of some unknown, consummate artist.

Then the feeling of unreality passed, and she looked into Jamie Hudson's eyes.

They were a rich, deep brown, and just as beautiful as the rest of him. But what startled Diana was the emptiness in those young eyes, the almost deliberate blankness with which Jamie Hudson greeted his world.

"Diana?" Reid inquired softly. "Is something the matter?"

But Michael Aninger stepped forward before she could even begin to react to the unexpected gentleness of Reid's voice. "Mr. Hudson? Mr. Reid Hudson?"

Reid swiveled his head in Aninger's direction. "You have the advantage of me." Now his voice was low, and imperious as always.

The reporter's fat fingers groped in his front breast pocket to once again produce his press badge. "Aninger, Michael Aninger," the man said briefly. Then, "Burns! In here, now!" The photographer immediately stepped into the doorway, effectively blocking Reid's passage out. His camera was already up to his face, searching for Diana.

"No!" Aninger ordered in a curt, excited voice. "This one! Get the boy, too!"

"What the . . . ?" But Reid's angry exclamation was lost in the blinding flash of the camera.

"Is this your little boy, Mr. Hudson?" Aninger was asking. "I understand you're enrolling your own son in Lyonhouse? Is my information correct?"

The camera flashed again, and Diana saw terror in the child's eyes. Her natural affinity with the young had all her concentration suddenly riveted on the small boy at Reid's side, even as Reid's eyes moved to Diana, all softness removed from them now. His gaze flicked over her with now-familiar derision.

"How about Miss Rowe?" Aninger's rough gravelly voice continued mercilessly. Burns had turned the camera to Diana once again; she saw the whiteness of the light too late to move her head. "Were you and Miss Rowe acquainted before this project began, Mr. Hudson?"

Diana began to feel dazed, as if she were in some particularly vivid dream. The white flashes continued to disorient her, and she was aware more than ever of the building anger of the dark man standing there so silently.

As the bulb flashed yet again, Jamie turned with terrified abruptness, and buried his head in the cloth of Reid's pants leg. His small frame was shaking uncontrollably, and he clung to his father's leg with all his might.

At the boy's unexpected movement, Reid's tall body stiffened, until he was stretched as taut as a rod. Diana saw his hands flex involuntarily, until they closed in rigid fists at his side. He flung his head up, so that his short, thick hair waved slightly from the jerking motion. His mouth tightened, and his eyes grew as dark as midnight.

Still Jamie clung to the stiff figure of his father, and the camera caught the strange tableaux. Reid shuddered, and his reaction seemed to waken him from some trance, so that he glanced down at the bowed, trembling head of his son. As if through force of will, Reid's features softened, his body relaxed, his hands unclenched.

"There, there," he said, patting the boy's head. "There, there." The voice was soft, as Reid Hudson's voice was always soft, but his eyes held the desolation of the damned.

The boy began to cry.

Reid bent down, and picked up the shaking child. Tears were running in rivers down the boy's checks, and his eyes were wide with unnatural horror.

Reid turned his body so that he was facing Aninger directly. "Get out," he said.

"Do you know just who Diana Rowe is?" Aninger ignored Reid's command. "Do you know she's Gregory Rowe's daughter?"

Outside the open windows a bird sang. From farther away, the muted noise of automobiles could be heard.

Inside Lyonhouse, however, all was suddenly, shockingly, silent. So silent that Diana thought she could hear the brains of the other reporters, thinking as furiously as they could. Even Michael Aninger quit talking, his ruddy complexion paling, as he realized he had just given away his own private scoop.

Diana felt a cynical smile creep across her face.

Only sag-face Burns remained active, his camera flashing as fast as he could make it go.

"You bastard," Reid said angrily, his low voice hard and terrible in his fury. "You're terrifying my son. The last time he saw flashbulbs he was being pulled out of the car where his mother lay dying. You shoot that thing one more time and I'll wrap it around your head."

"Oh," Burns mumbled, obviously startled. "Sorry." Dropping the camera to catch by the strap around his long, skinny neck, he deftly opened his second camera case. "This one doesn't need a flash," he said, before snapping a picture of the back of Jamie's golden head, now turned into Reid's shoulder.

"Get out of my way," Reid commanded Burns. "Better yet, get out of here completely."

Aninger had regained his impetus, and was practically jumping up and down with excitement. "You two go out at all?" he asked, his head jerking toward Diana. "Do we have a romantic interest here?"

Burns stayed in the middle of the doorway, and took another shot at Reid.

"Gregory Rowe *is* your father, isn't he, Miss Rowe?" Aninger asked. "The hotel billionaire who raised himself from the streets of New York? Is it true that the two of you are estranged? How long has it been since you've seen the big man, anyway? What did you two fight about?"

She was feeling cold again. She was once again the daughter existing only in her father's shadow. She saw her world, built so carefully, labored over so diligently, being destroyed just by the power of Gregory Rowe's name. She was as cold as ice.

"Gregory Rowe is my father," she said quietly.

"How much is he worth these days, Miss Rowe?"

She couldn't speak to save her life. The other reporters were scribbling like mad.

"What about it, Mr. Hudson? What's your relationship with Diana Rowe? You know she's as rich as a princess, don't you? An American princess, anyway? Our very own Princess Di. Princess Di of Day Care. How do you like that? What's she doing out here in Lansing, anyway? How long have *you* been here, Reid? Did she follow you out here? Is she offering you some comfort since the death of your wife?

Are the two of you sharing living space, or anything like that? Do you have plans for the future?''

Reid's eyes snapped toward Diana. His arms were around his son, one hand cradling the boy's sobbing head against his shoulder. Once again their eyes met, but she could read nothing in his dark gaze.

"Call the police, Diana," he said.

"Hey! Okay! Okay! Just doing my job, and all that. No need to make threats."

"Some job," one of the other reporters muttered.

Diana's paralyzing inertia fled, and in its place she felt a stinging anger. "Diana," Reid said again, his tone sharp with command. She nodded in response, and strode toward the door. Burns moved in a parody of polite accommodation, both his cameras now hanging limply across his chest. In the doorway Diana turned. Ignoring Aninger and Burns completely, she looked at the seven original reporters.

"You got more of a story than you bargained for," she said passionately. "And it doesn't involve Diana Rowe. Imagine this—you're four years old, you're visiting Lyonhouse for the first time, and you are greeted by hostility, frightening lights and terrifying tension. That is what happened to Jamie Hudson today. Write about that when you do your articles. Write about being a child in a world controlled by adults who are not always kind, or sensitive, or in any way concerned for your welfare. Not only is that the story you saw today," she continued, her voice low with fury, "it is the story of our century. Write about growing up in such a world. And then tell your readers what we are trying to do here, in our own small way. That, ladies and gentlemen, is your story."

She looked at Aninger, who was watching her narrowly. "If you are not out of this building as fast as it takes me to reach the phone," she said with icy calm, "you will ask any further questions you have of the police."

Aninger shrugged insolently. "I've got my story, anyway, Miss Rowe," he said, heading for the door. "You've been most...entertaining."

The other reporters were also filing out. Two or three shook Diana's hand, admiration and sympathy gleaming from their eyes. Then they, too, were gone.

Diana was left alone with Reid Hudson, who was standing in much the same place as he had all along, with the little boy whose sobs had gentled to whimpers in his arms.

"Bring him here," Diana said. "Now."

Without waiting to see if Reid was following, she walked to the windows that overlooked the parking lot.

"Look, Jamie," she said, allowing her anger to make her voice strong and sure. "That bad man is going away. Your father and I sent him away. He was mean, wasn't he?" She turned to face the father and son. Amazed comprehension flitted over Reid's features before he took a step forward. "Quick! Look!" Diana urged. "He's driving away. We made him go away!"

Jamie's head lifted tentatively, and he looked in the direction Diana was pointing. "See that blue car? He's in it. That man is leaving as fast as he can go. He doesn't belong here. I'm glad he's leaving, aren't you? Nobody liked him. Nobody wanted him here. Aren't you glad he's gone?"

The little tear-streaked face nodded vigorously.

"Now we can play and have fun. All the children that come to Lyonhouse have fun. We don't let bad people come here, because they don't like to have fun. We send all bad people away. Aren't you glad?"

Jamie was turned in his father's arms now, watching Michael Aninger's car until it was out of sight. He was still making little hiccuping noises, and his eyes were red with weeping, but some of the fear had left his haunted gaze.

"Jamie." Diana lowered her voice. "Jamie, look at me." The boy twisted further, until he was staring at Diana's face.

"I'm so happy that man is gone, Jamie. And I'm happy you're here. I'm so happy I feel like smiling. Don't you? Will you smile to show me how happy you are? I'll smile at you if you smile at me!" Then Diana gave the child the brightest, boldest smile she could.

Jamie's expression turned solemn, serious, as his unbelievably beautiful eyes locked with her own. Diana remembered how still Jamie had looked when he had first appeared at Reid's side, and she knew intuitively that his was a face unfamiliar with joy. She smiled harder.

Suddenly Jamie closed his eyes, tight. His little body stiffened. Then, with his eyes closed and his hands grasping for Reid's shirt, Jamie curved his lips upward very, very slightly. It looked like a grimace of pain.

Diana raised her eyes to Reid's face, forgetting that holding Jamie as he was, he could not see his son's expression. Instead he was watching Diana steadily, with something resembling confusion in his midnight eyes.

"That's a wonderful smile, Jamie," she said gently, with warm approval. "I love it when you smile." She touched the boy's face, and his eyes opened. "Let's go look at Lyonhouse, shall we? Do you want your father to carry you, or would you rather walk?" She looked at Reid questioningly. "That *was* why you brought Jamie today, wasn't it?" At Reid's slight nod she added, "Afterward, we can sit and fill out all the proper forms."

Jamie wriggled out of his father's arms and slid to the floor. Diana was not surprised when he walked over to her and spontaneously placed his hand in hers. She was used to receiving the trust of children—she had held a lot of little hands since leaving New York.

Reid, however, seemed startled at Jamie's action, and astonishment as well as a darker emotion—pain? grief? anger?—flickered deep in his blue eyes before he hooded them.

Then a long slow shudder coursed through her body. She was still in shock over the events of the past hour. Four years of anonymity and independence, she thought bitterly, gone with the tip of a writer's pen. Twelve months of preparation for Lyonhouse, only to have that work of substance overshadowed by the emptiness of unearned fame and inherited wealth.

Princess Di of Day Care.

She felt like barren soil, empty, without form of any kind. The old hopeless despair swamped her, sucked her down. She had to feel her own skin to be positive she existed.

Then she felt again the little warm hand in hers, and she glanced down to see Jamie waiting for her with his unnatural patience. She was important to this one, and many like him, who in their youth and innocence knew nothing of status or money or even last names. The strength of her sudden relief frightened her. *Who am I* she asked herself, *to receive comfort from a frightened and sad little boy?*

Reid was watching her, his eyes strangely intent. "Are you all right?" he asked, his harsh voice telling her just how unwilling his concern really was.

She took a deep breath. "Of course," she said, forcing another smile. "I'm afraid I was having a little reaction to that unpleasant scene myself." To her horror, her voice wobbled slightly.

"Perhaps it would be better if we came back another time...."

"No!" she said, more abruptly than she intended. But she needed the warmth of that small hand to help her feel real. She couldn't let go now. "No. Now is the best time for Jamie, and I am all right."

"Let's go then."

Lyonhouse resembled a small school. The administrative offices were to the immediate left of the big wide double doors that formed the entrance. To the right, directly across from the offices, was the After School Room, which they now left.

Four rooms were organized to hold the four major age groupings at Lyonhouse, and each room had a different color scheme. Infants would be surrounded by strong yellows and soft whites. The Toddler's Room incorporated bright red in its decorations. Kelly green was the primary color in the Five-year-olds' Room. She showed Jamie and his father the huge multipurpose room, and at the end of the building, the eating area directly off the kitchen—complete with child-size tables, low benches and twenty high chairs lined up neatly against one wall.

She finished in the Preschool Room, where Jamie would be spending much of his time. This room had a painted wainscoting of deep royal blue. As in the kitchen area, there were low, brightly colored tables with appropriately sized chairs. Photographs and paintings were hung three and four feet off the floor. Numerous large picture books filled one shelf. Other shelves held counting toys, stacking toys, toys that encouraged both large and small motor coordination. Building blocks had been provided, along with old telephones and a well-equipped play kitchen. An art center— complete with crayons, paper, scissors and paints—filled an entire corner.

It was a child's paradise. But young Jamie, still holding her hand, never said a word, or indicated in any other way that he was interested in what he saw.

Reid was just as quiet.

Diana's sense of disorientation was not quite so strong, and she became aware of the strange silence, not only of the boy, but the man at her side. She looked up to catch Reid staring at her face. She began to blush, and his eyes softened momentarily.

Deliberately she dropped Jamie's hand. "Why don't you two stay here and look around while I go to the office to get your forms? I'll be right back."

"We're done anyway," Reid said, his lips quirking as if he understood her desire to get away from him. "We'll accompany you to your office."

It was now after five o'clock; the staff members who had been in organizing their various responsibilities had long since gone. Lyonhouse seemed uncomfortably empty, a sensation that Diana had never experienced before. She felt again the pressure of acting cool and poised; she would be glad when Reid had gone, and she could once again know the sweet relief of being alone.

Motioning for Reid to sit in the chair opposite her desk, she took her own seat. Jamie sat on the floor at his father's feet. Remembering how Reid had interviewed her in his own office, she knew a sudden hysterical temptation to mimic his actions, complete with steepled hands and superior mien. Quickly, with desperate self-control, she curbed the impulse, knowing intuitively that to use arrogance to battle this man was to invite failure. Instead, she retreated into cool professionalism. As if this were a regular interview with any parent, she smiled at Reid politely.

Pulling a folder out of her desk drawer, she opened it calmly. "I have just a few questions, Reid."

Reid ignored her comment. "Does that kind of thing happen often?" he asked curtly.

She stiffened, knowing immediately to what he was referring. She met his eyes, but could read nothing in them. "Not since I left New York," she answered truthfully.

He was sitting casually, one leg crossed over the other. He seemed almost friendly, approachable, until he said next, in his soft voice that hid so very much, "Will Lyonhouse be overrun by nosy, obnoxious reporters from here on out?"

She understood only too well. Notoriety carried few advantages, and many liabilities. She knew from unhappy experience that Reid was probably reassigning her worth downward, and he was most likely rethinking his decision to hire her as well.

The palms of her hands became slick with perspiration as he gazed at her impassively. It was not her fault Aninger had showed up today, but she felt shamed just the same.

But she had built some defenses over the past years. Cool intelligence was her sword, and self-possession her shield. She would use these weapons now, and fight for what she knew was hers. Reid need never know how lost she really felt, nor how helpless.

"I sincerely hope there will not be a recurrence of what happened today," she said quietly, holding his eyes with her own. "However, since part of Lyonhouse's function is to serve as a model to the state, a little extra publicity certainly won't hurt us, if we handle it correctly. While I didn't seek to be singled out, the deed is accomplished, and cannot be undone. I suggest that we use my name to the advantage of Lyonhouse. Celebrities make good newsprint, and, for whatever reason, people are interested in what the rich and famous have to say." She paused, took a breath. "I think I can be lucid enough to say something of value, and I can probably play the part of a celebrity for three months."

She was sure she had spoken evenly, with no hint of weakness or defiance, so she was unprepared when Reid said with equal gravity, "You're over there shaking in your shoes, aren't you, Diana?"

Tears sprung thick and heavy into her eyes, and she blinked furiously. Refusing to bow her head, she faced him proudly. "Wouldn't you be?" she asked, not hiding her anger now. "It seems every time I turn around I'm fighting for this job. But whatever I do or say damns me in your eyes, Reid Hudson.''

"Not everything," he said. "Not all." He gazed at her then, until his eyes grew smoky and her breath caught at the message she read there. She sat absolutely still, not daring to breathe, not daring to move, just waiting...waiting...

Until he shook his head and passed a hand over his eyes. When he looked at her again, his expression was once more grimly expressionless.

"You had some questions?" he said.

She discovered her hands were shaking imperceptibly. For a moment she stared at the opened folder in front of her, the words on the page strangely blurred.

Finally, in a voice she barely recognized as being her own, she managed, "Has Jamie ever attended day care before, or preschool of any kind?"

"No." He paused. "At least, I don't think so."

She looked at him questioningly.

Reid shifted defensively. "His mother took care of those things."

Diana looked down, assimilating the strangeness of his answer. What kind of man was this, to take so little interest in the day-to-day activities of his only child? Hadn't he and his wife ever *talked,* for heaven's sake?

"Well, then," she said. "Maybe you could help me with some other basic information. Jamie's birthday is...?"

Reid looked at her blankly, a sudden chagrined helplessness appearing in his eyes. "I'm afraid I have forgotten."

Diana no longer tried to hide her surprise. "Perhaps Jamie knows." She smiled down at the boy. "Do you know when your birthday is, Jamie?"

The child shook his head.

Without looking again at Reid, Diana said, "Have you ever had a birthday, Jamie? A party? Presents?"

Again the boy shook his head.

She raised disbelieving eyes to silently question Reid, but he was looking out the window blankly. His body had gone rigid, and his hands were curled tightly around his chair arms.

She refocused her attention on Jamie. "Well, how about some other information. Do you have a favorite color, Jamie?"

This time the little head nodded.

"Can you tell me what it is?"

Jamie rose, looking around as he did so. Her office was done in soft roses and pale greens. Jamie walked first to one wall, searching the pictures she had placed there. Not finding what he wanted, he walked to the opposite wall, where Diana had hung an impressionistic picture of a bouquet of spring flowers. Jamie pointed to the vase.

"Blue?" Diana said gently.

Jamie nodded.

"Can you say the word, Jamie?" Diana asked then. "Can you tell me the name of the color?"

Jamie looked at her, his eyes filled with humiliation and fear. He moved closer to his father, reaching out to touch Reid's knee in a tentative gesture of need.

"Reid? What's going on?"

Reid gazed first at his son, then at Diana. His voice, when he spoke, was absolutely devoid of feeling. "Jamie has given up talking for a while," he said.

So. This beautiful, perfect child could not speak. And Reid had not told her, had not given her even a hint of warning. Her immediate compassionate response changed to a swiftly flowering anger, as she remembered Reid's apparent lack of involvement in his son's life. She waited with forced patience for Reid to offer a more complete explanation. When he did not, she said at last, simply, "Oh?"

He stood abruptly. "Give me the forms," he said bleakly. "I'll fill them out and send them to you later."

Standing also, she removed the office papers from Jamie's folder and handed them to Reid. "We need to talk," she said urgently.

"Some other time," Reid evaded. Then, "Come," to Jamie. With graceful obedience the boy rose from the position he had resumed upon the floor. Reid turned and walked toward the door, Jamie following him. They were just about out of her office when Diana said impulsively, "Jamie."

Reid paused, irritation flashing across his features. Jamie turned to look at her inquiringly.

"I was glad to meet you, Jamie. I'll see you Monday morning."

For a moment the boy stood still, gravely staring into Diana's eyes. Then he nodded, very briefly, before turning to follow his father once more.

Saturday morning the Lansing paper's front-page headline read: Local Day Care Center Headed By New York Heiress. With a sinking heart, Diana read the brief synopsis of her background and parentage. It was small consolation that the reporter had included a reasonable synopsis of the actual Lyonhouse tour, ending with a description of the scene Michael Aninger had caused.

"'All children need a safe place to play and grow,' Miss Rowe said, 'and they need to feel important and loved.' What all of us saw at the conclusion of her interview was a desecration of those ideals. Writing for this reporter only, I was more than ever aware of the excesses of my own profession, and I was ashamed. Kudos to Miss Rowe, who handled an ugly situation with poise, maturity and grace."

She only hoped the other reporters had been as kind.

By midmorning, Diana's phone began ringing with requests for interviews. She knew that just as a stone once rolling down a hillside does not stop until it reaches bottom, so the press would not quit until satisfied. As she told Reid Hudson, she would use the resulting publicity as well as she could to benefit Lyonhouse.

That afternoon she was back at the Center, repeating the tour to a much larger group of reporters, deflecting their personal questions as much as possible, returning time and time again to the subject at hand: day care. "I am not the star," she said, several times. "This building is. The children who will be here are. The everyday, ordinary people who will work here are the real stars. Interview them." The reporters nodded, sometimes smiled, and then asked Diana who her current boyfriend was.

Later that evening a national television network carried the story about heiress Diana Rowe working as the director of a day care center in Michigan. Twice the title was used: "America's Day Care Princess." The assumption was clear, if unstated: Wealthy Diana Rowe was playing at a favorite cause. Pictures were shown of Diana in her younger days, playing in other ways.

Sunday morning her father called. So great was her surprise, it was all she could do to hold on to the phone.

"I saw you on the tube," he said, without introduction, ignoring the four years' silence between them.

"Oh? How'd I look?" she asked at last, lightly.

"Four years older."

She didn't know what to say. In her entire life, she could count on one hand the number of times her father had actually called her.

"Surely you aren't serious about that day care thing?"

Reid Hudson had said much the same thing. She closed her eyes against the sudden pain his words caused.

"Diana?"

His voice was sharper now, and something in the inflection of his tone as he said her name told her what she needed to know. Gregory Rowe was furiously angry.

"Yes, Daddy?"

"What do you mean, making a spectacle of yourself like that? Your mother was quite humiliated."

"Oh? Why was that?"

His voice grew harder. "Who are all those people who send their kids to that place, anyway? They're nobodies, Diana. They're not worth your time or your effort."

Her fingers tightened around the telephone. "That's for me to decide, I guess," she said quietly. "It's my life."

"Diana..." Her father's voice was coldly authoritative. She could hear the old arrogance in it, the implacability that insisted upon immediate obedience. "There's a ticket to New York waiting for you at the airport. The plane leaves tomorrow morning. I expect you to be on it."

She took a deep breath. "I hate New York," she said.

"Diana..."

"Why don't you come out here, Daddy? To Lansing? Why don't you come and see what I'm doing?"

"How can I do that? You know the schedule I keep. Besides, you're making a damn fool of yourself out there."

"Are you ashamed of me?"

The silence on the other end of the phone was all the answer she needed. She had not spoken to her father for over four years, and now he was playing the same old games with her. She was filled with a nameless urgency, an insistent longing for something that had never been, could never be.

"I'm not going to quit, Daddy. I'm not going to come back to New York. But you feel free to drop in here, anytime. *You* can come see *me,* this time. When I'm important enough, you'll make time."

"Don't you be giving me ultimatums..."

"Goodbye, Daddy."

She hung up the phone slowly, and returned to her work. It was not until much later that she realized what had happened. She had spoken to her father, and had not once raised her voice in anger or, on the other hand, begged him to show attention to her in any way. Neither had she frozen up, until she felt cold and stiff and absolutely alone. She had simply hung up the phone, and gone on working.

Well, she thought, feeling the flowering of something warm and proud inside of her. *Well. Maybe I'm capable of being something of my own, after all. Maybe there will yet come a time that I can say "My name is Diana Rowe," and feel nothing but pleasure in it.*

The power of the peace that followed was unlike anything she had ever known, and stayed with her through the rest of the day, until she closed her eyes that night and drifted into a calm and restful slumber.

The next morning, Lyonhouse opened its doors.

Chapter Five

Monday morning dawned clear and gorgeously radiant. Diana awoke early, a keen sense of anticipation singing through her veins. This was it, then. In spite of Reid Hudson, in spite of Gregory Rowe, in spite of *everything,* Lyonhouse was opening today, and she—Diana Rowe—was in charge.

She drove into the Lyonhouse parking lot, aware more than anything else of an immense feeling of pride. Lyonhouse was hers, from its inception to its actualization. Her vision. Her dream. Her accomplishment.

She had dressed carefully for this opening day—wearing a practical but attractive red flared skirt, topped with a red-and-white striped oxford shirt. Her low pumps could easily be exchanged later on for flat sandals.

She knew she didn't look like an heiress—in fact, she had deliberately underdressed. She meant to be taken seriously.

And she meant to show Reid Hudson that he had not made a mistake in giving her this chance.

Nancy Cook drove up while Diana was still unlocking the doors. Diana had hired Nancy as her assistant director, choosing the matronly woman over several younger applicants with better academic credentials. She had liked Nancy's down-to-earth personality immediately, and she had trusted Nancy's fifteen years in home day care to give her the experience and wisdom that she herself might lack.

"Hi, there!" Nancy greeted her smilingly. "All set to start?"

"Think so." Diana wrinkled her nose engagingly. "At least I know *your* details are all taken care of."

Nancy's smiled faded slightly. "I saw you on TV the other night."

Diana paused and met the older woman's eyes. She could read nothing there but friendliness and calm acceptance. She nodded in rueful understanding. "Stupid boob tube," she said lightly. "Reporting all sorts of unimportant things." Then she added seriously, "Does it really make any difference, Nancy? Me being who I am?"

"It will to some people, and that's a fact. But I made up my mind about you the first day we met, and I'm not about to change it now. You're quality, through and through."

The simply stated compliment unnerved Diana momentarily. Then, as Nancy's words sank in, she felt a sudden hopeful lightness, a wonderful buoyancy. "Thank you for that," she said, grinning broadly. Impetuously she gave Nancy a warm hug. "It's going to be a wonderful day!"

An hour later Diana's opinion had not changed. It was almost seven-thirty; the Center had been open for thirty minutes. Several children had already arrived. Most, however, would come during the next half hour—just in time for their parents to punch in at eight o'clock.

"I'm so grateful to have my Anna close by while I'm working," a smiling mother was saying to Diana. "I've felt so guilty having her so far away. This center is an answer to my prayers."

"That's why Tom Lyon and Heritage House built Lyonhouse," Diana replied. "For working parents, like yourself. Please feel free to drop in during your lunch hour or breaks."

"You really don't mind?"

"On the contrary, we encourage parental involvement. Children have a sense of security when they know Mom or Dad is close by."

"I don't think I'd want to come over during the day," another mother commented nervously. "Chuckie cries like crazy whenever I leave him."

Chuckie was clinging to his mother now, his hands tight around her neck.

"He'll discover that when you leave, you'll also come back. Chuckie will learn to feel comfortable with that. Besides, believe it or not, the tears never last long."

Another mother said, almost timidly, "Are you really Gregory Rowe's daughter?"

Diana's smile didn't falter. "I'm afraid so. I hope that doesn't offend anyone?"

Anna's mother said firmly, "I think it's wonderful, you working here. I don't understand it, but I think it's wonderful just the same."

"Thank you," Diana said simply. Everything was going to be all right. Everything, she told herself, was going to be great.

She turned to see Reid Hudson standing just inside the doorway, his son Jamie in his arms.

"Hello there," she said softly, the warm friendliness in her voice surprising herself as much as it probably did Reid.

She watched his eyes narrow speculatively. "Did you bring the forms?" she queried hastily.

"Yes."

Maintaining her confident tone, she instructed him, "You know where Jamie is supposed to be. Why don't you take him there, and stop by my office on your way out?"

"All right. Though I won't be able to stay—I'm running late."

"This won't take long," she replied evenly.

Reid returned a short time later, and Diana led him into her office. He refused the chair she offered, and leaned instead against her doorjamb. His dark handsomeness was in direct contrast to her soft, feminine office; her pastel walls provided an unfortunate comparison to his lean form. He looked predatory, coiled, ready to spring. Totally male.

He took his time looking at her as she stood beside her desk, his gaze traveling from her carefully groomed head to her plainly shod feet. She fought to keep her response to his wordless communication invisible, but her confidence was already beginning to slip precariously.

"Did Jamie go to his group all right?" She knew relief that her voice was totally professional.

"Yes."

"He seems like a very obedient little boy."

Reid's expression darkened, and annoyance sparked from his eyes. "Compliant might be a better word," he said flatly.

His eyes were still taking deliberate inventory of her features. She fought the urge to turn from him, and willed the uncertainty from her eyes. "You do have the forms, I presume."

"Of course."

"Complete with birthday, and so forth?" She could not keep the challenge from her voice.

He stiffened, then pushed himself away from the jamb with his foot. "Don't needle me, Diana," he said softly. "I'm bigger than you are."

She looked down at her desk. "I'm sure I don't know what you mean."

"Don't lie, either." He walked with the grace of a panther to her desk, and dropped the registration papers on the exact spot to which her eyes were glued. "There they are," he murmured. "As requested."

She continued to avert her gaze. What was wrong with her anyway? Reid's voice was seductively persuasive, completely at odds with the tension she felt emanating from his tall figure. Unwillingly she felt her own response to the suggestive sensuality she heard in his tone. Her cheeks grew warm, and she was thrown totally off balance. "Thank you," she said, lifting the papers from her desk.

"You seemed to be handling everything quite well, out there." His voice had changed. If anything, he sounded slightly surprised.

Her head came up, and her eyes blazed at him proudly. "Did you think otherwise?"

But his face shuttered against her, and he shrugged insolently. "I don't know as I think about you very much at all, Diana," he drawled.

Something in her snapped. He was playing some cat-and-mouse game with her, and it was ruining her confidence and her morning. "I never thought you did," she bit out.

He continued to watch her closely, so that she felt herself becoming embarrassingly intimidated. Only the expanse of her desk separated them. He was taller than she by a good six inches, so that she was forced to tilt her head to meet his eyes. She became aware that his hands, held easily at his side, were not completely relaxed, that his smile was not mirrored in his eyes.

She remembered the impression of hidden anger she had gained the day he interviewed her. She remembered that he still didn't trust her, or even like her. But that didn't mean she had to be his whipping boy, or passively accept his male domination. She stood quietly, feeling with a sense of relief her own natural assertiveness seep back into her system, before she said with only a hint of defiance in her tone, "Talk to me about Jamie."

She sensed rather than saw his hands clench at his side. "What do you want to know?"

She stared at him in disbelief. If she had understood anything about Reid, it was his total possessiveness about what belonged to him. Four years ago he had gone to great lengths to protect his little sister. Most recently, during the Heritage House merger, he had personally come to oversee operations. Even if he didn't love Jamie, she would have expected him to feel that same sense of possession. That he obviously did not lent strength to an outrage that was growing by the second. "Tell me about him. Why isn't he talking? What can we do to help?"

"He isn't talking because he chooses not to. And there is nothing you can do to help."

"I don't believe that. What happened to him anyway? What's going on, Reid?"

His expression grew fiercely controlled, before he said with cool precision, "He hasn't talked since his mother's accident."

Diana felt as if she had just received a blow to her stomach. *Of course.* Jamie had lived when Cynthia had died. Even though Cynthia had not been kind to Lucy, Reid had probably loved his wife. Very much. And if he was denying his own grief, it was only natural he would find it terribly difficult to assume sole parenting of their son, especially if he had left most of that responsibility to his wife. Which he obviously had.

"I assume you've had him examined?" she asked huskily, trying to ignore the irrational stab of jealousy she felt toward the dead Cynthia. But she couldn't help but wonder what it would be like to be loved by Reid Hudson.

"Jamie's been examined by three different specialists. Nothing is physically wrong with him. I'm told he's in the throes of posttraumatic reaction."

"You sound as if you're having a hard time believing that."

"I believe it," he said. "Why should I not?" But the emptiness was back in his eyes, and beyond that, some bleak unhappiness.

"But you haven't answered my other question. Surely there is something we can do to help?"

"The theory is that if Jamie is around other children his same age, and as time passes and the memory of the accident grows more dim, one day he will just start talking again."

At that moment Diana had to fight the urge to reach out to him in comfort. "I see," she said instead.

"So simply treat him like you do everyone else."

"Of course."

His eyes widened slightly, as if seeing for the first time the depth of her compassion. "Diana," he said.

"Yes?"

"Don't get too involved. Let nature take its course. Don't make Jamie your pet project, or anything like that."

She stared at him, startled. "You don't want me to try to help Jamie?"

"I didn't say that. Just don't forget that you're leaving in three months. It would only hurt Jamie if he formed a lasting attachment for you. He's just lost his mother. Don't let him make you a surrogate."

It was the first time all morning Diana had thought about her limited stay at Lyonhouse. She was infinitely sorry that

Reid had mentioned it now. "Of course," she said coolly, trying desperately to hide the disappointment and resentment that flooded her at his rejecting words. Her chin came up. "You're right. I'll be leaving in three months, and it would be a terrible thing if Jamie learned to love me."

Ignoring any hidden sarcasm in her agreement, Reid added, "Good. Just so you understand."

She had sunk to her chair, her hands held against her stomach. "I understand perfectly, Reid," she said tightly, unaware that she was speaking through clenched teeth.

He looked at her, taking in her hurt and anger. "I'm not trying to be cruel, you know," he said evenly. "Just realistic."

"Fine," she said with determined brightness. "And I'm sure when I think about it I'll appreciate your...realism."

"If you don't need anything else, I really am late...."

"Goodbye, Reid," she said firmly, unbearably anxious for him to be gone.

His gaze encompassed her one more time, before he shrugged slightly, and turned on his heel and left.

After that, Diana never quite regained her sense of euphoric well-being. It was not fair that she was only going to be at Lyonhouse three months. It was not fair that little Jamie Hudson couldn't talk, and that his father couldn't love him, either. It was not fair that Reid was still grieving for his wife.

Still, the first day passed with no major problems. Diana was in another part of the building when Reid stopped to get Jamie that first afternoon. In the days that followed, she managed to avoid Reid most assiduously, which was not hard to do, since his times at Lyonhouse were limited to the minimum necessary to drop Jamie off, and pick him up again.

Jamie himself moved like a silent shadow through Lyon-house, barely participating in the games, often not responding when someone spoke to him.

In spite of her initial anger at Reid's words, Diana took his warning to heart. It would be unnecessarily cruel to form an attachment with the boy. While she was as friendly with Jamie as she was with all the children, she never went out of her way to treat him any differently than she did everyone else. She did, however, share what she knew of his history with her staff. She was relieved when Nancy Cook took a special interest, and spent time every day with the boy, even though he didn't seem to be responding to her efforts. Others tried to draw him out, but Jamie was not to be drawn.

One morning Diana was on the playground, watching pleasurably as the children played their games, when she sensed a movement at her side. Looking down, she was amazed to see Jamie Hudson standing close to her. He wasn't looking at her, and she thought his presence might actually be quite accidental. Except Jamie never voluntarily went close to anyone.

Unthinkingly she reached down to brush her hand against his beautiful hair, only to stiffen in amazement as his head leaned into her palm.

He wanted to be touched.

Without stopping to consider her actions, Diana knelt down beside the boy. He was dressed simply in pull-on pants and a brightly printed T-shirt. "Jamie?" she said questioningly.

His eyes flickered away nervously. She said the first thing that came into her head. "Would you like me to push you on the swing?"

He made no verbal response, but his small body grew immediately tense, a posture that Diana was at a loss to interpret. Did he want to swing? Did he want to be left alone?

Standing slowly, Diana reached down and took his hand in hers and headed toward the swing set. Docilely Jamie followed. She placed him in the buckled seat, then took her place behind him and gently began to push. She held her breath as she waited for a reaction. Surely he would let her know by some sign what he was feeling—joy, release, fear.

But Jamie did not. He sat holding on to the strips of chain supporting the seat, and made no sound.

Diana pushed him for a long time. When she stopped, she lifted him out carefully, holding him against her breast a little longer than necessary. "If you liked that, Jamie, and want to do it again, you will have to come and tell me. You will have to let me know somehow." But his eyes had not changed, and he stared at her blankly. Feeling frustrated and illogically angry, she returned to her office.

In the days that followed, Jamie never asked by word or movement to be pushed on the swing again, nor showed by any sign that he even remembered the experience. But it soon became apparent that wherever Diana was, Jamie would be with her if he could. If she was speaking with someone, he would stand quietly by, a silent ghost at her side. On the playground he would seek her out, and when he passed the office doors, his rich brown eyes would peer inside as he tried to get a glimpse of Diana. The staff began to refer to the boy as Diana's shadow.

But he never tried to touch her or communicate with her in any way. He never asked for attention of any kind. It was as if Diana represented some security for him, yet he never expected her to react to him at all.

And she tried not to react. She was going to be gone when the three months were over. She didn't want her parting to be one further wounding of an already wounded child.

But she found herself touching him more often than she should. And looking for him, to see if he was near. And thinking of him at night, wondering what was going on in the silence of Jamie's world.

Until finally Diana resigned herself to that fact that whether Reid was pleased or not, whether it was good or not, she had become Jamie's special friend.

Chapter Six

Lyonhouse was a beehive of activity. Enrollment, which had been at sixty-three on opening day, had grown in the two weeks since to seventy-five children. Diana thought in another two months the Center was likely to be operating at full capacity.

It was a cloudless summer day, and many of the children had found their way outside to the large, fenced playground.

Diana, dressed in neat jeans and a simple blouse, was taking a few minutes off from her administrative duties to help build castles in the sandbox. Jamie Hudson was sitting on Diana's left. Today the little redheaded boy was dressed in designer coveralls. He sat on the wooden frame of the sandbox, his hands in his lap, his face completely blank. Every once in a while Diana would reach over and give his hand a squeeze, hoping desperately that he would squeeze back. But he never did.

Anna Esterline, a four-year-old blond with a round face spattered with freckles, was on her right. Anna had just made a present of a shovel full of sand, dumping it at Diana's feet. Diana looked at the girl and smiled her thanks, before sitting back on her heels.

Usually she spent a good part of her day in her office, but today she was involving herself with the children as much as she could. She knew the reason for her behavior, although she was trying hard not to think about it too much. But ever since she had awakened this morning, she knew today was going to be a particularly trying one.

Today would have been Phillip's birthday.

At the swing set, a young mother on coffee break was pushing her son. Smiling slightly, Diana watched the hypnotic motion: back and forth went the swing, the little boy laughing with glee.

As she watched, the figures metamorphosed in front of her eyes. The mother became an eleven-year-old girl, the young boy someone quite different.

Push me on the swing, Di-Di. Push me please.
How high do you want to go, Phillip? How high?
As high as the sun. Can you push me that high, Di-ana?

Diana closed her eyes and shook her head, trying with all her might to shut the picture out, just as she had done with a hundred other memories this morning. She felt the edge of the Lyonhouse sandbox under her thighs, the sun warm upon her back. She reached down and grabbed a handful of sand, letting it sift itself through her fingers.

Phillip was dead. Had been for almost six years. Other people died, even she would die sometime. Why couldn't she let go?

Where did you get that dog, Phillip?

I found it by the road. Someone has thrown it away Diana. It's hurt. I want to help it get well.

You know you'll never be allowed to keep a mongrel, Phillip.

I'll hide it, then. Mother and Father and Horrible Pat won't find out. Please don't tell anyone, Di.

All right. It will be our secret. What will you name it?

It's a he. And I'm going to call him Odysseus.

He really is an ugly dog.

Odysseus and Horrible Pat. She had helped Phillip protect the one, and protected him from the other. But, she told herself fiercely, it's all done now, only memories. She turned to little Anna and began to help the girl with her sand cooking.

A shadow fell over Diana, and she looked up to see Nancy Cook staring down at her worriedly. "We have a problem," Nancy said. "You'd better come with me."

Dusting off her pants, Diana stood. "Don't tell me there's anything you can't handle, Nancy." But Nancy didn't even smile, as she said, "Only you can handle this one, Diana. Come right away."

The older woman did not speak again until they were back in the building. Then, looking deeply disturbed, she grasped Diana's hand.

"It's a three-year-old," Nancy said with quiet intensity. "Sarah Davidson. She's been acting strangely all morning—almost catatonic. Marcella was concerned that Sarah was ill, or becoming so. Then she touched the child's back, and the girl started to cry." Nancy paused, before continuing with unnatural evenness. "Sarah's back is full of welts, Diana. In some places the skin has been torn. Somebody beat that child last night."

Diana's abdomen wrenched painfully. "Where is she?"

"I took her to the nurse's station and had her lie down on her stomach. Sandy Buxted is with her now."

"Let's go then."

"I think we're going to have to call the police, Diana."

By this time Diana and Nancy were moving with swift urgency through the hall, and it was only seconds later that they arrived at the nurse's station.

The nurse's station was actually a small cubicle of a room, large enough to hold a sink, first-aid supplies and two cots. On the cot closest to the door a small figure lay huddled with her knees curled up to her chest, her back to the door.

The child had been dressed in a long-sleeved red turtle-neck sweater—in spite of the balmy weather—and long pants. Someone had pulled the sweater up to the tiny neck, so that Sarah's back was revealed to all. Diana took one look before coming to an absolute standstill, her hand reaching out to grip the door edge.

"Dear God."

Little Sarah Davidson's back was crisscrossed with fierce red welts. The skin had been cut in several places, and where blood was still oozing out, threads and lint from her sweater clung to her sticky body. Sarah was weeping quietly.

Diana's hands curled in on themselves. Her eyes met those of Sandy Buxted, the Lyonhouse nurse. "Have you taken her temperature?"

"It's not too high—just a degree or two."

"Has she said anything?"

Sandy shook her head, her eyes mirroring the distress that must surely be on Diana's face also. "I think she's in shock, Diana. Marcella said she'd been quiet all day."

Blessed numbness settled on Diana, so that she was able to kneel beside Sarah's cot without flinching. "Sarah," she said. The girl's eyes were cloudy, wandering aimlessly, and Diana wondered fleetingly what Sarah was thinking.

"Sarah," she said again, watching as Sarah slowly met her gaze.

As Sarah's eyes slowly focused on hers, Diana sucked in a jagged breath. Unbelievably, there was shame in the girl's eyes, and beneath that, stark terror.

Keeping her voice steady and reassuring, Diana continued, "You must have been very hot in those heavy clothes. I'm going to take off your pants now so you can be more comfortable."

The child offered no resistance as Diana gently removed her slacks. Diana's breath was in her throat as more marks were revealed on the upper thighs.

"Sorry, baby," she crooned, when Sarah flinched. "I'm so sorry." The little body began to shiver helplessly.

Diana covered the small, defenseless form with a sheet. Tears were falling soundlessly from Sandy Buxted's eyes. Diana turned to see Nancy Cook watching her, her expression troubled.

"You two stay here," Diana said. "I'll go make the necessary calls."

Blindly she traversed the short space to her own office. Without knowing what she was doing, she shut the door behind her. Her hands were shaking so badly she could hardly push the buttons on her phone. But she managed. She did what was required by law: she called the police, she called protective services, and last of all, she called Heritage House administration. Company policy dictated that management be notified whenever the police were summoned on Heritage House property. She put the call through directly to Reid's office.

"Reid's in conference," his secretary, Penny, told her. "He can't be disturbed."

She explained to Penny what had happened, and hung up. She sat at her desk, trembling slightly, staring blindly out the window. Her throat had swelled chokingly, and she felt her heart pounding fast and hard within her chest.

She would never forget this moment, this time. The sight of that bloody, bruised little back was burned forever in her memory. *That poor little girl,* she thought. *That poor child.*

What kind of monster was capable of doing a thing like that to a defenseless creature? She closed her eyes, trying to visualize the hand that raised itself against a child, but she knew that whoever had done this terrible thing would most probably look normal—just an everyday type of person. She thought of Sarah's mother—an attractive woman in her late twenties, and of Sarah's father, a jovial man who always had his hand out in friendship. Surely neither of them had been responsible for this brutality.

But someone had sent Sarah to Lyonhouse today. Someone had dressed her, covering those quivering wounds with rough fabric. Someone had...

She stood, intending to rejoin Sandy Buxted and Nancy Cook. But as she walked to her door she felt her own intense trembling, and realized her breath was coming in great, ragged gulps. She knew she had to calm herself. She was the director—she was the one who needed to react the most calmly. But every time she blinked she saw again the wounded innocence lying in that small bed. She saw Sarah's baby-blue eyes—so full of shame and guilt. How dare anyone put those things in that child's eyes? How dare they?

Things like this happen, she told herself sternly. This is the risk of the profession you have chosen. Lyonhouse is not exempt from the real world.

Yes, things like this happened, but never to anyone that she knew, never to one of her own, as she felt all these children belonged to her. She beat her fist into her open palm, as heavy shadows of helplessness and rage swept over her.

Who would beat a defenseless child?

She returned to the nurse's station, and looked in only briefly. "Help is on the way," she told Sandy and Nancy. Sarah appeared to be sleeping on her cot. "I'll wait for the police out front." Then she hurried away, averting her eyes lest the other two women read the truth there.

She did not *want* to stay in that room, to see again the evidence of her eyes, to feel once more the burning bitter knowledge of man's capacity to injure, to desecrate that which was most sacred, most pure, most full of hope. That child was only a toddler, yet already Sarah Davidson was ancient in her experience of evil.

She remembered something Tilly had told her in a long-ago conversation.

"It's all a part of the human condition, Diana," Tilly had said. "As long as man exists, there will be cruelty of all sorts: wars and rumors of wars, stealing and bribery, brutality of every variety. There will even be—" Tilly had eyed Diana carefully "—parents who don't love their children, who have no natural bonding with their offspring. There will be fathers who put down their daughters, and mothers who emasculate their sons. You, too, Diana, are part of the human condition. The sooner you assimilate that into your vast storehouse of knowledge, the better prepared you will be to make your own contribution."

It was a fine explanation, but somehow Tilly's words fell short when Diana was faced with the reality of Sarah Davidson. For this terrible sacrilege there were no words, no calm interpretation. There was only pain, and sorrow, and a great, powerless fury. *If this is the human condition,* Diana thought with hopeless despair, *I want no part of it.*

Thus Diana stood outside the Lyonhouse doors, waiting for help to come.

Reid glanced at his watch. The morning conference meeting had run late, and everyone had exited quickly to return to their own individual assignments. Only Mark Lyon was lingering.

Reid stifled a sigh. Much as he tried, he could not warm toward Tom Lyon's son.

"There is one other thing I wanted to mention to you privately," Mark said, almost lazily.

"Yes?"

"It has to do with that day care center and all the publicity. I think it's gotten out of hand, don't you?"

Reid leaned back in his chair, eyeing the other man. "What do you mean?"

"Surely you've noticed. Every day, something new appears in the paper, or on television. Even on the radio, believe it or not. My secretary told me a national news broadcast did a segment on socialite Diana Rowe just last night."

"So?"

"We've developed a three-ring circus over there."

Reid clasped his hands behind his head. "I saw the segment last night, and I thought the reporter did a very nice job reviewing the challenges of day care nationwide. And Diana spoke intelligently and professionally. The points she made were salient and timely."

"You don't think all this publicity is bad, then," Mark said flatly.

"So far I don't. After all, part of Lyonhouse's mission is to be the object of publicity. We might as well enjoy it while it lasts. And as a not unimportant serendipity, Heritage House is receiving some quality advertising—all of it free."

Reid looked at Mark as he spoke, and saw the anger and resentment flash in the blond man's eyes before he nodded in apparent easy agreement.

Mark Lyon continually amazed him. Lyonhouse had become Mark's own personal albatross, and several times the man had made negative comments about the Center or its director, Diana Rowe. That a man of Mark's position and responsibility should continue to bear a grudge against a program and the people in it, simply because the original decision had not gone his way, was almost unbelievable to Reid. And yet he was not so obtuse that he could not recognize his own personal irony: Whenever he defended Lyonhouse he defended Diana Rowe also.

And why not? She was doing an excellent job. She was professional, organized and got along well with all the people who worked at and used Lyonhouse. She was, in fact, one of the best managers he had ever seen.

And only twenty-four years old. He smiled slightly, remembering the way she had announced her age to everyone in the conference room, then waited with calm defiance for someone to say she was too young. Which he had done, of course. She was too young, and too inexperienced, and altogether too beautiful. And doing an excellent job.

A few minutes later Mark had gone, and Reid sat at his desk, his thoughts still with Diana. He was thinking about her far too much, but what red-blooded man wouldn't think of Diana Rowe? He thought of her long, smooth legs, of the graceful way she had of turning even the slightest motion into a dance of seductively fluid movement.

But she was Diana Rowe, for heaven's sake. He had her thoroughly investigated, four years ago, and the detective's findings had been appalling. She had more proposals of marriage than years of her life, and—if the report were to be believed—the dishonorable proposals were even more numerous. She had spent time with some of the world's most notorious playboys. Her picture had appeared frequently in glossy, gossipy magazines. She had appeared to have had the morals of an alley cat, and her habits hadn't seemed much better.

She had seemed, he sneered to himself, just like his dearly beloved Cynthia.

The thought was a stone around his heart. He had made a fool of himself over one woman; he would not do so again. But that didn't stop him from admitting that with every passing day he was becoming more obsessed with Diana Rowe.

He remembered the day he and Jamie had stumbled into her first press session, and Michael Aninger had caused such problems. He remembered Diana facing that small group of reporters, telling them what to write about. *The story of the century,* she had told them. He recalled again the way her eyes had blazed, proud and fiery as any true believer. He thought of how straight and still she had stood, reminding him of a soldier in some kind of holy war. He heard again her voice, low and passionate and angry, daring them all to question the justness of her cause.

She had been magnificent.

Almost he wished he had never met Diana Rowe until that exact moment. Almost he wished to erase from his mind forever his too complete knowledge of her unsavory past.

I wasn't in hiding. I was healing, that's all, Lucy. I was trying to change.

Maybe she had changed. It took courage to make a statement like that.

He found himself wanting…wanting what? A woman he could trust? A woman he could admire and respect? A woman who could make him whole?

Soundlessly he laughed at himself, but the feeling wouldn't go away.

He wanted Diana Rowe.

"Mr. Hudson?" Penny, his secretary, pushed open his door without knocking. Not waiting for him to respond, she rushed on, "There's some sort of emergency over at the Center. There's a child who has been beaten, probably by a parent, and Miss Rowe has called the police. She wanted me to let you know. Is there anyone you would like to send over?''

For a moment Reid stared at Penny blankly. Then he gave a short barking laugh. "I'll go myself," he said.

He was tired of avoiding Diana, as if he were some callow schoolboy terrified of her brightness. He was tired of chasing images of her graceful body from his brain. He was tired of dreaming strange yearning dreams at night.

He was tired of denying what he wanted most.

He wanted Diana.

Chapter Seven

Diana strode forward to meet the policeman when he arrived. He introduced himself as Edward Cosgrove. He was big, black, and carried both a gun and a stick. She put her hand on his arm. "Please," she said. "Protective Services is not yet here. Let's wait for a moment." Then she added, wanting to shield Sarah Davidson from any additional trauma, "Many children are frightened by uniforms and guns. This is going to be difficult enough already."

The big man chuckled, and the sound rolled like music in his chest. "I sure understand," he said, "but I'm as soft as a teddy bear."

Diana heard the words gratefully, but she was unable to relax. She felt tightly strung, almost suffocated. Still, she was relieved that the officer seemed so understanding. She doubted if this large man were as soft as he said, but his ability to say so reassured her. He would know better than to frighten an already damaged child.

Linda Jarvis from Protective Services arrived a few minutes later. "Hello, Edward," she greeted the policeman easily. She turned to Diana. "And you are Diana Rowe," she said, smiling. "I've been hearing about you in the news."

For once Diana felt no inner cringing at the open reference to the many reports about herself and her place at Lyonhouse. Who she was and what she represented had become suddenly, totally insignificant, overshadowed by the meaningless cruelty of a single, savage human act.

"Someone from Heritage House Administration has to be here, too," Diana said, wondering that it was taking the longest time for someone to arrive from the administrative building just a quarter of a mile away. But it was just seconds later that a car drove up, and Reid Hudson gave her one more shock by stepping out of it.

"I understand you've had trouble," he said, his eyes examining Diana carefully. She felt her trembling increase further.

She was not in control. The last person she wanted to see right now was Reid Hudson—she had never really thought he would come himself. She was terribly afraid she was about to lose any professional calm she ever had, and she didn't want him to see how much she had been affected by what was, after all, one of the hazards of her profession. Tearing her eyes from Reid's, she spoke directly to Linda.

"The little girl—Sarah—is at the nurse's station," Diana said, feeling totally incapable of returning Linda Jarvis's smile. "If you will come with me, please."

Sandy Buxted was standing by Sarah, rubbing the child's head gently. Diana stood aside so Linda could enter the small space. The policeman followed Linda, so that Diana was left standing in the background, with Reid at her side. She glanced at him warily, but for once his eyes were not focused on her at all. He was watching the scene unfolding before them.

Gently Linda Jarvis pulled back Sarah's covering sheet. Diana felt Reid go rigid beside her, as Sarah's body was once again revealed. The girl immediately started to whimper, and tried with little fluttering movements to pull the sheet back up. Linda stilled her with a single touch of her hand. For a moment she stood staring at the girl's back, then looked up to meet the police officer's eyes. "Have you seen enough to stand as witness?" she asked emotionlessly.

He nodded gravely. "I'll write it all down, so I won't forget," he said. With a weary resignation that told of other crimes at other times in other places, he asked, "You got a home to place this child in?"

Linda shrugged. "I'll find someplace." Then she knelt down so that her face was even with Sarah Davidson's.

"Sarah?"

The little girl looked at her.

"My name is Linda, Sarah. I would like to be your friend. I'd like to tell you about what I do. I have a very special job. Would you like to know what it is? My job is to help children who have been hurt, and to protect them—make sure they don't get hurt anymore." Linda paused. "Did someone hurt you, Sarah?"

The child said nothing, and Diana wondered at Linda's assumption that the girl would tell her anything at all.

"You know what it looks like to me, Sarah? It looks like you got spanked. You must have done something last night, huh? When I was little I got spanked sometimes. I got spanked when I stole something from the store, and I got spanked when I went to my friend's house without asking. Once my mother spanked me when I was playing in the street. Why did you get spanked, Sarah?"

Linda's litany must have reassured Sarah, for she responded, although her voice was too soft to be heard.

"*Why* did you get spanked, Sarah?" Linda asked again, her voice gentle but firm.

This time the timid voice was a little louder. "Spilled my milk."

Linda's eyes showed neither shock nor anger, only friendly sympathy. "Ah," she said. "Who spanked you, Sarah?"

"My daddy."

"Uh-huh. Now Sarah, I'm going to tell you something very, very important. Your daddy should not have spanked you as hard as he did. *Your daddy was wrong, Sarah.*"

Sandy Buxted was still rubbing Sarah's head. Diana and Reid were standing quietly in the doorway. Sarah Davidson continued to watch Linda's face, and Diana thought she could discern some small difference in the girl's features, some relaxing of tension.

She's only three years old, Diana thought. *How much can she possibly understand?*

Then, in the waiting stillness, Sarah spoke, her eyes locked with those of Linda Jarvis. "Daddy hurt me," she said, almost wonderingly.

Diana expelled her breath sharply—only then did she realize she had been holding it. She was conscious of Reid standing at her side. Somehow his arm had found its way around her waist, and when he pulled her close, she went unresisting.

"Yes, he did," Linda said. "That's why I'm going to take you with me, Sarah. I'm going to take you someplace where you will be safe." Then Linda smiled at Sarah, and Sarah smiled shyly back. "Yes, please," she whispered.

Everyone in the room seemed to relax as Linda stood. "I'm going to move this child by ambulance," she said to Diana. "We have no real way of knowing if she's sustained any internal injuries until she's been examined."

Sandy Buxted nodded her agreement. "I was going to suggest the same thing myself."

"I need to speak to you, Diana," Linda continued. "And Edward, can you stay for a moment? Mr. Hudson, perhaps you would like to join us?"

"We can talk in my office," Diana said, feeling an enormous sense of relief that Linda Jarvis was here, and so obviously knew exactly what to do. She led the small group to her office, conscious of the weight of Reid's arm still about her waist. Motioning for everyone to sit down, Diana pulled away from Reid to take her own chair at her desk. Linda took the chair closest to Diana's desk, but Edward Cosgrove and Reid remained standing. Reid's eyes rarely left Diana's face.

"Who usually picks Sarah up?" Linda asked calmly.

"The father," Diana answered, adding, "around five-thirty."

Linda turned to Officer Cosgrove. "Edward?"

"I'll come back then, just in case there's a problem," Edward Cosgrove replied.

"Thank you," Diana accepted gratefully.

"Do you know the father well?" Linda asked Diana.

"No. Sarah's mother came alone to the initial interview, but the father has been dropping Sarah off and picking her up. He's the one who works here at Heritage House. I think the mother works as a secretary downtown. But I've never had a real conversation with Mr. Davidson."

"He's one of our most trusted foremen," Reid said, speaking for the first time. "I've had several talks with him. I'm afraid I'm finding all this just a little hard to believe."

"Believe it," Linda Jarvis said flatly. "And I'm sure you're going to have a real conversation with Archie Davidson today, Diana. But having Edward here should help."

"Perhaps I should be here also," Reid said from where he was leaning against a wall.

"No," Linda said. "That's probably not necessary, and there's no reason to antagonize the man more than he will be already."

Nancy poked her head into the office. "Ambulance is here," she said succinctly.

"Good," Linda said, rising. "Just tell Mr. Davidson that I've taken Sarah, and give him my card. You don't have to make any accusations, or deal with him in any other way. Remember, Edward will be here to support you."

A stretcher was being brought in through the front door of Lyonhouse, and Linda Jarvis hurried away, Edward following.

Diana was left alone with Reid.

He studied her with slow deliberation, before he moved to shut her office door. "I'm going to lock this door for a moment," he murmured gravely. She heard the lock slide into place, before he turned to face her once more.

Outside, she was aware that the sun was shining brightly as usual. Inside, she could hear the noises of Lyonhouse—children's laughter, little feet running, a group of children somewhere singing a song.

Everything was the same, she told herself somewhat hazily. Nothing had changed.

Except that a blameless child had been made to suffer. Except that Diana was shaking again, quite uncontrollably. Except that Reid had stood with his arm around her, and was even now staying with her.

Everything had changed.

"Well," Reid said calmly. "That's something that doesn't happen every day."

"Thank God," Diana replied shakily.

"You're upset."

"Yes."

"Come here, then."

She looked at him out of shadowed eyes. She tried to remind herself that this was Reid Hudson, who scorned her.

"Come, Diana."

She closed her eyes, rising unsteadily. She knew what he was offering. She needed comfort, badly, and he was offering some. She thought again of Sarah Davidson, and slow tears began to wind their way down her cheeks.

He opened his arms. "Diana," he said.

She went mindlessly into him, and buried her head against his rocklike strength.

He wrapped his arms around her. She felt his fingers bury themselves in her hair. He shuddered slightly.

He was incredibly warm. She hadn't realized until that precise moment how cold she had felt. She burrowed against him, her tears wetting his shirtfront, her hands creeping around his waist. "Warm me," she said. "Please."

He stiffened at her words. One of his hands began a slow mesmerizing movement over her back. "I'll warm you."

Her trembling increased. She would have fallen if he had not been holding her. "She was hurt, and I couldn't help her! I couldn't fix her! I doubt if anyone will be able to fix her, ever again!"

Reid crooned to her quietly in understanding.

"How *dare* he?" she demanded furiously, her hands in fists at his back. "How dare he hurt his little girl like that?"

He had shifted his body against the wall, widening his stance as he did so. He pulled her against him, so that she was leaning into him between his legs.

"How about you, Diana? Were you hurt once?"

She went absolutely still in his arms.

"Tell me," he urged, shaking her a little.

She shook her head.

"Tell me."

"Not like that," she said at last, her voice very low. "I wasn't hurt like that."

"But you were hurt."

"Yes." He had to strain to hear the single word.

"And you're afraid that you will never be fixed, either, aren't you?"

A great shudder moved through her body, and he pulled her even closer. She couldn't seem to stop crying. Was what he said true? Was she afraid? Was something so wrong with her that it could never ever be fixed? From deep inside her most secret heart, a dark terror began to grow.

Unfixable.

"No!" she cried. "It's not true. What you say is a lie!"

"Shhh. Hush, Diana. Don't worry. Don't worry. Relax. You're safe here. I'll take care of you."

His tone of voice soothed her almost as much as his words did, and she gentled against him. For a long time she stayed there, unaware of anything except his voice speaking soft and low above her, and his hand moving up and down her back.

After a while, though, she began to notice other things. Reid was wearing a piney cologne—its scent tickled her nostrils. She could feel the skin of her cheek pressed against a button of his suit coat. His legs were practically wrapped around her own; there was more strength in them than she would have guessed. And his lips were speaking words of comfort against her temple. She could feel them move against her, even as she felt his warm breath in her hair.

He was offering comfort.

Blindly she turned her face into his. She felt him pause for a moment, but she refused to meet his eyes. "Please," she begged. "Warm me." He needed no other invitation before his mouth moved to cover her own.

The feel of his lips jolted her further. She was hungry, so incredibly, unthinkingly hungry. So filled with *want*. She opened her mouth eagerly, inviting him in, clinging to him mindlessly. This was comfort. This was power. This was escape.

His hand was against her breast, brushing it through the fabric of her blouse. Another hand was still in her hair, holding her head tight, tight. She moved against him, felt his legs shift once again as his body hardened, felt herself hauled against him in a frenzy of need. She heard a moan, and could not tell whose throat had made the sound.

And then she remembered something else. A promise she had made to herself a long time ago. And such was the strength of the promise that she allowed her body to go limp against him, even though everything in her was clamoring for release.

He was having none of it. He moved slightly, his hands embracing her, his mouth devouring her. "Give to me," he murmured. "Give."

She could not, even though she wanted to. Slowly, with great effort, she tried to pull away.

A low growl sounded in his throat.

She removed her arms from around his waist and worked her hands between them.

"Reid," she pleaded, when she was at last able to turn her head. "No, Reid."

She sounded hesitant, unsure. She would not blame him for not listening. He probably couldn't even hear her.

"Reid," she tried again, a little louder. "We're in my office, Reid. I want to stop. Please."

He stared at her, his eyes black pools of darkness. Until comprehension dawned. "Good Lord," he said. Gradually his body calmed, the hold of his hands relaxed. He put her from him almost roughly, so that she—still weak herself— stumbled. His head reared up. He ran an angry hand over his head, before he went completely still, watching her.

"I believe . . . I believe I lost . . . control," she stuttered.

"It wasn't your fault."

She drew a great shuddering breath, and forced herself to meet Reid's dark, hooded gaze. "I *am* sorry," she said.

Anger, sharp and bright, flared in his eyes. "Don't be," he said fiercely. He reached out and touched her cheek lightly.

And then he was gone, leaving her shaken and quite alone, with Archie Davidson still to face, and memories of a wild and wanting kiss fresh in her mind.

Edward Cosgrove was supposed to arrive at five-fifteen; Archie Davidson would come shortly thereafter. Anyway, that was the plan.

Only Archie chose to leave work early that day, so that he arrived at four-thirty to pick up his daughter, and the police officer was not yet there. Diana was left to face Sarah's father alone.

He took her completely by surprise. She had spent the afternoon trying to convince herself that everything was really all right, that she had regained her self-control. But she didn't believe it, not for a moment.

The moment of madness in Reid's arms was just that— madness, she told herself, and she was determined that it would never, *ever,* happen again.

She was filling out reports in her office when Sandy Buxted came racing in. "Mr. Davidson's here, Diana. Forty-five minutes early. Can you talk to him?"

Wondering what else could possibly go wrong today, Diana stood wearily. "Send him in."

Archie Davidson was a slim man of moderate height. Diana put his age in his mid-thirties. His dark hair was combed back from his face, and grew longer in back, giving him an almost rakish handsomeness. His ruddy complexion spoke of outdoor hobbies.

"You wanted to see me?" he asked politely.

"Mr. Davidson..." She took a deep breath. "Please come in and be seated for a moment." After he had done so, she told him what had happened to Sarah.

It took him a moment to understand what she was telling him. When comprehension finally sank in, his face grew red as fury. "What are you talking about?" His voice progressed swiftly from a low growl to an outraged roar. "What possible right do you have to take my child away from me? I'll sue you! I'll smear the name of this place all over every paper in town, every paper in the country! I know you, Diana Rowe! So does everyone else. A filthy rich society girl do-gooder, that's what you are! With precious little brains to go with your glamorous little body—"

"Mr. Davidson..." Diana tried to cut into the tirade, trying to make sense of his reaction. Archie sounded so righteously angry that she would have believed him herself had she not seen little Sarah with her own eyes. "Mr. Davidson, please be quiet for a moment..." He stood, glaring at her venomously, before he rushed from her office, tearing down the Lyonhouse hallway, looking in every room for his daughter.

Only when he was positive that Sarah was really gone did he come back to Diana, his fury growing more irrational by the second.

Nancy Cook was hovering protectively in the background, and Diana turned to her, saying unthinkingly, "Go call Reid Hudson. See if he will come over here."

She forgot that she had vowed to have as little to do with the man as possible. She forgot the shame she had felt after their kiss.

Nancy looked out the window. "He's just driving up now, here to get Jamie, I suppose. I'll go tell him what's going on."

Diana nodded as Archie came closer, then leaned over her desk, his tight-fisted hand shaking threateningly in her face. "Tell me where she is," he said, loudly. *"Now."*

Diana thought of a three-year-old girl, her eyes filled with terror and humiliation, her body shaking as she was examined. She remembered a little tender bottom bruised, a back that was cut open and bleeding.

She looked at the man in front of her, ranting at her with such self-righteous anger.

She stood up. "Mr. Davidson..." she began.

He waited, thinking he was going to get the information he wanted.

"I wouldn't tell you where Sarah is even if I knew, which I don't. Linda Jarvis, from Protective Services, has Sarah. She's taken her someplace where she can be safe. Which she obviously isn't with you. Why are you so upset? You should be relieved Sarah's gone. Now you can't hurt her anymore!"

"Why you..."

"Archie Davidson," Reid said from behind him, in the quiet way he had of getting someone's attention. Diana's eyes flew to Reid's face. She had not even heard him come in.

Immediately Archie Davidson stilled, his ruddy complexion, paling. He stood upright and turned around slowly. "Mr. Hudson," he said, and for the first time Diana heard a very human desperation in his tone. Then, warily, "Sir. Am I glad to see you."

"Oh?"

Archie took a deep, calming breath. "There's been a terrible misunderstanding here, and I'd be much obliged if you could use your influence to help straighten it out."

Reid's eyes flicked to Diana's outraged face before he came all the way into her office, shutting the door quietly behind him. "I was here, Archie. Earlier. I saw Sarah my-self. She was taken away, *by ambulance.*"

Archie slumped then, as if all the air had been knocked out of him. "You were here?" he croaked.

"Yes."

"You let them take her away?"

"Yes, Archie."

Slowly Archie lowered himself into a chair. Unbelievably his eyes welled with tears. "They've taken my little girl away?"

"Mr. Davidson," Diana interrupted. "Here is Linda Jarvis's phone number. If you do not call her, I'm sure she will be calling you." In spite of her earlier anger, she found herself feeling an unwilling compassion for this man. "I know you're upset, Mr. Davidson, but your daughter had been badly hurt, and in addition, is scared. I suggest you get your mind off of protecting yourself, and start thinking about Sarah, and what you need to do to—somehow—make amends."

"Diana..." Reid said warningly, and she realized too late that her assumption of Archie Davidson's guilt was like waving a red flag in front of the man. For a moment he stared at her blankly, before his face once again grew apo-plectic, and stark fury blazed out of his eyes. He leaned forward in his chair, then half rose from it. "You know I'm upset," he mimicked her. "*You know I'm upset?* Tell me what you know, Miss High-and-Mighty Rowe. Tell me how your bleeding heart understands what it's like living week to week, waiting for a damn paycheck that never quite covers your bills. Tell me you know what it's like driving old cars because you can't afford new ones, or that you understand supporting a family on a workman's pay. Tell me more. Do, Miss Rowe. Tell me you understand how it is to come and pick up a daughter, only to be told she's been taken away, and there's not a damn thing you can do about it!"

"I may not know all about those things, Archie," Diana said furiously. "But I know this—other people have those same problems, and they don't beat their children. It's not Sarah's fault, and you shouldn't have beat her."

Archie fell to his chair again, and buried his face in his hands. For a moment the room was absolutely silent.

Outside, Edward Cosgrove was just pulling his police car into the parking lot. Archie raised his head in time to catch sight of the marked vehicle, and fear returned to his eyes. Turning toward Reid, he said, "This won't affect my job, will it, Mr. Hudson? I've worked here ten years...."

Reid's face showed neither compassion nor condemnation. "Your job is the least of your worries, Davidson," he said. "If your work here is satisfactory, of course it won't be affected."

For the first time since hearing his daughter had been taken away, Archie Davidson's eyes seemed to clear. "Yes, sir," he said, almost calm. "Thank you."

"And Davidson?"

"Yes, sir?"

"You'll find the company willing to help if you need counseling."

Archie stared at the floor. When he looked up, misery was written on the planes of his handsome face. "Thank you, Mr. Hudson."

There was a knock on Diana's office door. Reid opened it to admit Edward Cosgrove. There was pure steel in Edward's gaze, and Diana wondered now how this giant of a man could have ever referred to himself as a teddy bear.

"Mr. Davidson was just leaving," Reid said calmly.

Edward looked at Archie measuringly. "Good enough." Then, to Diana's surprise, Edward put his arm around Archie Davidson's shoulders. "Hey man," he said. "It's been a tough day, but I've handled cases like this before, and I wondered if you'd care to talk it out...."

Diana was once again left alone with Reid. She realized she was still standing, and took her seat. For a moment she sat quietly, looking down at her hands, which were clasped on her desk. She knew her cheeks were flushed, and that her hair had come loose of its clasps.

She remembered, too late, that she had vowed to have nothing more to do with Reid Hudson. She was just opening her mouth to tell him so when she caught him staring at her, almost rudely. Yet beneath his dark expressionless mask she sensed the same burning she had experienced this morning, the same fire that was still threatening to blaze out of control. Almost unaware of her own movement, she shook her head, responding to his yet unspoken question.

His eyebrows lifted questioningly.

"Well," she forced herself to say. "I hadn't meant to see you again so soon. I hadn't meant to see you at all...." The words trailed away. Her voice was really shaking now, and she was trembling. She felt unsteady and terribly frightened and strangely like weeping.

"Diana," Reid said very quietly. "What time are you leaving tonight?"

"Probably around seven-thirty," she mumbled unthinkingly. She had been coming early and staying late.

"Perhaps..." he said, "...perhaps it would be best if I drove you home."

"There is no need," she said, filled with desperate trepidation. "I'm all right, and my car is here."

"You're not all right, Diana. And I want to drive you home."

"No."

He walked over to the side of her desk, standing so close she could have leaned her head against his thigh. The temptation to do so had her practically swooning. "Look at me," he commanded.

Drawn by a force greater than her own control, she raised her head. His eyes were dark—darker than she had ever seen them. And they were on fire. Slowly his hand came out, and touched her face. He stroked her cheek once, twice. His thumb touched her lower lip, gently. Unable to help herself, she bent her neck, so that her head was resting in the curve of his hand.

She heard him say, very softly, almost tenderly, "I want you, Diana. Let me take you home."

It took a minute for his words to penetrate, and took even longer still for her to react. She felt hazy, dreamlike, so that even when she straightened her head and reached up to move his hand away, everything seemed slow and far away.

She forced herself to stand, to move away from him. She turned her back, and looked out her window. She remembered his words to her when she had fought for the job he didn't want to give her.

It's absurd for someone with your background to be working with children, who are, above all else, still in a state of innocence.

He thought... had always thought... she was easy. Finally she turned to face him, finding her voice with supreme effort.

"No," she said huskily. "I... thank you, but no." Ridiculous words with which to turn down such a proposition. But she could say nothing else.

He looked strangely vulnerable, standing there, watching her. Until his eyes flared once more, hot and burning and hungry. His hands clenched at his sides. She thought he meant to continue to persuade her, but he merely said, in a voice so cold and stiff it belied the heat of his eyes. "Of course. It would be folly, wouldn't it?"

"Yes," she whispered. "Folly."

"But you'll be careful driving home? And you'll do what you can to relax tonight?"

"I will," she said. "I'll do that."

He nodded then, briefly, and she watched him go out her door, watched him turn down the Lyonhouse hallway, going, she knew, to get his strangely silent son. And she was glad no one was in the outer office, for tears were running down her cheeks, and her own arms were wrapped around her body. She walked to the window and stared out blindly, waiting for the moment of grief to pass, waiting for her natural self-control to impose itself, waiting for her heart to grow calm again, cold again, protected again.

It was Phillip's birthday. A little girl had been beaten. Reid Hudson had *wanted* her.

She stared out the window, and felt as if she were seeing for the first time the world as it was. It was harsh and forbidding to her, cruel and ruthless. And she cried for things that happened, that could never be fixed.

Then her heart quieted once more, and retreated into its own private hiding place. For it had been broken a little, its voice silenced, and its warmth denied.

Diana took a deep shuddering breath. There was nothing to be gained by standing here. There was much to do, and hours to go before she was able to leave Lyonhouse and go home.

ACCEPT FOUR BRAND-NEW

YOURS

We'd like to send you four free Silhouette novels, worth more than $13.00, to introduce you to the benefits of the Silhouette Reader Service. We hope your free books will convince you to subscribe, but that's up to you. Accepting them places you under no obligation to buy anything, but we hope you'll want to continue with the Reader Service.

So unless we hear from you, once a month we'll send you six additional Silhouette Special Edition® novels to read and enjoy. If you choose to keep them, you'll pay just $2.96* per volume—a saving of 33¢ each off the cover price. There is no charge for postage and handling. There are no hidden extras! And you may cancel at any time, for any reason, just by sending us a note or a shipping statement marked "cancel." You can even return any shipment to us at our expense. Either way, the free books and gifts are yours to keep!

ALSO FREE!
VICTORIAN PICTURE FRAME

This lovely Victorian pewter-finish miniature is perfect for displaying a treasured photograph—and it's yours *absolutely free*—when you accept our no-risk offer.

Perfect for a treasured Photograph

Plus a FREE mystery Gift! follow instructions at right.

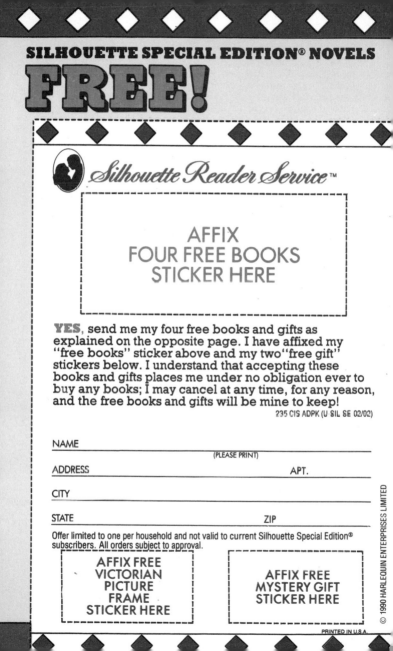

WE EVEN PROVIDE FREE POSTAGE!

It costs you *nothing* to send for your free books — we've paid the postage on the attached reply card. And we'll pick up the postage on your shipment of free books and gifts, and also on any subsequent shipments of books, should you choose to become a subscriber. Unlike many book clubs, we charge *nothing* for postage and handling!

Chapter Eight

Reid and Jamie were having dinner, if you could call it that. Reid wasn't really much of a cook. Jamie seemed to have a fixation with peanut butter and jelly sandwiches anyway. So Jamie ate his sandwich, and Reid heated a frozen dinner in the microwave.

During the course of the meal, Reid kept up a one-sided conversation. "I picked out some new furniture designs today," he said. "Pretty nice ones, too. Should do well in the marketplace." He took a bite of green beans.

"Knotingsly seems to be doing okay, too. Kind of takes the air out of one to know things can go so smoothly when you're away." Reid waved his fork. "Wasn't always that way, though."

The boy ate his sandwich quietly, looking down at the table.

"Would you like more milk, Jamie?" Reid asked. "How about some potato chips?"

Jamie held out his glass for a refill.

"All right. Now it's your turn. How was life at day care, hmmm? What did you do today?"

Jamie looked at him unwaveringly, almost challengingly, with his clear golden-brown eyes that were reminding Reid more and more of Diana Rowe's. There was no expression there, no hint at what the boy was feeling.

"Did you play outside? On the slide?" Reid made a sliding motion with his hand.

Jamie ate a potato chip, his eyes never leaving Reid's face.

"Enjoy the playground, do you? What else did you do today? Did you color?"

Jamie made no sound, except for the quiet *crunch crunch crunch* of the potato chip.

"Mrs. Cook gave me some of your artwork. It's still in my briefcase." Reid rose, giving his unfinished dinner one last, disgusted look. He walked to where his briefcase rested on the sofa. Opening it, he pulled out three sheets of paper, all with children's drawings on them. Then he returned to the table.

Jamie's expression shifted, and Reid thought hopefully that there was some eagerness there, hiding behind that unnaturally blank gaze. "I like this one," Reid said, referring to a brightly colored picture. The huge circle took almost the whole page, and underneath were some recognizable trees and flowers. "Mrs. Cook told me this was a picture of the sun. Was she right, Jamie?"

Jamie stared at the picture.

"And this one, according to the knowledgeable Mrs. Cook, is a . . . is . . . what *is* this one, Jamie? Can you tell me about it?"

Jamie glanced away.

"No, I guess you can't, Jamie. But you will, someday. You will talk again, you know, as plainly as anybody. All the doctors said you could talk, and I believe you can, too."

Jamie took another bite of his sandwich.

"Talking is kind of fun. You can make your voice loud or soft. You can be angry or happy. You can name all sorts of things." Then, "Don't you want to talk, Jamie?"

As if he had not heard the question, Jamie got up from the table and walked into the living room, where he pulled out a book. Reid sighed.

The formula he followed every night with Jamie was one prescribed by a top New York psychiatrist. Talking to Jamie that way actually made him feel rather foolish, but he certainly didn't have any better ideas. Dr. Wheaton had also hoped that placing Jamie in an environment with other, normal children would loosen the boy's tongue, but so far he had not said a word.

And nobody could explain why Jamie had suddenly quit using his voice. Accident trauma was the most popular theory. Reid, however, had his own opinion.

He thought the boy was angry, more than angry. He thought the boy was in a towering rage, and the overpowering fury that inhabited that small form was more than a four-year-old could even begin to comprehend. Reid had some comprehension of it, though. In the last ten years Reid had become accustomed to reading other men's minds; second-guessing had become second nature. The same intuitive knowledge that told him whether a man was lying or speaking the truth, whether a purposefully bland face was content or seething with anger, told him that Jamie Hudson's wrath was directed at *him,* the man Jamie thought was his father. As completely as if Jamie had been years older, the boy was deliberately repudiating Reid, freezing him out by the force of his silent rejection.

Only when that louse of a photographer had started flashing pictures had Jamie turned to him, terrified by the bright lights, which—Reid knew—had reminded the boy of the night of his mother's accident, when reporters were taking pictures like mad. That day at Lyonhouse had been the only time Jamie had voluntarily turned to Reid for anything at all.

Jamie's rejection made Reid feel terribly guilty. Maybe he should have been more a father to the boy. Maybe he should have overlooked Jamie's illegitimacy much earlier. Maybe he should have...

It's not Sarah's fault, Diana told Archie Davidson.

Jamie's bastardy wasn't Jamie's fault, either.

Reid looked again at the pictures in his hand. They were actually quite sophisticated for a four-year-old boy, Nancy Cook had told him. Jamie used the whole page, incorporated a variety of colors, and put in more detail than any other child at the Center. Nancy thought perhaps Jamie was gifted.

But they just looked like child's drawings to Reid. He lifted the last picture. He had not asked Jamie about this one, for he knew all too well what it was. The head wasn't too recognizable, but the silver hair colored in down to the shoulders was a dead giveaway. And the shirt was yellow.

Diana Rowe had worn a yellow blouse today.

He taped all three pictures up on the kitchen wall.

Later, after he had given Jamie his bath and put the boy in bed, that third picture began to bother him. It was as if his conscience was up on that wall, staring down at him disapprovingly.

He had treated Diana badly today. He had given in to all kinds of dishonorable impulses.

And she was trying so hard. Even a fool could see that Diana was doing a wonderful job at Lyonhouse, and Reid was no fool.

She had been truly upset by the incident with Sarah Davidson. Hell, he had been upset himself. No one could look at a child like that and come away unmoved. So he had reacted. He had kissed Diana a lot more...more *passion-ately* than he had intended. A lot more.

Even so, the strength of her response had staggered him, had pushed him beyond the limits of his own control. Even now, remembering the feel of her lips beneath his, his whole body grew rigid with desire.

He clenched his hands, and shutting his eyes, he laid his forehead against the kitchen wall. From beneath his closed lids her eyes stared back at him: soft and brown, confused and tormented. And cloudy with her own, answering long-ing.

He had wanted to kiss her eyes.

Folly, he thought. Folly. Folly. Folly.

He tried to think of something else.

Five minutes later, he remembered how her voice had trembled when she turned him down, and he groaned aloud.

Ten minutes after that, he was rubbing his fingers to-gether, as if Diana's hair was still resting against his hand.

Later still, sitting in the living room easy chair, trying to review his plans for the coming week, he thought of Archie Davidson shaking his fist in Diana's face, and his own ex-pression grew tight and angry. *I'll smash Davidson's face in,* he thought, *if he so much as touches a hair on her head.*

Abruptly impatient, he set aside his papers, closed his briefcase and stood up.

Folly.

He decided to take a shower. When the water was pour-ing down on him, hot and steamy, he remembered the opera, and the way Harry Reichenbach's arm had curved around Diana's waist in calm, intimate possession.

We have reservations in the city.

Who was she? What was she? Why did she obsess him so?

Out of the shower, he felt his chin. It was rough, stubbly. He started to shave.

No, she said. *I ... thank you, but no.*

"Yes." He spoke the word aloud, and was startled by the sound of his own voice.

Folly, she whispered.

"Then let it be folly," he said.

He used the bedroom telephone to call his old friend, Tilly Martel. She answered it on the first ring.

"Tilly? Reid here."

"Hello, Reid." Warm affection was in Tilly's voice. "What's up?"

Like a drowning man, he fought for air. "Are you by any chance free tonight?"

"Absolutely."

"I . . . I have a big favor to ask. Something has come up, and I need to leave for a while. Jamie is asleep, of course, but obviously I can't leave him alone. . . ."

"Say no more. I'll be there in twenty minutes."

His heart was slamming painfully against his chest. "Thanks, Tilly. I'll owe you a big one for this."

She laughed lightly. "I won't forget."

"One more thing. This may take a while—perhaps it would be best if you came prepared to spend the night."

There was a pause then, as Tilly said with slow innuendo, "You'll owe me a very big one, Reid Hudson."

"Sure Tilly. Anything . . . And thanks."

You're a first-class fool, Hudson, he told himself. A prize idiot.

Folly.

Diana was asleep when the buzzer rang. In the deep sleep of her dream the harsh, insistent summons seemed part of a scene far removed from reality, and at first she simply ignored it. When it rang again she became frightened, disoriented. She finally recognized the sound on the third peal, and resisting it, she covered her head with her pillow.

But it rang once more, and then again.

It was mid-June, and her apartment was not yet completely dark. Swinging her legs off her bed, still in a slumberous haze, she walked to the mouthpiece by the side of her door. Clearing her throat, she spoke into it. "Who is it?"

For a moment she thought she had waited too long, for no one answered. And then she heard: "Reid."

She closed her eyes and leaned against the wall almost drunkenly, her hand raised automatically to her suddenly pounding heart.

"Go away," she said, without thinking.

"Diana," she heard. "I've brought you some flowers." His voice sounded thin and metallic over the intercom. "Let me in, Diana."

It was a warm evening—she was wearing a short nightgown; nothing else. She peered at the clock on her bookshelves. Nine twenty-three. "It's late," she said. "And you have no reason to be bringing me flowers. Go away." Then she turned off the intercom.

A few minutes later it buzzed again, long and loud. She thought of Reid Hudson, standing three stories below. She thought of how tired she was, how inexpressibly weary. She thought of the ache she had carried in her heart all evening, until she had finally sought the relief of early sleep. She thought of all that was wrong in her world.

Reid Hudson was wrong in her world.

The buzzing stopped. Unable to help herself, she walked to her window and peered out. She saw Reid's tall form walk across the street to a black sedan. He looked at a bouquet of daisies he was holding in his hand, before he hurled them violently into the street. She saw him slide into the driver's seat, then sit with his head on the steering wheel.

Soon he would be driving away, and she knew intuitively that he would never come again.

She found a robe, and slipped into it. She dropped her keys into her pocket. Barefoot, she sped down the three flights of stairs. Shoving the front door open, she ran across the street.

Reid was just starting his engine, and didn't see her. She pounded on his window.

His head turned toward her, and before surprise obliterated everything else, she saw something glad and leaping in his eyes.

For a moment he stared at her through his closed window, making absolutely no movement. Then, still staring at her, he reached over with calm deliberation and turned his ignition off. She stepped back, and he opened his door and got out.

"All right," she said to him, wrapping her robe tightly about her. "You can come in. But there is something you need to know." She paused then, and stood tall and proud in the middle of the street, her silver hair tousled from sleep and blowing in the light summer breeze, her body only partially dressed and barefoot. "No man sleeps with me here. If you have come for that, you have wasted your time."

A pause the space of a heartbeat. "I can't say that's not why I came, Diana. But God help me, I accept your terms."

She turned and walked back into her building, treading on strewn daisies as she did so, and he followed her. When she had to stop to unlock the bottom door, he stood so close she could smell his after-shave and hear him breathe, but he did not touch her. She turned to him. "Don't crowd me," she said, and he moved away.

She left him in the living area of her apartment, while she went into the bedroom to change. She dressed carelessly, in worn jeans and a casual shirt. She ran a brush through her hair, then swept it to one side and pinned it back with a comb. The entire process took less than five minutes. When she returned to Reid, he had not yet sat down.

He was looking around at her apartment, and she tried to see it through his eyes. It was comprised of two spacious rooms, with a huge walk-in closet and a kitchenette behind louvered doors. The ceilings were high, and the walls clean and white, providing a brilliant background to the colorful posters and prints she had framed and hung throughout. A large potted tree stood by the windows. The effect was peacefully simple, neat and bright.

"I can afford it," she said flatly, "on twenty-four thousand a year."

He raised an eyebrow. "Actually, I rather like it."

For a moment their eyes locked, before she turned away. "I'll make some coffee."

"No," he said. "Not yet, anyway. It's a warm night, Diana, and still early. Jamie is . . . someone is with Jamie, and I have a little time. I wondered if you would like to walk with me for a while."

Her hand stilled on the kitchen faucet, where she was about to run some water. His voice sounded different, almost diffident. If she did not know better, she would think Reid Hudson was feeling shy.

But a walk would be fine with her. Better than Reid sitting in her apartment, with Diana playing hostess in some crazy new game in which she had no comprehension of the rules. She turned to him, only to find herself facing his back, as he studied with seeming fascination an Art Institute print on her wall. She had purchased it the weekend she had spent with Harry, in Chicago.

"A walk would be nice," she said quietly.

The taut spread of his shoulders visibly relaxed. He turned and looked down at her gravely, no trace of shyness in his expression, but then she could read precious little in his closed, shuttered face. "Let's go then."

Diana's street was a quiet one, and the lamps on the corners shed a shadowy glow over trees and pavement. Reid shortened his stride to fit hers, even as he scrupulously avoided touching her in any way.

At first they walked in silence. After a while he said, "I'm sorry about today, Diana."

She didn't know what to say, so she said nothing. He had wounded her this afternoon, more than he knew, and she still felt raw and sore from it. When she didn't comment, he continued, "You're doing a fine job at Lyonhouse, too."

"I'm sure you found that a surprise," she said lightly, yet the underlying bitterness was there, just the same.

Out of the corner of her eye she thought she saw his hand clench briefly. But when he spoke again, his voice was calm and level, and he talked of other things. "When I was a child," he said, "my family would spend summers at Cape Cod. My father and I used to take walks together at night. He was something of an amateur astronomer, and he taught me the names of all the constellations."

She knew he was trying to dispel the rising tension between them, and she forced herself to reply in kind. "I can't see any stars tonight."

"No. The streetlights are too close, and the clouds too low. But they're out there. Ursa Major and Ursa Minor. Perseus . . . Aries . . . Pisces . . . Delphinus. Leo and Gemini. And more, much more. All out there, just the same as they were centuries ago. My father used to say staring at the stars helped him keep his own life in perspective."

"Lucy told me your parents died when she was still very young."

"She was ten, and I was twenty-two."

They turned a corner, and she stumbled slightly. Almost reflexively Reid put a hand under her elbow until she steadied, then moved away from her once again.

"What else did your father teach you?"

"Simple things: To tell the truth, to honor my name, to accept responsibility without shirking."

That was Reid Hudson, honorable to the core, she thought, with some bitterness. He was not like her—he had no dissolute behavior hiding in his past, no dishonesty, no wildness. It was hard to live up to someone who had maintained such high standards all his life.

"My father was the most honest person I have ever met," Reid continued with quiet pride, and there was something else in his voice, something deeper, something Diana had never known with her own father. "He was more than honest—he had integrity of character."

"And so you've lived your whole life in his shadow, trying to be his duplicate." She supposed it was jealousy, pure and simple, that made her sound so spiteful.

His gaze slid to hers. "I wouldn't have put it precisely that way."

"No?"

"No." But his mood had shifted again, and she could sense his hidden despair, and wondered at it.

How long they walked after that she did not know. In the shifting shadows of the night she began to feel transparent, slightly unreal. Reid was no more than a dark phantom at her side, lost in his own secret thoughts. So that when he asked, his voice low and clear in the night, "And you, Diana, how do you feel about honesty?" she felt faintly startled, and answered with quick truthfulness.

"Sometimes I think it is more important to be careful than honest."

"Yes," he said slowly. "That is exactly how you are with me. Careful, and not very honest."

The part of town they had entered was unfamiliar to her, and seemed vaguely threatening. "I want to go back," she said.

"No," he said. "Not yet. Let's not go back yet." Then, as if he had made some decision, he reached out and took her arm. It was a light touch, somewhat tentative, as if he were merely testing, waiting for her reaction. When she made none, his fingers tightened almost imperceptibly.

But where he touched her she was burning, on fire. She had not known how cold she was until now, and she began to tremble. She knew he would feel her trembling, even though the night was warm, and draw his own conclusions.

"If I were not who I am, Diana," he said, his tone surprisingly pleasant, "and you forgot for a time to be careful, so that you trusted me just for a while..." He left his thoughts hanging in the night air.

She drank in the night breeze as fine wine, and felt light-headed with it. Everything seemed strangely abstract, far away, except for that hand upon her arm. "What would you like to know?" she asked distantly.

"Who is Harry Reichenbach, and what is he to you?" His voice was low, but she could hear the unmistakable anger, the accusation. And then she knew that nothing had changed. She tried to pull away from Reid, but he guessed her intent, and held her firmly.

"He is a friend," she said, and sensed his disappointment.

"You are still being careful."

"I want to go back," she said again.

"We'll try another subject. Something simple. Tell me about your family, Diana."

Something simple, she thought, almost wildly. *Just tell him you don't have a family anymore.*

But she could not deny Phillip, not today, his birthday. "I...once I had a brother." The words sounded stilted, strange, and she held her breath.

He moved closer, and he shifted his arm until it was around her shoulders. Their legs brushed each other as they walked. "Had." The word was an acknowledgement of his understanding.

"He died six years ago." Then she added, "Today was his birthday."

He leaned toward her, and she could feel his breath, warm and sweet upon her face. "What was his name?"

"Phillip. Phillip Michael Rowe."

She was conscious of an enormous feeling of relief. All through this horrible day Phillip had been there, in the back of her mind, yet never once had she spoken his name, or allowed her memories of him to linger. That it was Reid Hudson who had freed her did not seem to matter one whit.

"Tell me about him."

She gave a little husky laugh, suddenly perilously close to tears. "Once I got started, it would probably take all night."

"I have all night."

Traffic in the street had increased. She looked up and saw that they were in the downtown district. "We have come a long way," she said wonderingly.

"So we'll take a taxi back to your apartment now. You can make me that cup of coffee you offered earlier, and I'll listen to you tell me about your brother."

"Why?" she asked him, abruptly conscious of the way his arm was encircling her, of the way he was bending his head, so that his mouth was just above her ear. "Why are you being kind to me?"

He chuckled ruefully. "I believe I'm a kind person."

"Not to me," she said flatly. "You have not been kind to me."

"No. I'm sorry, Diana. I'm sorry for today. I should not have . . . touched you as I did."

"You're touching me now."

"Yes. I can't seem to help it." Wry resignation was in his tone. "But you're not pulling away, either."

"That does not mean I am giving you permission."

"A small technicality. I am here, holding you, and you are not fighting. You've had a terrible day, part of which was my fault. So I will go back with you, and comfort you, and listen to you."

"And then? Will you remember what I said earlier, when I am weak and vulnerable from such attention? Will you remember your honor then?"

She lifted her head and tried to look into his eyes, but the night was too black.

"I will remember. I promise. I swear it."

And—at last—she recognized the gift when she saw it. This was Reid Hudson, as he was with his sister Lucy the night of the opera, before he looked up and saw her there. This was the man she had heretofore only guessed at, the one who was not dark and brooding and bitter, the one whose presence could electrify a room, whose smile could melt the coldest heart.

Her heart had been cold for so long.

And it *was* Phillip's birthday. On tonight, of all nights, she could use a little warmth. "All right," she said. "Find the taxi. It's time now to go back."

Later, in her living room, they sat together on her white sofa, and she no longer found it strange that it was Reid Hudson's arm that was around her, that it was his chest she was leaning against, that one of his hands was buried in her hair. And she was talking, softly enough, but the words were pouring from her, as if from a swollen river whose dam had finally burst. She spoke of the time Phillip, then only eight years old, had found a beaten almost-dead puppy by the side of the road, and how together they had hidden it, and nursed it, and fed it, until their governess had found out and—when they were both away for the day—had the dog taken to the pound, where he was destroyed. Phillip had been inconsolable, though she had done her best to comfort him, in spite of the fact that she was only two years older herself, and equally devastated.

And there was real pride in her voice as she told of Phillip's exceptional brilliance, how he was reading at the age of three, how at twelve he had been placed in accelerated math classes, how he had always called her when he wanted to share the pride of his latest achievement.

She talked of Phillip's relationship with her parents. They had his life all mapped out, she told Reid. He was going to be a financial wizard, and multiply the family fortunes over and over. Only Phillip wanted to be a zoologist, something her father could never understand.

She talked of lazy summer days, of a brother and sister bonded close in mutual need, of laughter and innocence and loyalty and love.

She talked and talked, until she was at last empty and felt newly cleansed.

Reid asked very few questions. "Where was your mother?" he said once. "Your father did that?" he commented later. And finally, when she had grown silent and was almost asleep against his broad strength, he asked, "How did Phillip die, Diana?"

"It was so stupid," she said. "So senseless. He was a first-class horseman, and had started jumping in shows when he was twelve. But the horse he was riding was temperamental and balked at one of the jumps. Phillip fell, and his body hit the ground a certain way, so that his neck snapped. Dead. Just like that. Dead."

In six years it was the first time she had told anyone exactly what had happened, although five thousand people had witnessed it. But never before had she been able to speak of what she had seen with her eyes, so that she found it strange that there were no tears on her cheeks, and that instead of feeling desolate with loss, she felt a peace growing warm and strong inside her.

One of Reid's hands was rubbing her back, the other moved up to cup her face. As if it were the most natural thing in the world, she kissed his palm. "Thank you," she said huskily.

His hand moved against her face, touching her everywhere: her eyes, her lips, her brow. Gently it moved lower, and his fingers stroked her neck. Unthinkingly she arched her head back, and he bent down and placed a kiss on the smooth, tight muscles of her throat, so that her skin jumped in response.

"You are so beautiful," he murmured.

Instantly her new, fragile peace was shattered. "No," she said. "I'm not."

He laughed a little then, tracing the line of her collarbone through the thin layer of her shirt. "How can you say so? Don't you ever look in the mirror, Diana Rowe?"

"All the time. I look at myself and think, how odd—Only I know how far from beautiful I really am."

She began to cry then, and he lay down on her sofa and pulled her next to him on it, leg to leg, thigh to thigh, chest to chest. Heart to heart. "Lie with me for a while," he said, but he didn't undress her. He held her, and stroked her, and planted kisses on her face, until she quieted at last.

"Diana," he said. "You are beautiful. Inside and out. You can believe me when I tell you so."

"I hear the words, but you are Reid Hudson, and it's hard for me to believe you," she said with stark implacability.

His hand touched her mouth, quieting her. "I, too, know what it's like to lose faith, Diana. But you lie when you speak so harshly. You believe. Every time you look at a child, hope and belief shine out of your eyes."

No. He was wrong. She loved the children, because *they* still believed, not because she did.

He stopped talking and shifted instead, so that her body slid between his legs. His hold on her changed subtly, and he raised himself above her. "Diana," he said. "I'm going to kiss you. Kiss me back." Then he lowered his head.

After that, all was sensation, a joining of mouths and tongues and hands in a search of exquisite exploration, in a gaining of knowledge that had just been hinted at in her office today—this was what it was like to kiss Reid Hudson, to be held by him, to be desired by him and to hold nothing back. And she was hot, so hot, blazing and burning and hungry and crying.

When he pulled away, his eyes were as black as smoke. He sat up abruptly, dragging her up also, pulling her head once more against his chest. "I promised," he said, each word dropping like a blow against her heart. "I gave my word."

They sat like that for a long time, so that after a while Diana recovered herself. "Where do we go from here?" she asked. "What do you want from me, Reid?"

For a moment he didn't answer. Then, very carefully, he said, "What you told me tonight, have you ever told anyone else? Of all the men who have known you, which ones have you talked to like this?"

"No man," she said, then added, "No one."

"Then that, Diana, is what I want."

She understood. He was asking for her soul, naked and unprotected. He was asking for whatever trust she had left. He was asking for her dreams, to be spread out before him as on a silver platter.

"And you?" she whispered. "What will you give me in return?"

He looked at her for a long silent moment. Then he said, "I will give you my heart, Diana."

He was beguiling her with words, and they were more powerful than any physical seduction. He was offering her forbidden fruit, and she thought nothing in the world was more desirable.

The temptation was strong to say yes, to do exactly as Reid wanted, to surrender to his dark potency. It was the strength of her own craving that terrified her, and sealed her lips against that irretrievable word.

But she had no strength to say no, either.

For a moment she lay against his chest, and felt the beat of his heart. She inhaled the manly fragrance of him, and could think of no other aroma that was so tantalizing. She sensed his unnatural stillness, and knew he was controlling himself with terrible restraint.

But her own resolve was strengthening. This is Reid Hudson, she told herself. Remember how much time he has spent disliking you, despising you. Surely neither of us is ready for this thing that is happening between us.

It was the warning of cold reason, ever her protective armor. She had spent too many years listening to its voice to deny it now.

She pulled away from Reid, and stood up. Immediately she felt a wrenching sense of loss, so that she swayed slightly. "You ask too much." Her voice was husky with longing.

"You're going to send me away." There was harsh disbelief in his tone.

Perhaps that was what she should do, but she could not. "I . . ." she began, only to find her voice lost in the heat of his blazing eyes. She took a step backward. "I just want some time, Reid. I think we both could use some time."

"How long?" The question lashed at her, threatening her precarious self-control.

"A week. I want you to leave me absolutely alone for a week."

He stood also. His hand came up to touch her hair. "A week," he repeated.

Her will was returning. "I won't be rushed, Reid," she said, and heard with relief the new determination in her tone.

Reid Hudson was in torment. *Seven days.* Everything in him screamed a denial. He had her *now.* Now was the moment of his power, and he felt frustrated with her refusal to submit. Not to see her again, not to touch her again, for seven days... and anything could happen in a week. It seemed he had waited a lifetime for this moment, and to turn it away...

He looked at her, and there was such steadiness in her eyes that it took him a moment to recognize that hiding behind her steely resolution was a very real fear.

Feeling an unfamiliar compassion, he sighed. "All right," he said. "A week. No longer."

Her eyes filled with tears, and she smiled her thanks. He felt his heart grow lighter. Those seven days would be gone in no time, he told himself. Nothing could happen that would spoil the certainty of this moment. She would be his—if he would wait.

Diana Rowe was worth waiting for.

His hand was still on her hair. Using his other one, he drew her closer, so that her head was resting against his shoulder. He felt a new and wonderful fullness, a different kind of strength, a rare luminosity that warmed without consuming.

"I'll wait," he said huskily. "But we have wasted so much time, Diana. So much damn time." Then he added, "And you *are* beautiful, Diana Rowe."

She shuddered against him, and he thought how fiercely difficult it was going to be to leave. It took all his strength to do so, putting her from him, leaning down to place a gentle kiss on her forehead, walking out her door and down to his car, all the time seeing her drenched and troubled eyes, wanting to once again comfort her, reassure her, and knowing that he could not, without betraying the promise she had extracted from him.

A week. The next seven days were surely going to be the longest of his life.

Later that night, lying sleepless in his bed, Reid Hudson finally understood what had happened tonight. For he felt lighter than he had in years, and more powerful. All this time he had felt himself flawed, somehow condemned, unable to choose anyone who was faithful and loyal. But no matter what Diana had done in the past, no matter how she had lived, the essence of her ran deep and true. He need no longer feel ashamed of his desire for her.

In his new buoyant state of mind, everything seemed crystal clear. Diana's past—all those men she had known— could actually be an asset. For she would surely understand the only kind of relationship that was possible for him. He had no wish to marry again, after all. He was a man who learned from his mistakes, and tried never to make the same one twice. But Diana, with her experience and intelligence and sensitivity, would surely never insist on such a thing as a marriage certificate. Everything was going to work out just fine.

He frowned, feeling an unwelcome twinge of doubt. She had never really answered his question about Harry Reichenbach. This coming week, when he was denied even conversation with her, Reichenbach could talk to Diana anytime he liked.

It was unthinkable.

But he had given his word, and he was a Hudson. Somehow he would have to bear it.

Chapter Nine

The next day was Saturday, and Diana slept late. She had been up only a couple of hours when the doorbell rang, and she accepted a single red rose, delivered in a rare and superbly crafted cut glass vase. There was a note: *the first day.*

She shivered slightly as she placed the vase on her dining table. Last night seemed like a dream to her now. But the rose was all too real—reminding her of all it would surely be better to forget. She closed her eyes and moaned slightly as she recalled how she had trembled in his arms, how she had kissed him with such abandon.

You are so beautiful.

She wanted to believe it, so badly.

She walked into her bedroom and stared at the full-length mirror on her closet door. She was wearing a pair of royal-blue slacks, topped with a white T-shirt. Her hair was pulled back in a careless ponytail. She peered at herself more closely.

Her eyes were brown, just plain brown, she thought defiantly. Her brows were normal—*everybody* had eyebrows. Her lips were naturally pink, it was true. She looked at her eyelashes. Someone—a man—had once told her they were exceptionally long. He had written a poem about her eyelashes.

Eyelashes, for heaven's sake.

She was tired of having her worth measured by the length of an eyelash. Or the shape of her lips. Or the color of her very ordinary brown eyes.

The truth was, all her life she had been judged by such things, and now she was terrified that Reid was using the same yardstick—that for her, no other judgment existed.

She sat at her table, chin on her folded arms, and stared at the rose.

I want you, Diana Rowe.

Who did he want? Last night she had felt desire for him and in him, yet still the last words he spoke were of physical beauty, and today he sent her a rose—that eternal symbol of earthly perfection.

What do you want from me?

He wants your soul.

She laughed softly. What did Reid Hudson know of her soul?

On Sunday there were two silk roses, in a different vase of even greater beauty. *The second day,* the note read. And under that: *I miss you.*

She spent the day cleaning her apartment from top to bottom. She scoured her sink and her oven, cleaned out her refrigerator and laundered all her clothes. She changed the sheets on her bed, and imagined Reid lying there with her.

Where would it lead? They were still strangers to each other. She was long past the stage of wanting an affair, but she had no idea of Reid's views on commitment. All this time there had been this smoldering tension between them, and she was afraid that all he wanted was simple relief. He would come back, next Friday night, and there would be no talk of him sleeping elsewhere. The assumption had already been made, and accepted.

I will give you my heart.

On what terms? she thought as she reorganized her closet. Reid Hudson was an intellectual man, a coolly reasonable man. The words were pretty indeed, but saying them didn't mean he had the least idea of what they meant.

But he *had* been kind to her. He had listened to her and comforted her.

Only because he wanted her.

On Monday she returned to Lyonhouse, her apartment immaculate, her state of mind painfully jumbled. She was in the hallway when Reid brought Jamie in. The redheaded boy left his father immediately, to come to Diana's side. Tossing Reid an openly defiant look, she knelt by Jamie, put her arms around him and kissed his cheek in welcome. His gold-flecked eyes flickered for a moment, before they resumed their habitual blank expression.

When she began to rise, she found a hand at her elbow, assisting her. She turned to Reid to thank him, only to be ravaged by the desire burning from his midnight gaze.

Her breath quickened involuntarily, her lips parted slightly, her body trembled. Until a satisfied gleam appeared in Reid's blue-black eyes, and he gave a slight nod and left her, his son still standing quietly by her side.

The three roses that came to Lyonhouse that afternoon were created of incredibly delicate blown glass. This time the note read: *How can I see you and not touch you?*

She made it a point to be hidden in her office when he came for Jamie that evening.

* * *

At Tuesday's staff meeting, Sally Nussbaum, the pre-school supervisor, spoke of Jamie Hudson. "I'm worried about him," she said. "He's becoming more and more withdrawn. I know Mr. Hudson thought Lyonhouse would help Jamie, but the opposite seems to be happening. He doesn't speak, he doesn't play with any of the other children, he doesn't react much to any of us who are trying to help him."

"What do you suggest?" Diana queried.

"I think Mr. Hudson has got to be told what's happening here. I think it should be suggested that he make other arrangements for Jamie."

"I would hate to see that happen," Nancy Cook spoke up. "It's true we haven't seen much progress with Jamie, but to force him into another change now certainly can't help the child."

"I agree," Diana said.

"Why don't you work with him, Diana?" Nancy said deliberately. "He obviously feels some comfort when you're around. Why don't you see what you can do?"

She thought about that. Lyonhouse had been open for three weeks, which left her only nine more, under the terms of her original agreement with Reid. No one among the staff knew that Diana's time at Lyonhouse was limited, so she could hardly explain her hesitation to them.

On the other hand, with Reid in hot pursuit, perhaps she could bargain with him for more time.

She immediately discarded the unworthy notion. Besides, such sexual bargaining would only muddy waters that were already murky enough.

Sally Nussbaum was still waiting for a response. "I'll consider it," Diana said at last. She thought again of Jamie as she had first seen him, so beautiful, so innocent, and then crying in Reid's arms only moments later. "I'll spend some time with him myself before I make a decision."

Later that day she received a beautifully mounted and framed colored photograph, of four brand-new rosebuds, just opening up, hanging with dew and quivering in the wind. The tag listed a well-known New York studio, and she knew the picture must have cost the earth. And on a little white embossed card, the words: *Four days gone, over half the week over. Stop avoiding me, please.*

Wednesday morning Diana was changing a display on the hallway bulletin board when Reid and Jamie walked in. They were at least half an hour earlier than usual, and Diana knew with certainty that Reid had changed his schedule so as to catch her unaware. That he succeeded was evident in the construction paper flowers that went flying from beneath her hands. Covering her sudden confusion, Diana knelt to pick the flowers up from where they drifted to the floor. But then Reid's polished, expensive shoes appeared next to her, and she felt his hand upon her head.

Her whole body stilled. Involuntarily her eyes closed. The weight of his hand momentarily stunned her senses, and she waited, kneeling at his feet, for him to move on.

Instead, his hand slid down her head onto her shoulder, then on down her arm as he knelt beside her. "You seem to have dropped something," he murmured. "I'll help you gather these...masterpieces."

The wry humor and dry tone coupled with the ordinary activity helped awaken her out of her sudden stupor. Trying to avoid Reid's eyes, she quickly gathered up the rest of the flowers. But when she reached for the shapes in Reid's hand, he held on to them, forcing her to look up and meet his gaze.

Where was all her old defiance, her cool self-control? Just when she needed her old weapons the most, they had abandoned her, leaving her open and vulnerable. And she knew with helpless certainty that the depth of her hunger and her fear was revealed in her brown eyes.

He touched her cheek. "Better," he murmured. "You don't have to be afraid of me, Diana." Then his finger rubbed her lips, gently. "Two more days," he said.

They stood simultaneously. At least the hallway was empty, and Diana knew grateful relief that no one had witnessed this scene of unconcealed intimacy. There was only Jamie, sitting quiet and still, on a bench on the other side of the hallway.

Only Jamie. Compassion welled within her. He was so unnaturally patient, so uncommonly contained in his muteness. She left Reid to walk toward his son. "Hello, Jamie," she said gently. "Would you like to walk with me to your room?"

Jamie looked at her as she put out her hand confidently. The boy's eyes flicked to his father before he placed his hand in hers. Squeezing his hand reassuringly, she walked with Jamie down the hallway. With every step Diana could feel Reid's eyes boring into her back, until she turned the corner and was out of his sight.

Later that morning Diana rearranged her office so that there was space for a rocking chair. Humming lightly, she brought in a pegboard and attached it to her wall. Then she went to find Jamie.

He was sitting in a corner of the preschool room, staring at a blank wall. His hands were clenching crayons so tightly that his knuckles were white; several pieces of paper were thrown on the floor around him.

Other children were gathered across the room, sitting enthralled while listening to Sally Nussbaum use puppets to tell a story. Diana's heart went out to Jamie as she absorbed his rigid, lonely posture.

Casually she walked across the room, before sinking cross-legged beside the boy. "Hello," she said. "Did you want to go over and listen to Sally's story?"

Jamie made absolutely no response.

"Well then, maybe you would like to show me your pictures." Not waiting for a reply, she picked up a sheet of paper from the floor.

Jamie had drawn the figure of a man, big and dark against the white paper. The picture was filled in with quite an amazing amount of detail for so young a child, but that wasn't the only thing that caught Diana's eyes. Big wide angry slashes covered the figure, as if Jamie, having once drawn the man, had deliberately tried to destroy him.

The anger in the drawing was terrifying.

Then she noticed a much smaller shape in the bottom left hand corner of the paper. It was simply a face, with no connecting body. It had features, too: red hair, nose, eyes. It took her a moment to realize the mouth had been left off.

She looked at a second piece of paper. There was a man there, too, this time on the far side of the page. He was doing something—although Jamie's drawing was unclear as to what. Diana thought perhaps the man was reading a book, or writing. His hair had been colored black, and it took very little guesswork for Diana to know that Jamie was drawing pictures of his father. As far away from him as was possible and still be in the same drawing was another figure, again much smaller, and with bright red hair. Many of the features were lacking this time, but the eyes were carefully drawn.

The third picture was of a woman, and Diana could not help grinning when she saw it. The woman had silver hair, was wearing blue pants and a red shirt, and was smiling. She was holding the hand of a child. In this picture the small figure was all mouth, shaped into a huge smile.

She remembered telling Jamie she loved it when he smiled.

She picked up other drawings off the floor. Dark slashes covered several pages, fanning out in every direction, pounded into the paper so that holes and tears were abundant.

Diana looked at Jamie, who had shifted slightly so he could watch her.

There was no doubt in Diana's mind that Jamie was gifted, talented far beyond his years. The intense emotion and detail included in his art would be the envy of many an aspiring artist. But more importantly, Jamie was in pain. She could hardly believe that she had been so involved with Jamie's father that she had ignored the greater, more important need of his son. But she made a solemn promise, sitting there next to this beautiful, perfectly formed boy. The father would not be more important than the son. She would not send Jamie away from Lyonhouse. Not yet. She knew too well what it was like to live in silence, although she could talk well enough. She understood loneliness, and terrifying anger. She would not think of the weeks that were flying by. Instead she would try to help this child, before it was too late.

She held up the picture of the woman. "This is a lovely drawing, Jamie," she said softly. "And I think I know who this is. I think you drew a picture of you and me, didn't you?"

At first she thought Jamie was not going to respond at all, and knew true relief when he gave a tiny, almost imperceptible nod of his head.

"It's a beautiful picture. I like it because we're holding hands, and because you're smiling. Can I keep this picture, Jamie?"

Again that faint nod.

"Would you like to come with me while I hang it in my office? Then you could see where I'm going to put it. And every day you can come and look at it, if you want to."

Jamie stood, and before Diana had made the motion, held out his hand. She took it in hers, and together they walked back to her office.

She pinned the picture right in the center of her peg-board, knowing that Jamie was aware of her every movement. Then she turned to him, wanting to explain everything so that he would not be caught unprepared. "I like being with you, Jamie. I brought a rocking chair in my office just so I could hold you for a while. Sometimes I need to hug somebody, and today I want to hug you." She picked him up, and seated herself in the rocking chair.

Jamie offered no resistance to her action, but didn't actively participate, either. He was like a rag doll in her arms. She settled him on her lap, and wrapped her arms around his small frame. Then she began to rock gently.

For a space of about ten minutes she was silent, communicating with Jamie only through touch. She held him against her, letting him feel her acceptance while she gently ran her fingers through his hair. After a time she felt the life come back into his body, as he shifted against her, and placed a hand on her surrounding arm. All the while she was thinking of the things Jamie needed most to hear.

At last she spoke. "I love you, Jamie," she said. "You are special to me. I don't care if you talk or not. After all, talking doesn't make you special. What's inside of you makes you special. So I love you whether you talk or not." These were the words she planned to use every day, until Jamie Hudson understood that he was of priceless worth, no matter what his handicap.

But she was not prepared for his reaction. Jamie went absolutely rigid, every small muscle, every tiny sinew stiffening. He would have fallen from her lap had she not held on to him tightly.

She continued to rock, back and forth, waiting to see what would happen next. It didn't take long before her arms ached from the effort of holding his taut form. She tried to turn him to a more comfortable position, but with all his small strength he resisted her. That was when she realized he was stiff with terror, and her own mouth grew dry as she tasted his fear. It was then she knew that Jamie's anger and fear were directed more at himself than Reid.

Immediately she began to do what she could to reassure him. Softly she began to sing, "Hush little baby, don't say a word, Mama's gonna buy you a mockingbird..." She rocked and rocked, and sang and sang, until the words no longer made any sense, and her arms felt as though they were going to fall from their sockets. Finally Jamie's body relaxed, and he slept against her breast.

That afternoon she received five perfectly formed, intricately carved wooden roses. They were smooth and cool to the touch. There was no note.

When Reid came to get his son that afternoon, Diana was in the preschool room, speaking with another parent. She looked up to see him standing in the doorway, dressed in his dark suit, his eyes on her face. She could not control the blush that immediately suffused her features. His eyes flared briefly, and she glanced quickly away, her gaze coming to rest upon Jamie, who was sitting at a small table, his hands in his lap. An open picture book was in front of him, but during the entire time Diana had been in the room, Jamie had not turned a single page.

"Jamie," Reid said.

Immediately Jamie closed the book, and rising from his chair, walked to his father's side. Diana watched as Reid's gaze traveled slowly around the room, so that when their eyes met again, it seemed almost coincidental, although she knew it was not so. He inclined his head, and said quietly, "Good evening, Miss Rowe," and she wondered if anyone else heard the amused familiarity there.

"Have a nice night," she replied inanely, as she would to any parent. Then he was gone, Jamie at his side. She did not realize until much later that father and son had never once touched. Nor, except for Reid saying Jamie's name, had they communicated with each other in any way.

Thursday when Diana went to get Jamie he came willingly enough, and rested in her lap easily. "I love you, Jamie. You are special to me. I don't care if you talk or not. Talking doesn't make you special. What's inside of you makes you special. I love you whether you talk or not."

Jamie looked at her out of his golden eyes, reminding her of nothing so much as a doomed hero in a fairy tale. But he didn't go rigid again, and he allowed her to rock him. She told him a story about a frog who was kissed by a princess, and turned into a prince himself. Then she kissed his cheek, and led him out to the playground, where Sally Nussbaum stood waiting. "Here is a prince," Diana said. "Prince Jamie. He would like to be pushed on a swing." Sally smilingly assented and, grasping Jamie's hand firmly in her young strong one, took him to the swing set.

Thursday afternoon Diana received a paperweight. Encased inside were half a dozen tiny white roses. The card read: *Tomorrow.* She let the stiff white paper flutter to her desk, before she picked it up again and crumpled it in her hand. She knew that she was once again trembling.

She was terribly afraid. She no longer knew what she wanted. Everything seemed so cloudy and confused.

That night Jenny Sevilla called. "I just wanted you to be the first to know," she said. "Harry and I have set a date: the first Saturday in November."

"That's wonderful news," Diana said, genuinely pleased.

"We're planning a small wedding. Harry hates pomp and circumstance, and I couldn't care less myself. But we thought we'd have a best man and maid of honor. Will you stand up with me, Diana?"

"That's the nicest compliment I've had all week. I'd love to, Jenny."

How simple life seemed for Harry Reichenbach and Jenny Sevilla: They met; they fell in love; they got married. Happily ever after, she thought. For some people it really worked.

Tomorrow was Friday. Tomorrow Reid Hudson would want to touch her again, kiss her again. Tomorrow he expected...things, and she had done nothing to change his mind. She had accepted his roses, and seen the hunger in his eyes, had felt his hand upon her head.

But she had no peace. As the week had progressed, so had her anguish. There was going to be no happily ever after for her.

Friday morning Jamie climbed into her lap willingly. As she rocked, she told him again that she loved him, repeating her words of the previous days as their own private liturgy. She lifted one of Jamie's hands, and spread his fingers out.

"Look, Jamie. You have two perfect hands, with five perfect fingers on each hand. Your hands are a gift, Jamie. You can do so much with them. You can clap your hands, and wave them. You can wash your face with them, and touch other people with them. But most of all, Jamie, you can make beautiful pictures with these hands. You are special indeed, because the pictures you make are so wonderful."

Jamie looked at his hands.

Encouraged, Diana continued. "And your eyes are perfect, Jamie. They are made exactly right, and they're clear and can see a lot of things. Your eyes tell you what to draw, don't they? It would be hard to draw without your eyes, wouldn't it? And your eyes are perfect."

Jamie had pulled away from her slightly, had sat up straight on her lap. She knew he was listening intently.

"Nearly everything about you is perfect, Jamie. That's why I'm not worried that you are not talking right now. Everyone at Lyonhouse loves you whether you talk or not. I promise you it's true. I promise."

She had said the words before, over and over. Except for that very first time, Jamie had never given any sort of indication that he had heard them. But now he gave a great shudder, and as if some chain had just broken, he threw his arms around Diana's neck and began to sob.

Diana reacted instinctively, without thought. She wrapped her arms around Jamie, and rocked, and talked. "That's right," she said. "Cry all you want, little boy. It's hurt, hasn't it? And you've been scared, haven't you? Nobody was listening, and you were all alone. But we're listening now, all of us. And we love you, Jamie. I love you."

It wasn't long before Jamie's sobs quieted to a newly contented peace, and when she looked down into his little face, she saw a brand-new smile of satisfaction stretched across his features. Her heart swelled within her breast, warring with a strong feeling of remorse for having left Jamie alone for so long.

While she had been busy organizing and managing Lyonhouse, while Reid Hudson had been turning her life upside down, this little boy had been slowly dying inside, separated from everyone else by a wall of silence. How easy it was to ignore a child, and yet how simple had been the solution: a little kindness, a little love. The locked door needed no other key. Suddenly she felt like singing.

"Jamie," she said, continuing her game of a few minutes earlier. "You have two perfect feet, with five perfect toes on each foot. You can run and play with your feet. You can run as fast as the wind. You can even dance with the clouds. Have you ever danced with the clouds, Jamie?''

When he shook his head, she stood, lifting him in her arms. "I didn't think so. I'll show you how. We'll go outside and dance with the clouds, and we'll teach everyone else how to do it, too."

Still carrying Jamie, not wanting him to lose the reassurance that only human touch can bring, Diana went to the playground. She stood right in the middle of the playground, between the swing set and the sandbox, and told Jamie to raise his hands to the sky. "Like this," she said, holding on to him with one arm, and raising her other arm as high as she could. Then she began to recite:

> "The clouds dance fast,
> The clouds dance slow,
> But I am so
> Small and low
> It's hard to reach the clouds,
> You know.
> So I stretch high
> As I can go
> And dance with them.
> The clouds so fast,
> The clouds so slow,
> Until it seems
> That they must know
> That I am here
> On earth below."

All the time Diana was turning in a slow circle, her free arm stretched high, her head tilted upward, her voice clear and strong. Several of the other children gathered around, and even the playground staff looked up to see what Diana was doing.

"Did you like that poem, Jamie?" Diana asked. At his nod, she said, "Would *you* like to dance with the clouds?"

When she tried to lower him to the ground he shook his head vigorously, and clung to her. "All right!" Diana said, in the voice of one who was starting a game. "Who wants to dance with the clouds? Come on over here, and Jamie and I will show you how to do it. Come on, Jamie, stretch out your arms...." She shifted him so that he was held securely at her waist. "Everyone ready? The clouds dance fast..." Her voice was clear and strong and full of joy.

To an adult unfamiliar with the workings of a child's mind, it was a ridiculous game. There were no rules, no patterns of movement, no order. Just a dozen or more children, all looking up at the sky, their arms stretched out every which way, their feet moving in circles, or up and down, or running, but all of them dancing with the clouds. Several of the other providers had joined in—Wanda Smith, Sally Nussbaum, even Nancy Cook. All had caught the spirit of the moment, feeling again as they had when they were young; that if they reached far enough and hard enough, they could somehow touch the sky.

It was a moment of magic, and when Diana had recited the little poem twice, and ended the game, Jamie Hudson laughed in her arms, and clapped his hands.

Nancy beamed. Sally Nussbaum gaped at them. Wanda Smith, only nineteen herself, mimicked Jamie, and clapped her own hands.

Diana spoke again, loudly. "Listen up, everyone. Everyone needs to tell Jamie that you love him, *even though he doesn't talk*. Jamie thought no one liked him here, but we all know that's wrong, don't we? Who will come and give Jamie a hug? Who will be the first to give Jamie a hug?"

There was a riot of movement. All the children loved to hug and touch, and soon Jamie, now standing on his own by Diana's kneeling form, was surrounded by other children, who gave him hugs and quick "I love you's." And Jamie was smiling ear to ear.

Jamie had been at Lyonhouse for three weeks, had been silent for almost seven months. How long is three weeks to a child? Diana wondered. Surely it must have seemed like years. And how long is seven months? She already knew the answer: a lifetime.

Nancy Cook came to stand by Diana. "That's that," Diana said. "We'll need to give Jamie special reassurances on a regular basis, but he can definitely stay at Lyonhouse."

Nancy looked at Diana with new admiration. "How did you know what to do?" she asked. "You didn't learn that in any textbook."

Diana shrugged. "We all have our gifts. Understanding children is mine. The fact that others don't have the same knowledge sometimes catches me by surprise."

Later that evening a messenger from Heritage House brought her a large brown interoffice envelope. Inside was an oversize sealed red envelope, addressed simply, *Diana*. On the enclosed card he had written, *I have waited as you asked. But no longer.* Then: *Tonight. Seven-thirty. Dress for dinner out.* The signature was a scrawling *R*.

The picture on the front of the card was of seven blood-red roses.

Reid Hudson sat at his desk and looked at the clock. Five-thirty. Soon this interminably long week would be over.

He no longer knew what he felt for Diana Rowe. He had spent a good portion of the week in an absolute rage, so that several of the people who worked for him at Heritage House were avoiding him, and he had developed a reputation for being "temperamental." Which only infuriated him more, when he considered that in New York he was known for his even, fair disposition.

On top of that he was living in a constant state of frustration. He had developed a good old-fashioned case of lust, such as would be the pride of any eighteen-year-old boy.

Tonight, he thought, and the single word became a sacred oath. Tonight, he would see Diana, and ease at last the tension threatening to explode inside him. And next week would be different. His fever would be cooled, and he would be himself, once again.

Everything would be all right, after tonight.

Chapter Ten

That evening Diana dressed carefully, in a simple modest white dress that had a high neckline, fitted sleeves that stretched to the wrist, and a hem that reached below her knee. The waist was cinched with a matching cloth belt. She draped a silver necklace over the fine tailored collar.

Looking at herself in the mirror, she smiled somewhat grimly. Her appearance was certainly innocent and virginal. There was even fear in her eyes.

Indeed, she was more frightened than she had been in a very long time. There was so much she wanted to say to Reid tonight—about Jamie, about herself. But she was filled with an apprehensive nervousness that had her wringing her hands tremulously.

Reid Hudson was planning on spending the night with her tonight.

But she was terrified that the person he wanted was a figment of his imagination, and the person she really was would not be strong enough to deal with Reid's sure power.

She thought of how she trembled when he touched her. She remembered how she had cried out his name when he kissed her. And she closed her eyes tight, knowing that somehow the time had passed when she could tell him no. Last Friday night she could have said it, perhaps. Or anytime during the past week. But not tonight, when he would arrive dark and eager on her doorstep. Tonight was not the time.

Breathing slowly, she opened her eyes. Her arms were wrapped tightly around her own waist, and there were shadows under her eyelashes.

Was an affair with Reid what she really wanted?

Her hands shook slightly as she pulled her hair back with silver combs, from which short strings of pearls dangled gracefully. She applied just a touch of makeup—a dash of loose powder, a bit of gloss on her lips, a tiny amount of brown shadow.

She was ready early. She could think of nothing to do, and sat like a stone waiting for her doorbell to sound, rehearsing to herself what she meant to tell Reid. But she wondered if he would really ever understand.

When Diana had first come to Lansing, she had brought very little with her from New York, and much of what she had brought was now gone. Her Corvette had been sold to pay for college tuition. Many of her clothes had literally been worn to shreds during her college days, so that except for a handful of haute couture dresses, and some favorite jewelry, nothing was left of a wardrobe that had once been worth a small fortune. She had also brought from New York about thirty books, but even these had been replaced in her affection by others she liked even better.

So that now there was very little left to remind her of her previous life.

Still, she never forgot that desolate time and clung to the lessons she had learned. That the loyalty of a friend was more to be treasured than the kiss of a lover, and the regard of her peers more to be esteemed than ten Corvettes. She had learned that respect for herself was the beginning of freedom, and to magnify her own talents the source of true pride. And there was another thing that she knew, although she could not tell when she had learned it, or who had taught her the lesson. When she touched the hand of a child, she felt, for a time, beautiful.

Reid arrived at precisely seven twenty-six.

"I'll be right down," she said into the intercom. She didn't want to start the evening with Reid in her apartment, where the memory of the hunger that had exploded between them, just one week ago today, would be strong indeed.

She found Reid standing with deceptive patience a few feet away from the front door. He had discarded his formal business attire for black summer slacks and a deep paisley-print silk shirt, opened at his neck.

"Hello, Diana," he said gravely, his face impassive.

"Hello, Reid."

He took her arm and led her to his car, opening her door and helping her ease inside. Hunkering down on his heels, he tucked her skirt around her legs. Then he walked around the hood of the sedan, opened his own door, and slid in.

For a moment he sat there silently. She waited for him to start the car, but instead of doing so he turned his head and looked at Diana. His short dark lashes were incredibly thick. His blue-black eyes were brilliant with barely suppressed emotion.

Then, quite deliberately, he lifted his arm until his hand encircled her neck. Without hurrying he leaned over the space between the two seats and drew her closer. With sure determination he lowered his head to hers, and even though she had plenty of time to prepare, she was still caught in a state of unreadiness. His lips brushed hers once, twice, then stayed for closer examination.

His lips were warm and dry. She could smell the faint scent of his after-shave upon his cheeks. His mouth, when it opened on hers, tasted deliciously sweet. His hand upon her neck tightened momentarily as his kiss deepened—she could feel his strength of purpose there. Her ears were filled with the sounds of his breathing, of the brush of his arm against her car seat, of the small sounds that were coming from her own throat.

She felt her body soften, grow pliant, and knew with a sense of utter helplessness that her own seduction had begun.

He took her to an exclusive, out-of-the-way restaurant, where everything was lit by candles, the atmosphere was slow and languorous, the service subdued and deferential.

Reid treated her with utmost courtesy. He pulled her chair out when she sat down, and the brush of his hand against her neck seemed almost accidental. He sat directly across from her, his foot carelessly placed against her own. He asked her preference when ordering, and she knew she gave him an answer, but later could not remember what she had wanted.

She sat there, and all the words she meant to say died in her throat. Instead she was strangely tongue-tied, aware more than ever of Reid's male beauty. In the dim light of the restaurant, he looked like an ancient pagan god. His skin glowed bronze in the flickering candlelight, his eyes were dark and brooding. She felt the muscles in her abdomen begin to tighten, even as the rest of her body grew relaxed, almost sleepy. She looked at Reid out of slumberous eyes.

He stared at her, and there was awe in his night-blue gaze, and hunger, and possession.

She forced herself to ask him questions—about Knotingsly, about Heritage House. But his answers were brief, almost curt, as if those subjects had little interest for him, and held no relevance to the present moment.

Diana found she had no appetite.

"Has Archie Davidson bothered you anymore?" Reid asked suddenly. "Has he said anything else to you that might be construed as threatening?"

She shook her head. "I haven't seen either Archie or his wife. But I'll have to testify at the initial hearings, which will be next month."

Something of her feelings must have communicated itself to him, for he commented, "You're not looking forward to it."

"No."

"What will you say?"

She shrugged, looking down at her food, aware more than ever of the feel of his foot gently touching her own. "I will tell what I saw, no more, no less."

His eyes flashed, and she knew she had somehow made him angry. She looked away from him, glancing at the other patrons in the small dining room, then turned back.

"What language can I use to describe the things that we saw?" she said at last. "Words mean nothing! What phrases are there that do justice to the brutalizing of an innocent child? What answers to *my* questions will there be in the courtroom? Will there be wisdom there? Or understanding? Or healing of any kind?" She bit her lip then, fearing that she sounded incredibly naive, that she was making a fool of herself.

"What questions do you have, Diana?"

She shook her head, suddenly embarrassed, and was quiet for a long time. The candles on their table burned steadily.

Around them she could hear the conversations of others, pleasant and subdued. To her right someone got up to leave; to her left a party of four were laughing quietly together.

Questions. She had a few. Maybe if she told him what they were, he would understand...what? That she was afraid of what was happening between them? That they were really strangers to each other?

When she finally spoke, her voice was calmer, more controlled. She gave a little, self-deprecating smile. "My questions have no answers, I'm afraid. But someday, somehow, I would like to know *why?* I remember a professor put that question on an exam once, and the correct answer was *because*. For every why there was a because. But I can never find an answer to my whys."

He reached out and took her hand, brought it to his lips. "This," he said. "This is the why." And he kissed her palm.

"No," she replied huskily. But her voice was trembling with the need she could no longer keep hidden.

Reid was still holding her hand, rubbing her palm gently. "And where better to find the whys than in the arms of a friend?"

Only she was still not sure that Reid Hudson was her friend. She looked at him, but his face was hidden in shadow, and she could not see his eyes.

He took her dancing, and she laid her head upon his silk paisley shirt, her silver hair spread against it like the moon's rays in the night. His arms were strong and muscular; they held her close, close. She felt the rising desire in him; his body communicated it to her with every breath he took, and she knew her own answering hunger. Her breathing grew shallow, her legs weak. And she thought, I am without strength. I am afraid of what is happening between us, but I have no power to stay the flood. The time to speak was days ago, the moment of safety was lost, and now she had no alternative except to flow with this dark tide.

After a while Reid said, his voice low and surprisingly tender. "Let's go now. I'll take you home." And she knew he meant to stay with her there, all night long.

She was not at peace. Even as his arm surrounded her, and she melted against him, she knew no harmony. For the words she had spoken were true, seven days ago. No man had ever slept with her in her apartment. No man had slept with her for over four years. She had spent her time changing, trying to make something of herself—something of worth, of value—and she had almost succeeded. Almost she had believed in her own consequence.

Reid Hudson knew nothing of that long struggle.

Later, she was silent, and they were in the car, speeding heedlessly through the night, and nothing was clear between them. They had made no promises. No word had been spoken of the future. She was not even sure they were friends.

Soundlessly she began to cry.

He didn't notice until he had parked in front of her building and opened his door to get out, flooding the car's interior with light. Turning to smile at her, he frowned instead, seeing the moisture on her cheeks. "Hey," he said softly, "What's this?" He reached out to touch her face.

She felt his fingers upon her skin, wiping away her tears. "Reid . . ." She choked, unable to speak further.

He leaned over and kissed her, and her tears dried as he comforted her with his lips. "Don't worry," he said. "It'll be all right."

How did he know that? He didn't even really know her. She was afraid nothing would be all right.

They went upstairs to her apartment. Reid took her keys from her shaking hand and unlocked her door. She automatically reached for her light switch, but before she could make contact, he caught her hand, and turned her instead in his arms. "No lights," he murmured. "Not yet."

"But we have not talked..." she said, sounding indistinct and uncertain.

"Later." His voice seemed suddenly harsh, as he sensed the time of his waiting was over. "We'll talk later."

Then he was kissing her, and she was drowning in a sea of weakness and pleasure. He laughed low in his throat as he removed the combs from her hair. "I've been wanting to do that all night," he growled against her neck. "You've been driving me mad." And she hadn't really meant to, but her hands were buried in his hair as she bent his head down to her. She had no intention, but she was suddenly pulling at him, pulling him down, so that they were lying on the carpet of her living room, their legs entangled. And her hand was against his bare chest, and his fingers were touching her naked breast, and she had no choice... no choice...

"Diana," he said huskily. "You are so beautiful."

Remember, Diana, men will like you when you are beautiful.

She closed her eyes at the searingly painful memory. What was she doing here? What had she allowed?

Four years ago she had made a choice.

She spoke unthinkingly. "Stop!" But her voice was buried in the darkness.

Her blood was running hot and fast, her legs had lost all their strength, she was shaking from head to toe. Reid's head was at her breast, and involuntarily she arched toward him, wanting... wanting what? Release? Ecstasy?

She felt Reid's body against her own. She felt the skin of his back, smooth and slick with sweat. His chest hairs brushed against her trembling stomach as his mouth found her swelling breast. She felt his hand underneath her skirt, stroking, stroking.

She felt tears upon her cheeks. She felt her body grow cold, and ice form within her heart.

What have I done? she thought in terrible self-reproach. I am being swept away, but the choice was not really mine. What am I doing, here on the floor, panting and eager for a man who has made me no promise, except that of a night's pleasure? I promised myself this would never happen again. I promised myself...

She tensed her muscles, and tried to sit up, but Reid's arms were on either side of her, and the weight of his chest was against her own. He had raised his body, and now his lips were seeking hers.

"Reid," she said, turning her head. "Stop, please."

His hand moved over her, stimulating, promising. She heard herself moan, and knew a moment of true panic. It was surely too late....

For four years she had held her body sacred, inviolate. And ten minutes from now it would all be for nothing. She had run a long race, but she was going to end where she had begun. Her traitorous body writhed, responding to the message of Reid's hands.

His lips touched her neck, her ears, her chin. He drew in a breath, before his throat rumbled wordlessly in hunger and triumph. He bent his head and kissed her eyes.

And tasted the tears there.

His hand stilled against her waist. His body stiffened over hers. "Diana?"

She stared at him, saying nothing.

"Diana, why are you crying?"

"I..." she whispered, groping for words. "I'm sorry, but I think... I've made a terrible mistake, Reid."

His head came up as if she had struck him, and his eyes seemed like black holes of darkness. He looked at her in utter disbelief.

"I'm sorry," she whispered. "I'm so sorry, Reid."

He sat up, still staring at her.

She did likewise. Not bothering to cover her nakedness, she buried her face in her hands. She was trembling still, hungry still. She felt like a fool.

"I wanted to talk," she managed. "I wanted to explain, but I could not get the words out."

"You wanted to explain," he repeated coldly.

"I...I haven't done this, Reid. Not since I left New York. I promised myself long ago that next time—" she took a deep, shuddering breath "—next time it would mean something besides...besides lust. I promised myself that next time it would be a gift, something special. That there would be true love..."

"Love." If possible, his voice was colder still. He stood up.

She reached for the dress that had been pulled down to her legs, and tugging it upward, covered her breasts.

"Do you think..." Her voice was no more than a wistful whisper. "Do you think we could ever be friends, Reid? Just get to know each other, and be friends?"

He laughed, low and bitter. "You ask me that, at a time like this? No, Diana. There is no possibility of friendship between you and me."

"I see."

He was shrugging into his shirt. She struggled to rise, still holding her dress against her. "Don't bother," he said frigidly. "I'll let myself out."

"Reid..."

He paused, a mere shadow in the darkness.

"There's one more thing, Reid. It's Jamie. He needs you so much. He needs to know you love him. He needs you to touch him. He needs to know he's...beautiful on the inside, Reid."

She wasn't really certain what she was trying to say. Thoughts were all mixed up in her head, but somewhere she had the idea that she wanted to tell Reid that what had happened between them was unimportant in the light of his greater calling. But his words stopped her.

"I'm afraid Jamie will not learn those things from me."

"You're his father. Who else will teach him?"

His body grew rigid, even as his voice became bleak as a drought-swept plain. "I have no son, Diana. Jamie is Cynthia's bastard. Born two years after we made *our* promises, *our* vows. I have no idea who his father really is."

She stared at him then, her silver hair loose and wild upon her bare shoulders, tears glistening from her eyes, until he turned from her and went quietly out the door.

Sunday evening Diana called Tilly. "I need to talk," she said gracelessly. "Can I come over?"

Tilly lived in a farmhouse on the outskirts of the city. She had three acres, which she mostly let grow unrestrained. The house itself lacked any definite style. It had started out as one big all-purpose chamber, and over the years had been added on to, one room at a time, so that pieces of building stuck out at odd angles.

Inside was just as bad. Tilly was widely traveled, and quite a collector. Everywhere Diana looked were memorabilia of some trip or other. And Tilly believed in stacks: stacks of paper, stacks of dishes, stacks of clothing.

Tonight Tilly was dressed comfortably in hot pink sweatpants and an oversize T-shirt. Large block earrings dangled to her shoulders.

Diana could not help but smile. "Is this the woman," she teased gently, "who speaks with power before legislatures, who persuades with the voice of an angel, who commands respect wherever she goes?"

Tilly shrugged, her earrings swaying with the motion. Even though her eyes were twinkling, she answered with her usual seriousness. "I learned long ago that living up to other's expectations took more energy than it was worth.

Ultimately the only person who matters is the one who stares back at you when you wash your face in the morning." Then she reached up and gave Diana's cheek a quick kiss. "But you haven't come to talk about me, my dear. I've put on a pot of tea, and we can sit and chat as long as you like."

The tea was warm and sweet; the evening air coming in through the open windows laden with the odors of summer; and the house itself was quiet. In spite of all the clutter, Diana had always felt a real sense of peace at Tilly's house.

"Perhaps the most important person is the one seen in a mirror," Diana began, "but there have been times when the opinion of others mattered to me more. *Your* opinion has kept me going during some pretty hard times."

Tilly smiled gently, accepting the compliment. Then she said, with a discernment that never ceased to amaze Diana, "So whose opinion has been bothering you lately?"

For a moment Diana did not answer. Then she looked up and met Tilly's eyes. "Reid Hudson's."

"Uh-huh. I must say I'm not in the least surprised. Would you like to tell me about it?"

Diana wanted to. Ever since Reid had walked out her door Friday night she had felt heavy, confused— surrounded as it were by a thick mist, where nothing could be seen clearly. She knew she had made a complete fool of herself. She had, after all, committed the unforgivable female sin—she had led a man on and then cut him off at the last moment. She had no excuse; she had understood the rules of the game for a long time.

To Tilly she said, inadequately, "I went out with Reid last Friday night."

Tilly simply raised her eyebrows and looked at Diana curiously. "Did you now?" Then, seeing the tears in Diana's eyes, she added, "You'd better tell me about it, dear one."

And it was sweet relief to tell all, from the first time Lucy had introduced them, to their fiery parting four years ago. She told of the continuing tension between Reid and herself, and how he had come uninvited to see her just a little over a week ago. She explained that she asked him for some time to sort things out. She spoke of the daily presents, of the physical hunger, of the changes in Jamie, all of which had culminated in Friday night's disaster.

"I feel like an immature fifteen-year-old," Diana said. "But the truth is, Tilly, I don't know how I will continue to face Reid, until my time here is over. I can barely face myself."

"He really didn't leave you alone, you know."

"What?" Diana asked blankly.

"Reid. The roses, the daily reminders, the way he touched you whenever he saw you. Either he didn't understand what you were asking for, or he simply didn't give it any respect."

"The time to sort things out, you mean."

"That's right. You asked for some time, and he didn't give you any. He didn't honor your request."

Diana had spent so much energy remembering her own faults that she had not thought to look at Reid's actions very critically. Now, however, something in her eased a little. "I suppose you're right," she said slowly.

Tilly smiled. "I know I am. And you were thinking more with your heart than your head."

"With my hormones, you mean."

"No, my dear. You care for Reid more than you are admitting. The trouble is, you don't care for yourself enough."

"What do you mean?"

"I mean you let things go as far as you did because you thought to do otherwise was to invite rejection. You felt afraid to make your own demands. You said that you kept thinking of the things you wanted to tell him, but you never said a word, just let things go on as they would. Probably that's because, deep down, you still don't feel that you're worth sticking up for."

Diana absorbed Tilly's words silently.

"But what you did was right, Diana, even if it was a little late. You did the right thing."

"You're going to make me cry."

"Truth has that capability, my dear. It's so rarely spoken, it will bring the strongest man to his knees."

"Reid believes in truth. He told me so."

Tilly rose then to retrieve the teapot from the stove, and refilled their cups. "Reid believes only in what he knows and understands. He does not yet comprehend that there may be other truth, still outside the realm of his own experience."

"You like Reid, don't you, Tilly?" For some reason the answer to that question was incredibly important to Diana.

"Yes, I do. Would you like to know why?"

At Diana's nod, Tilly continued firmly. "Reid tries. He has set a high standard for himself, and he is valiant in trying to reach it. This gives him his nobility.

"But he also fails, and every time he falls short he wounds himself a little. He's covered with scars from his battles with life, Diana. He has always seemed an almost tragic figure to me, battling his windmills like a twentieth-century Don Quixote. And for that reason, more than any other, I think he's worth fighting for, Diana."

"Have you ever loved a man, Tilly?"

A look of wry acceptance crossed Tilly's face. Then she shook her head. "No. In fact, I could probably count on one hand the dates I've been on, and they were years ago. Many men have called me a friend, but I've never had a lover. Never been propositioned, never been asked to be married, never been in love. I guess whatever men want romantically in a woman is missing in me."

There was no hint of self-pity in Tilly's tone, which fact gave Diana permission to say, "Doesn't it bother you? Haven't you ever felt that something was missing?"

Tilly gave a short bark of laughter. "Of course. I used to think something terrible was wrong with me, that I was somehow defective. But with years comes a little wisdom, hopefully, and one day I woke up and knew that I had intrinsic value, just me, Tilly Martel, all by myself. If no man wanted me, I didn't have to spend my life languishing in despair. I had intelligence, I had a sense of humor, and I had a definite desire to be useful, to live a purposeful life. So I put myself to it, and I've never looked back." She smiled. "You don't have to have a man to be happy, Diana. Happiness comes from within, not without."

"Yet just a few minutes ago you told me to fight for Reid Hudson."

"And for only one reason. The same reason I fought for you, my dear. Because I *loved* you. When you were in high school I fought for you. When you came out here to be with me in Lansing, I was fighting for you all the way. You're special to me, Diana. And not because of any outside beauty, or wealth. I loved what you were on the inside. And that is what you see in Reid Hudson. The man on the inside. The person worth fighting for."

Diana stood abruptly, overturning her chair as she did so. She thought she could not bear Tilly's words. To be loved for what was within . . . it had been her hunger for so long, it shocked her that someone else understood. And then she thought, perhaps Reid had the same hunger. Perhaps that is the common need, the universal cry. Love me, not for who you see, but for who you are.

She turned and righted her chair, sat herself on it. She gave Tilly a watery smile. "Thank you," she said.

Tilly smiled back. "Of course. Anytime. But Diana, there's one more thing. A bit of advice from an old woman."

"Surely, Tilly."

"These past years, during the time you've spent in Lansing, you've fought a hard fight, and I've been enormously proud of you. Don't turn your back on all you've learned. In your struggle with Reid, use the strength you've gained here. Cling to what you know, as if to a rod of iron. Never let go."

"And will Reid love me then?"

"I cannot predict the future. But remember what I said and you will love yourself, no matter what happens."

After that their conversation moved on to other things. Tilly was beginning a new book, and was excited about starting a different project. Diana spoke of the publicity Lyonhouse was receiving. The first of the quarterly media open houses, she said, was likely to be big indeed. And Tilly smiled and commented gently, "Good. You'll handle everything beautifully, I'm sure. After all, you're a person of exceptional capability and great worth."

And still later Tilly cleared some papers off the living-room sofa and made up a bed, so that Diana could spend the night. Just before Tilly went off to her own bedroom, Diana asked, almost pensively, "Did you always want to be a writer and children's advocate, Tilly? Was this your goal from the beginning?"

Tilly shook her head. "In the beginning I had no goals. Like you, I have evolved." She paused. "But why do you ask, Diana? What do you want to be?"

And then, because Diana felt warm and calm and safe at last, she told the truth. "It sounds so silly, in our day and age. But more than anything else, I would like to be a mother." She looked at Tilly, trusting her friend not to laugh. "I want to do better than my own mother did. I want to have a child, and raise her to believe in herself."

Tilly leaned forward, and put her hand gently on Diana's arm. "Being a true mother is a most exemplary aspiration."

Diana looked at Tilly then. Only one lamp was burning in the living room, and the planes of Tilly's face were soft, and there was love in Tilly's eyes. In that moment Diana felt there was no one in the world more beautiful.

"You are my mother," she said wonderingly. "My true mother."

"Yes," Tilly agreed. "I am." She reached out and smoothed Diana's brow. "I always wanted a daughter, and long ago I adopted you. Didn't even ask your permission, either."

And for the first time Diana understood the bond that is felt between mothers and daughters, between sisters and friends, and was comforted. She smiled at Tilly, and Tilly smiled back, before turning out the light and leaving her to sleep. And the dark of the night was soft, and the sofa seemed like a cradle, and the creakings of the old house was a lilting lullaby.

Diana slept.

Chapter Eleven

But what seemed clear and easy in the gentle peace of Tilly's house turned to bewildering confusion on Monday morning. Reid never brought Jamie to Lyonhouse that day, or the next day, either.

On Wednesday Diana had Nancy Cook contact his office. "He's gone back to New York," Nancy reported. "Nobody seems to know for how long. Guess he's taken the little tyke back with him."

Diana tormented herself with guilt and worry. Jamie was gone, and she had never once told Reid about the progress they had made with him here at Lyonhouse. She had spent all that time with Reid, and instead of telling him what was truly important, she had acted like a complete fool. Now he had no idea how Jamie had soaked up the love here like a sponge; how he had cuddled with her in the rocking chair, listening to her stories and promises, how he had laughed and clapped his hands and danced with the clouds.

She should have told Reid.

I have no son. Jamie is Cynthia's bastard.

It doesn't matter, she thought fiercely. He's yours, just the same.

On Thursday evening she had dinner with Harry and Jenny. "You're looking haggard," Harry said bluntly. "What's up?"

Yet even with her closest friends, Diana found she could not completely dissemble. "Lyonhouse has been more of a challenge than I suspected," she admitted instead. "And with only two months left before someone else takes over, I feel as though there is so much for me to do."

"You need a break," Jenny commented. "My folks have a vacation home up north. Would you like to use it sometime? How about the long Fourth of July weekend?"

She was about to refuse, when Harry added, "Think about it, Diana—a chance to get away from everything. Imagine three days of utter peace and quiet. No telephones. No Lyonhouse. No children. And..." he added, "...no bosses."

It *was* tempting. "Won't someone from your family be using it?" she asked Jenny.

The dark-haired woman shook her head. "We all have a big family party to attend in Ohio. My mother's brother is hosting a reunion, and everyone will be there. My parents would probably be relieved to know someone was using their place for a few days."

"I'll think about it, then," Diana said.

On Friday Diana received a letter from Lucy Hudson. Lucy was going to be in Lansing the first of August. Would Diana care to get together with her then?

Of course, Diana wrote back. She'd be delighted.

And so her fourth week at Lyonhouse passed. That weekend she drove herself back to Chicago, and spent an entire day walking around the University of Chicago campus. Come September, she thought, this will be my home. I might as well see what it feels like.

The following Monday Diana was watching one of the Lyonhouse providers tell the three-year-olds a story, when she suddenly realized her cheeks were wet with tears. Wiping them away quickly, she hurried from the room. You're falling apart, Rowe, she told herself sternly. Get your act together. But the same thing happened to her later as she was working at her desk, and again the next day when someone put an arm around her in casual camaraderie.

"Are you all right?" Nancy Cook asked her. "Is there something I can do?"

"I'm afraid not," Diana replied. "But thanks for asking." To herself she thought, What is happening to me? All my ice is melted, and I have no protection left. She thought of old fairy tales, when time would stop, and everything would be absolutely still. She wished her own life could do the same, that she could keep time from going forward, until she had found a way to once again freeze her heart.

But time has its own inexorable way of moving onward, and the warm summer days passed, until it was yet another Monday. And Diana, sitting at her desk, began to write Reid Hudson a letter.

Dear Reid, she began. *I know I'm probably the last person you want to hear from, but I thought I ought to tell you some things about Jamie...*

Only when the letter was done, and safely in the mail, did Diana begin to feel a small portion of peace.

Reid Hudson was finding no peace. He had been in New York for two and a half weeks, and nothing had gone as he wanted.

He had rediscovered, to his hidden chagrin, that Acting Director Bill Tyrell was doing an exceptional job at Knotingsly. During the two months Reid had been in Lansing,

Bill had handled a new advertising campaign, had streamlined operations in Knotingsly's four retail stores, and had faced the unpleasant task of firing a senior executive.

Bill Tyrell was doing very well indeed. Knotingsly was lucky to have such a capable, efficient man as second-in-command. The only problem was he made Reid feel redundant in his own company.

That was not, of course, Reid's only problem.

Reid had meant to impose upon his godparents again and leave Jamie with them. After all, he was gone much of the day, and Knotingsly certainly didn't have a New York Lyonhouse. It only made sense, he told himself, for the boy to stay with Pete and Mary.

But then he had looked in the expressionless, golden eyes of the boy, and remembered his last, unfortunate conversation with Diana Rowe. *It's Jamie. He needs you so much.* And he had found himself unable to do that which would have been, after all, easiest—get Jamie out of his life for a while. Instead he had contacted a temporary nanny service, with the result that now he had in residence a mid-forties woman who cooed at him in the mornings and fussed over him at night. Mrs. Florabelle Attison was driving Reid crazy, and he found himself staying away from home as much as possible.

And then there was Diana. He could not get her out of his mind. Even though he told himself that his desire for her was dead, once and for all. Even though he knew that whomever and whatever Diana Rowe was, she sure as hell wasn't for him.

Last Saturday night he had actually gone on a date. Except for his two evenings with Diana, this was the first time he had been out with a woman other than Cynthia since before their marriage, over six years before. He found the experience curious. The woman of his choice was well-known in the city, was calm and serene to be with, and was certainly mature in her understanding of male-female relationships. Yet before the evening was half over he had been bored silly, and was able to refuse her offer of a nightcap with only marginal charm. He had gone home to dream of Diana Rowe.

Damn her.

It was Wednesday evening. His day at Knotingsly had been incredibly tedious. Bill, knowing his place, had been in and out of Reid's office a dozen times to confer about decisions he was perfectly capable of making himself, until Reid had said irritably, "Quit toadying, Tyrell. You know and I know you don't need my advice. I have better things to do than be a rubber stamp in my own company." So then Bill Tyrell, with ill-concealed relief, left Reid alone.

He had spent the afternoon touring his manufacturing plant. Everything was going smoothly there—no major problems. He knew that when he visited his stores tomorrow, as he planned to do, he would find the same thing to be true.

The truth was, Knotingsly was incredibly healthy. Its profits were up, its production lines hummed, its stores did a fine trade. He missed the challenge he had found at Heritage House when he had worked at merging the two enterprises as smoothly as possible.

He was in constant telephone contact, of course, with Mark Lyon, who told him nothing more than he thought Reid wanted to hear. Yesterday Reid had spoken with David Stone, and there had been an odd hesitancy in the man's voice. All of Reid's nerves had gone suddenly alert.

He was going to have to return to Lansing. No, he amended—he *wanted* to return to Lansing. He was bored here, in New York. He wanted to be where the action was and for now the action was in Lansing. There was still so much to do there. In fact, he really should not have stayed away so long.

He frowned momentarily. He had allowed his involvement with Diana Rowe to interfere with what he knew was good business. He had left Heritage, and Mark Lyon was still in charge.

Still, he would wait another few days. There was the tour of the stores planned for tomorrow, and he knew the managers involved had been working to spruce everything up for his inspection. There was an important meeting on Friday, at which his attendance was probably a necessity. And he had, unfortunately, hired Mrs. Attison through the Fourth of July. Still, when these commitments were done, he would leave immediately. He would not spend another full week in New York.

He reached that decision as he turned into the driveway of his three-story brownstone. For once he had arrived home at a reasonable hour.

Upon entering his home, he knew immediately from the odors wafting through the house that Mrs. Attison had prepared another of her completely indistinguishable dinners. He had not expected that his temporary nanny would act as cook, also, but the woman had insisted. He privately thought that her results were only nominally better than the frozen meals he usually picked up at the supermarket. And at least with frozen fare, he knew what he was getting. He was never quite sure about Mrs. Attison's offerings.

Reid valued his privacy; he hated having someone live in. Just a few more days, he promised himself. The next time he was in New York, Jamie could go to Pete and Mary's, and the hell with Diana Rowe.

Automatically Reid headed away from the kitchen. Usually he would sit and look at his mail and quietly sip a glass of wine. But tonight he felt an odd restlessness. He decided to look for Jamie instead. His conscience had been pricking him. He really had paid very little notice of the child. In fact, now that he thought of it, he realized it had been three days since he had even seen the boy.

He found Jamie in his bedroom, sitting on the floor, his back against his bed, his legs angled out in front of him. The television was going, but Jamie wasn't paying any attention to it. He wasn't paying attention to anything else, either.

The room was as neat as a pin. The toys Reid had purchased sat with precise order on the shelves, and Reid doubted if even one had been removed from its place all day. The crayons and colored pencils were still in their boxes, and the stack of drawing paper Reid had provided was completely unused.

"Hello, Jamie," Reid said, but he was somehow unsurprised when he got no response. Not with so much as a flicker of an eyelash did Jamie acknowledge his presence.

Reid looked at the neat room, at the television playing mindlessly on, at the little boy sitting motionless on the floor. He felt his gut twist painfully. It had been so easy to assume that Mrs. Attison was taking good care of the boy. He had been more than glad to leave the caretaking of Jamie to someone else.

A mixture of guilt and rage settled over him. He turned on his heel and went to find Mrs. Attison.

She was taking some sort of muddy-looking casserole out of the oven, and Reid felt his stomach turn in immediate unease.

"Mrs. Attison..." he began.

She looked up at him rather vaguely. "Oh. Hello, Mr. Hudson. Dinner will be ready momentarily. And your mail is on the front table."

"I am not interested in dinner," he said, keeping his temper under tight control. "I think I'll pass tonight."

"Missing meals is bad for the system," Mrs. Attison said righteously.

Reid rubbed his head. His anger was growing more explosive by the second. "Mrs. Attison, put the… dinner…down. On the table. On the stove. Anyplace. I want to talk with you. Now."

Her eyes widened slightly, but she did as he asked. The casserole dish was placed carefully on the stovetop. "Well, of course, Mr. Hudson. How can I help you?"

He pulled up a chair and sat down at the kitchen table. "Tell me about Jamie, Mrs. Attison. What has he done today?"

"Done today?"

"That's what I said. I want to know what he's done—what you've done with him. Did you take him to the park, for instance?"

"The park?" She blinked owlishly.

"Yes. There's one right around the corner."

Mrs. Attison shook her head vigorously. "Oh, no, Mr. Hudson. Not in New York. It's really too dangerous for me to be out with a helpless child like that."

Reid closed his eyes, shaking his head disbelievingly. How could he have been so blind? He was *responsible* for that boy, dammit. He was furious with Mrs. Attison, but even more furious with himself. He stood suddenly, scraping his chair back, and glared at the nanny.

"Jamie isn't helpless! He just doesn't speak, that's all. But he can hear perfectly well. He can walk and run and play like any other child. So tell me, Mrs. Attison, what has Jamie done today? Has he looked at any books? Has he drawn any pictures? How long has that damn TV been on anyway?"

Mrs. Attison found one question she could answer. "Why, I turned it on first thing this morning. *Fun on Magic Street* is such a nice program for children."

"I see," he bit out. "At what time does this *Magic Street* program begin?"

"First thing. Eight o'clock, I believe."

"And Jamie has done nothing except watch television since eight o'clock this morning?"

Mrs. Attison backed away slightly. She was just beginning to understand how truly angry Reid was.

"Well...ah...that is...I've been busy cleaning your home, Mr. Hudson. That takes time, you know. I dusted all the shelves, and put new sheets on your bed, and of course there was dinner to make..."

"Mrs. Attison, you came to me from Nannies International, not some maid service. Your primary function was to take care of Jamie."

"Why, I do take care of him, Mr. Hudson. Poor little guy. It really is too bad he's so backward, to put it plainly sir...."

Reid took a deep breath in an effort at self-control. "You're fired, Mrs. Attison. Right now. This minute I want you *out* of my home."

He smiled grimly as the woman looked at him blankly. All he could feel was relief.

"But...but..." Florabelle Attison was actually sputtering. "You can't *do* that, Mr. Hudson. It says on my contract that I was hired through the end of next week."

"I'll pay your damned salary then. Earn it cleaning your own house, not mine. *But don't come back here anymore!*"

Reid turned abruptly from Mrs. Attison's now red face and strode back to Jamie's bedroom. He jerked the television cord from the wall socket, as he cursed all televisions to hell. He grasped Jamie and raised him in his arms. "Let's get out of here," he said.

Passing Mrs. Attison, who was gathering her purse and a few other belongings from the kitchen, he headed to the front door. "We're eating out," he told Jamie, making sure his voice carried through to the now ex-nanny. "We'll go someplace that caters to kids, and you can have anything you want.''

Jamie made no response, but later that night, after they had returned to a peacefully empty house, and Reid had prepared Jamie for bed, he stood looking at the boy as he lay under the light summer blanket. Jamie's hair was red-gold against the white pillowcase, his skin was so fair as to be nearly translucent, and his brown eyes looked up at Reid almost tranquilly.

He remembered Diana kneeling beside Jamie, putting her arms around him, kissing him. He remembered watching as Diana and Jamie walked hand in hand down the Lyonhouse hallway. *Jamie needs you so much. He needs to know you love him. He needs you to touch him. He needs to know he's beautiful on the inside, Reid.*

Slowly, and very awkwardly, Reid bent down and gave the child a kiss on the cheek. ''Good night, Jamie,'' he said. ''I won't leave you with Mrs. Attison again.''

The boy smiled slightly, turned on his side and went to sleep.

On his way to the living room, Reid almost passed without noticing the stack of mail on the hallway table. But something in the fine feminine hand of the top letter caught his attention, so that he stopped to examine it further. There was no return address.

But he knew who the letter was from, even though he had only seen Diana Rowe's handwriting once before, in a memo she had sent him when Lyonhouse first opened.

He carried the still unopened envelope to his easy chair. Holding it lightly in his hand, he sat quietly for a long time. Periodically he glanced at the plain white envelope. There was only one lamp burning, and it was low, so that his face became a study in darkness—all sharp planes and jagged edges. His mouth twisted sardonically.

It was close to midnight before he slit the seal. Holding the single sheet out to the dim light, he read the carefully penned words: *Dear Reid, I know I'm probably the last person you want to hear from...*

Then she told him about Jamie. Her words were clear and concise, lacking embellishment of any kind, yet without any effort at all he pictured Diana Rowe, rocking a stiff and frightened boy until he slept against her breast. He could hear her voice as she talked to his son, low and determined. He could see her in the play yard, teaching Jamie to dance with the clouds. She told him about Jamie's pictures.

I just wanted you to know, she wrote earnestly, *what had happened here at Lyonhouse, and what a special boy you have. I am positive Jamie is unusually gifted. But even if he is not, he is still a child who is truly worth loving, Reid. I hope you can find it in your heart to do so.*

The she concluded: *As for our own terrible misunderstanding, I take full responsibility. I cannot tell you how sorry I am to have behaved so irrationally. Perhaps someday you will be able to forgive me.*

She had signed the letter, simply, *Diana.*

So Reid sat in his chair in New York and pondered the bitter irony of his fate. Down the hall a little red-haired boy lay sleeping. In his hand he held a letter from Diana Rowe, and her only concern was for that child.

Time passed, so that the noise from the street faded into an occasional car passing by in the shadows of night, and still Reid did not move. His eyes were open, although he saw nothing of the furniture and appointments of his own home. His mind was on other things.

As if it were yesterday, he could see her clearly, her soft woman's body pliable and willing next to his, her hands reaching out to him, her voice crying his name.

But she had pulled away at the last possible moment. And even though there was a name for women who behaved like that, Reid could not force himself to apply it to Diana Rowe.

She had no idea, but at that very last moment, while he had stood harsh and condemning and stared at her cruelly, a sudden wash of moonlight had come in through her window and lit her face, showing it to be tear-streaked and full of anguish. The light had glanced off her bare shoulders, causing them to gleam like alabaster, and her hair had shone like magical silver strands.

The memory had his blood singing. And he knew, with utter hopelessness, that he wanted Diana Rowe still.

The letter she had written was clenched in an abruptly fisted hand, as he balled the paper and threw it with angry force across the room.

Damn her.

Vows, she had said. Commitments, she had said. And even though he no longer felt shame for desiring Diana Rowe, he knew he would never in a million years consider marrying her.

He thought of Harry Reichenbach, and did not hear his own groan of pain. He knew intuitively that Reichenbach had respected Diana's integrity, that *he* had not tried to force her to give what she was unwilling now to share. Reid remembered the night at the opera, and he fought down a wave of jealousy so hot that he could feel his hands and face burning with it. When he looked at his hands, they were twisted into tight, painful knots.

He was a fool.

Reid was thirty-two years old, a man of respectability and honor, a man who had long ago forgotten what it was like to be young. Nothing in his life had prepared him for the obsession that poured over him and through him, until he ached with it, and—like a child—longed to cry his need aloud. Of course he was a grown man, and could do no such thing, not even in the sleeping privacy of his house, where no one could possibly see him. So he sat there instead, holding himself rigid until all his muscles hurt, and willed the hours of the night to pass.

When morning came, he packed Jamie's things, loaded a suitcase for himself, cancelled his meetings and caught the first available flight to Lansing. He had read between the lines of Diana's letter, and knew that he held the ultimate weapon with which to break through Diana's considerable defenses.

He had the boy, Jamie.

Friday morning Reid returned with Jamie to Lyonhouse. Diana was in her office, as usual. Paperwork was one of the burdens of her position, and Diana was finding she had less and less patience for it. Her gift was understanding children—not pushing forms around some desk. This was one aspect of her job that she would not miss.

Such was the nature of her thoughts when she looked up to see Reid Hudson standing in her doorway, Jamie by his side. She was then so startled that the impatience that had been reflected in her brown eyes changed to joy before she could control herself. Reid smiled slightly, and nodded in acknowledgement.

"I got your letter," he said softly.

Color flooded her face, and she looked away. Her hands, resting upon her desk, trembled slightly.

"Shy, Diana?" he asked, amused.

Her gaze came back to him then. "I'm not sure what I feel," she replied honestly. "You should have told us you were taking Jamie away. All of us were very concerned."

Reid and Jamie walked into her office, and Reid closed the door behind him. Diana rose from her chair, and came around to kneel down in front of the boy. She touched his face lightly. "I'm glad to see you, Jamie," she said. "I missed you."

Jamie merely stared at her, and made no reaction.

"Jamie?" she said. "Will you smile for me now?"

He looked at her blankly.

She wrapped her arms around the child, and lifted him as she stood to face Reid. "What has happened?" she asked, accusation clear in her tone.

Reid was watching Diana carefully. He had been right, of course. Except for that first happy flash in her eyes, there had been no glad greeting for him. Diana had felt no need to touch *his* face. Jamie got the banquet of a king, while he stood here and accepted crumbs.

Shame swept through him. He had injured them both, woman and child, and that knowledge had him almost changing the course he had planned in New York. Then Diana's eyes sparkled angrily, and he was again lost.

God help him, he wanted that woman.

So Reid shrugged. "The past few weeks have been hard on Jamie, and before you wrote me, I had no idea what was happening with him here at Lyonhouse. I was pretty busy in New York, and the nanny I hired turned out to be completely incapable. I wasn't home much, and I'm afraid I didn't notice his withdrawal until just before I got your letter."

"Oh . . . I probably should have written you sooner."

He was without mercy. "Probably you should have."

She flushed again, but she kept her head up and back straight. "And you should have been more perceptive about your own son."

His eyes narrowed, and she knew she had made him angry. Still, she was unprepared when he reached out to touch the smooth line of her cheek. Holding Jamie as she was, she made no reflexive movement. Reid's fingers wrapped themselves around her face, and his thumb traveled leisurely from her brow to the tip of her nose, and then downward to her lips. Her gaze flew upward to be caught within his, and she recognized the look of a predator in his blueblack eyes.

"*I* missed *you*," he said, rubbing her lips softly.

What game was he playing with her now? What cruel revenge had he devised? Not for a minute did Diana believe that Reid's movements were spontaneous, unplanned. But she quivered beneath his hand just the same.

"Stop, Reid," she murmured huskily. "Whatever you're playing at, please stop now. I've already apologized the best I know how. Don't punish me further, please."

His hand held her head a moment longer, before it fell away. His lids dropped, so that they hooded his eyes almost sleepily. "You're right, of course," he said mockingly. "All the passion is dead between us, isn't that right, Diana? While I was gone, you never thought of me and I never thought of you. Is that how it was?"

She was afraid now. She had expected many things, whenever she saw Reid next, but she had not thought he would attack so quickly and with such thorough devastation.

He shook his head. "Maybe that's how it was with you, Diana, but that's not how it was with me. I saw your face a thousand times a day, and I dreamed of you at night. Then you wrote me, and I came back." His eyes swept her trim figure. "There's unfinished business between you and me, Diana. I want to finish it."

"I cannot give you what you want," she whispered.

"You no longer know what I want."

Then, at the silent, agonized question in her eyes, he said, very quietly, "I want you to think of me, and I want you to help my... son." He paused, and his lips curved briefly, though the smile somehow failed to reach his eyes. "That's all, Diana. That's all I want."

Jamie had laid his head against her shoulder, and his arms had crept around her neck. She felt his weight against her as he relaxed more fully against her breast.

Reid had called Jamie *son*. And he had asked for help. Yet something hard and doubting caused her to say, with more skepticism than she intended. "For how long?"

That which was cold and black burned in his eyes, before his expression softened and he said with exquisite carefulness, "You said you wanted to be friends, Diana. Let's start with that, shall we?"

He put out his hand, and she took it, so that they shook hands gravely. When she would have spoken, he put a finger against her lips. "Shh," he said. "Don't worry. Trust me." Then, "Help Jamie, please."

He really means it, she thought unbelievingly, even as a song began to loose itself within her heart. She had done the unforgivable, and Reid had still come back, prepared to begin again. He didn't hate her, after all.

She was full of an almost reverent gratitude. Her lips curved in a smile against his fingertips, and his eyes darkened. "All right," she said. "Friends."

"Good, then."

He rubbed Jamie's back then, gently, tentatively. "I'll see you this afternoon, Jamie," he said, but his eyes were on Diana.

She had stars in her eyes, and a glow in her smile. She felt suffused with happiness and relief. Everything was so suddenly, surprisingly, fine. Everything was going to be all right.

But Diana could not know how the softness left Reid's face immediately as he turned from her, how a heavy darkness settled on his heart as he left Lyonhouse. He knew only too well what he was doing. He was using Diana's weaknesses for his own benefit. He knew such action was neither honorable, nor right.

She wanted promises.

He had no promises to give.

The honorable thing would be to leave Diana Rowe absolutely alone.

But for the first time in his life, Reid Hudson simply didn't care. He had made up his mind. He would have Diana Rowe. On his terms. On his time. He would not be made vulnerable again.

Diana worried about Jamie all weekend. His regression had left him worse than he had begun, so that he responded little to the hugs and warmth surrounding him. By the end of the day on Friday, she felt ready to weep with frustration.

Whatever she felt for Reid Hudson, however strong this thing was between them, she could not blind herself to the fact that his trip to New York had practically destroyed this little boy.

But Reid *had* asked for help. Every time she remembered that fact her heart swelled with hope. And hope clarified Diana's thinking, so that she was able to seek new possibilities, new solutions.

Next weekend was the Fourth of July. Jenny Scvilla had offered her the family cabin, two hundred miles to the north. It was quiet there, and secluded. There would be no interruptions.

Reid Hudson had said he was willing to be friends.

She would invite him and Jamie to spend the weekend with her. Together she and Reid would seek to reach Jamie, and through the striving for a mutual goal, would also gain friendship. She was sure it would happen, exactly as she planned.

And Reid would see, once and for all, that she had changed, truly changed. Perhaps he would learn to love her a little, on the inside. Perhaps there would be a future for them, after all.

Perhaps, like Harry and Jenny, their own ending could be a happy one. Perhaps dreams really did come true, and happily ever after even happened to Diana Rowe.

But it was Tuesday afternoon before Diana gained the courage to share her plans with Reid. She was both confused and relieved at the alacrity with which he fell in with them.

"This is for Jamie's sake, and for friendship," she continued.

"Did I say anything else?"

But his eyes said something different. His eyes said hunger and anticipation. So that Diana suddenly felt younger than she had in years, and incredibly foolish, and wished she could take her words back, that the invitation had never been issued. Then Reid put his arm around her in a caress that was almost brotherly, and gave her a slight hug. "It's a good idea," he said. "Quit worrying."

She wanted to, but the old anxiety was back. And at night she grew soft and languid, so that she was unable to sleep. Several times she had told herself she should retract her invitation, but she did not.

The days passed, and there was no change in Jamie. Nancy Cook mentioned a boarding school in Detroit, whose clientele was made up exclusively of emotionally handicapped kids. "We're not set up for Jamie here," Nancy said reasonably. "He needs special help."

But Diana feared Jamie had suffered too many separations in his young life. To remove him from Lyonhouse again could be the final shattering blow to his still unformed soul.

"Wait," she said. "We'll wait a little longer."

Friday came, and she bundled Jamie into her car. Reid was not going to be able to leave for a couple of hours, and would meet them later at the cabin.

A single tremor made its way through Diana's body— whether of fear or expectancy she knew not. She was going to spend a long weekend with Reid Hudson and his boy. For better or for worse, they were all three of them committed now. Whatever was going to happen, would happen.

Diana pointed the hood of her car northward, and drove on.

Chapter Twelve

The Sevilla vacation cabin was really a seven-room dwelling of modern design, artfully placed among a stand of trees so that it seemed totally isolated from encroaching civilization. The land surrounding the home was mowed and carefully tended, but where the short grass met the trees, the underbrush sprang up thick and wild. The trees themselves included several varieties: spruce and white pine, oak and wild apple, honeysuckle and willow.

There was a large expanse of white, sandy beach. The lake was deep, so deep that it absorbed the colors of the sky. There were sea gulls on the beach and over the water. The birds soared, their flight effortless, their movements incredibly graceful. The day was sunny and almost windless; the waves lapped upon the shore in their own ceaseless, ancient rhythm.

Diana was seated on a large rock, her bare feet buried in the fine sand, her hands placed for balance on the stone on either side. Several feet away Jamie was standing, looking out at the water.

She wished she knew what he was thinking.

At the beginning of the trip she had explained to Jamie carefully and in language he could understand where they were going and how long they would be staying. She told him his father would be joining them that evening. She repeated some of the things she had said before, how special he was, how loved he was. Then she told him stories. For the entire two and a half hour drive she had told Jamie one tale after another. At first the stories had been frivolous, unsubstantial, but then she had moved into the older tales. In these a boy could meet a giant, and slay him with his superior strength and cunning. A brother and sister could be left in the woods to die, and there meet a wicked witch, but still overcome all to succeed at last. She told him of an ugly duckling, who grew to be a beautiful swan. And she told him again the ancient version of an old tale, wherein the prince was the one that slept in silence, until he was discovered by a princess, who kissed him and made him whole again.

Jamie sat quiet and without reaction beside her, but she knew he was listening, for these stories—with their courage and pathos and eventual happy endings—were full of power. It was with tales such as these that she meant to reach Jamie, wherever he had fled.

She was going to find Jamie's most secret hiding place, and comfort him there. She was going to go with Jamie into his darkest nightmare, and show him that even in that bleak place, a ray of light shone through. She was going to find the small, frightened person within, and teach him that he was valued more highly than the most golden prize.

But now her voice was still, the old tales silenced for a while, as she watched Jamie stare at the water. He was standing with his unnatural motionlessness, but there was around his small frame an aura of tension, of strained expectancy, as if at any moment, he, like the birds, would break into flight.

"Touch the sky, Jamie," she whispered. "Reach out, and touch the sky."

But he just stood there, unmoving, until she eventually slid off her rock and walked to his side. Taking his hand, she said, "Let's go inside, shall we? Maybe we can decide which bedroom will be yours."

Reid arrived at eight o'clock.

She had prepared a simple dinner—fresh garden salad, baked potatoes and steaks, with a small hamburger for Jamie. Reid talked easily of the work he had done in New York, of the continuing changes being made at Heritage House. He asked Diana endless questions about Lyonhouse, and listened attentively to her answers. Then he shifted the subject. "Tell me about your college years, Diana. How did you end up at Michigan State?"

She shrugged. "Tilly was in Lansing."

"A remarkable woman."

"My best friend."

"She was a college roommate of my mother's," Reid commented. "But I never knew Tilly knew you, Diana."

"She taught at my boarding school."

"It's obvious that Tilly thinks a lot of you." The words were spoken lightly, yet very carefully. "And so do I."

Her eyes flew to his, and held. There was nothing but calm sincerity in his tone, and she wondered at her own continued feeling of discomfort. But there was something in his eyes that mocked her still, and it was to that dark force that she responded, "I don't think you really know me, Reid."

"That can be remedied. Isn't that what this weekend is for, after all? Getting to know each other? Friendship?"

"This weekend is for Jamie," she said. "We're here for Jamie's sake."

"And for our own," Reid's voice was low, like a caress. "Don't leave us out, Diana. We're here for us, too."

Later that evening, after Jamie was tucked in bed and the sun was a low golden ball only half visible above the tree-tops, Diana and Reid sat on the porch swing and discussed the coming days. Diana told Reid of her plan to use stories to reach Jamie. "Fairy tales have been utilized with great success to heal children with all kinds of serious emotional disorders," she explained. "The stories have a strength and understanding of a child's predicament that is not always duplicated in modern children's literature."

"How will you know which story helps Jamie?"

"I'm going to try to get him to tell me. Tomorrow I'll start by repeating the names of the stories I've already told him, and asking him which ones he wants me to tell again. If we can discover his favorites, we will have the first key to knowing what's going on in Jamie's head."

"We?"

"You're a part of this, too, Reid. You asked me to help Jamie, but I can't do anything without your cooperation. Whatever Jamie and I are doing, you should do, too. If we're picking up rocks, you need to be right there with us. If we're feeling the water on our bare feet, you need to do the same. And you need to tell your share of stories."

"I don't know any fairy tales."

She looked at him pityingly. "Then you will need to listen, so you can repeat them later."

As if he had only just then thought to do so, Reid reached over and took Diana's hand. In the fading light he examined her fingers. They were finely tapered, well-manicured, but without decoration of any kind. "No rings," Reid mused. "No artificial color." For a moment his fingers stroked hers lightly. Then he raised her hand and brought it to his lips. His mouth was warm and dry against her skin; she could feel his breath as he nibbled gently on her fingers and knuckles.

The swing swayed gently with the combined weight of their bodies. From the trees came the evening song of a bird. In the yard a rabbit paused in its forward motion, raising its nose to sniff the aromatic breezes. Everything was calm and incredibly peaceful.

Except, of course, the beating of Diana's heart.

You invited him here, she thought. This weekend was your idea.

He lowered her hand to his thigh, and stretched his arm along the back of the swing. "Come here," he said.

She slid her body over until it fit snugly against his. His arm dropped down around her shoulder, holding her close. She laid her head against his chest, and waited for him to make the next move.

For some time he did nothing, except keep the swing going with the weight of his heels against the porch. After a while her heart slowed again, and she began to relax.

When Reid spoke, his voice was low and clear in the night. "That time at your apartment... You wanted to talk, Diana."

"Yes."

"Tonight let's talk."

"All right."

"But first, I want to know about Harry Reichenbach, Diana. What is he to you?"

It took her a moment to answer. Perhaps, she thought, the time for games was truly over.

"Harry is my friend," she responded slowly. "He's getting married in four months. This cabin belongs to his fiancée's parents. I'm to be her maid of honor."

For several minutes he said nothing. The swing continued to sway lazily across the porch. "He touched you, that night in Chicago."

"He was pretending. He knew who you were, he sensed your interest, and he was protecting me. I promise you, Harry has never touched me like that before or since. He's like a brother to me."

"Like Phillip," he said flatly.

"Not the same. Diffcrent. But a brother, nonetheless."

"You spent the entire weekend with him, and you swear to me you are just friends?"

"Yes."

"I don't understand such friendship." His tone was disbelieving, hard.

She had begun to move her hand against his leg in little stroking movements. "I'm a fool to say so, but you have no need to be jealous of Harry."

He reached down and stopped the movement of her hand. "You love him, don't you?"

"Of course."

"That is reason enough for envy, Diana."

She felt the roughness of his shirt against her cheek, heard the beating of his heart against her ear, and thought, I could love you, too, Reid Hudson. And it would not be the love of a sister for her brother.

Then she heard him say, his voice heavy with angry sarcasm, "This *friendship* with Reichenbach ... I am afraid I can neither believe it, nor bear it, Diana. You have known too many men to play the innocent now."

Diana immediately went stiff beside him.

Reid heard his own statement with appalled disbelief. He had meant to play the seducer, tonight. He had meant to try again for his prize, tonight. When Diana had curved against him, so soft, so trusting, he had felt his own need swell inside him, and knew what he had wanted, tonight.

He was going to promise her anything she wanted. He was willing to lie, and deceive, until he had what he desired, at last.

Instead, her explanation of Harry Reichenbach had filled him with fierce, irrational anger, so that he had lost control, and blurted out the ungraceful truth. So that there was no hope of seduction now, or comfort, or relief. He tasted bitterness in his throat, and knew he had just lost everything. So he did not react when Diana went still against him, nor did he move when she pulled away and stood before him.

"Then I cannot bear you," Diana said, and her voice was a song of grief in the quiet night. She touched his shoulder once, lightly. "When you look at me you see memories and mistakes and arrogance. What I have to offer is all within, and that is the person you still cannot see." She paused and took a breath. "You're right, of course. I am not innocent. I had lovers. I was young and confused and alone, and I sought comfort in all the wrong places." She walked to the edge of the porch, her back turned to Reid. She wrapped her arms around herself and stared at the dusky sky. "I came away more empty than before. But I paid the price, in loneliness and despair. I spent my days hating myself, until I found that healing came in the understanding of a friend, and belief in the love of a mother. I do not need you to condemn me now."

She left him then, and he did not know how much she had understood, and how close she had come to giving him everything he wanted.

Saturday morning Diana discovered Reid carrying his single suitcase from his bedroom. She watched him silently for a moment, before asking, "What are you doing?"

He turned to her, his face shuttered. "What it looks like. This weekend is never going to work, Diana. This is your vacation. I'm going to take Jamie and leave you to it."

"And do you think I will enjoy my time here with you gone?"

"Yes. That's what I think."

She took a deep breath, even as she moved a quick step forward. It took all her courage to meet his eyes, but she did it. "You're wrong, Reid. I would be miserable. I would like you to stay."

He went quite still and expressionless, his only movement a sporadic ticking in the vein at his throat. He stared at her intently. Then he dropped his suitcase and said, almost wearily, "What do you want from me, Diana?"

"I told you. I want you to stay here in the house with me."

He gave her an all-embracing look. She was dressed in rose silk pajamas, with a matching robe pulled over her shoulders. Her hair was loose and uncombed, her face absolutely free of makeup. She looked about seventeen years old.

Her brown eyes stared at him with a subtle mixture of challenge and vulnerability. He sighed, and his mouth quirked upward in almost weary resignation. "All right. I would like to stay, also."

"We have still to become friends, after all."

"Yes."

"And Jamie needs to hear more stories."

"If you say so," he said gravely.

She smiled, filled with sudden happiness. "Thank you," she breathed. "I'm so glad!" She felt light again, and full of hope. Today was the Fourth of July, and it was going to be wonderful.

* * *

After breakfast, Diana told Reid, "It's time for you to begin."

He looked at her warily. "Begin what?"

"Helping with Jamie, of course. Playing in the sand. Telling him stories."

"You tell the stories. I'll listen."

"We'll start with that, anyway."

The day was still young when Jamie indicated with a nod of his head that he wanted to hear *Hansel and Gretel* again. Diana told the tale simply. "Once there was a poor woodcutter, who had two children..." Jamie listened intently, his eyes on Diana's face. And Reid listened, and also watched Diana.

After that, every time a story was started, Jamie would shake his head vigorously. The only tale he wanted to hear was of the woodcutter, and the children abandoned in the forest.

Later, in the afternoon, Diana slipped into her one-piece black swimming tank and a beach shirt. Reid had already spread a blanket on the sand, and had also changed into swimwear. When she joined him he motioned for silence. "Look!" he whispered.

Jamie was playing with a truck and shovel in the sand.

For a moment she stood and stared. "Oh my," she said. "Oh my." The boy looked up at her words, and smiled quite naturally.

For over a week Jamie had been totally unresponsive to any stimuli whatsoever. He had eaten, he had gone where he was told, he had been absolutely obedient. But he had not once danced, or drawn a picture, or played with any toys.

Now he was building castles in the sand.

She reached for Reid's hand and squeezed it hard. "Oh my," she said again.

The sun was hot. Diana spread sun block all over Jamie's fair young body. When she was done, Reid's shadow appeared over her. "I'll do the same for you," he said. "With your skin you'll burn in minutes."

"I can manage," she replied awkwardly. "I can reach everything except my back, and that's covered by my shirt . . ."

"And aren't you going in the water at all, Diana? Surely you're not really so shy."

She flushed, and removed her shirt. To her surprise his hands did not linger as he spread the lotion on her back. When he was done, he handed the bottle back to her. "Return the favor," he said, and she did, just as quickly and efficiently.

She thought him totally unaffected until he turned to her with a quick word of thanks. But his eyes were dark and hungry, and they flashed at her, before he moved to the water's edge and dived in.

He was an excellent swimmer. She moved to sit by Jamie, and watched Reid move in the water. She again wondered at how beautiful Reid was. His body was nearly perfect, hard and slim and intensely masculine. His chest was covered with dark hairs, his legs well-formed and muscular.

When he rejoined them some time later, she said guilelessly, "You have a beautiful body."

She could see at once that she had startled him. She wondered if no one had ever told him how wonderful his body really was.

After a while they moved the blanket to the lawn, and spread it under the shade of an old oak tree. She used her beach shirt for a pillow, and lay down, enjoying the sun and the warmth and the sheer laziness of having nothing in particular to do.

Jamie joined her, and promptly fell asleep. She fashioned a tent for him, then placed a kiss upon his brow. "Get better, Jamie," she said. "Please get better."

Reid was lying on her other side, his head cradled in his arms, watching her.

"Why does Jamie want to listen to only one story?" he asked.

"He's reacting to some element in it. Somewhere in the story is the problem he's dealing with, and its resolution. And in the fairy tale, the ending is always happy, the hero always successful. So the child has hope."

"You think he's identifying with Hansel, then."

"Probably.

"Hansel was abandoned by both his parents."

"Yes."

"And don't look at me with those knowing eyes, damn you."

She lay back down, on her stomach, and turned her head away from him.

Reid cleared his throat. "Would you mind," he said, "If I put my hand on your back?"

She raised herself upon her elbows and looked at him. "We've come a long way," she said, "for you to ask permission."

But his hand was already there, against her skin, rubbing it lightly. "Shh," he said. "Lie down. I'm just going to rub you for a little while."

And for the first time that she could remember, there was no fear in being touched by him, no torment in the pleasure she received at his hand, no doubt in the movement of his fingers against her skin.

She lay there, feeling the palm of his hand move against her back, gently massaging her neck, between her shoulder blades, down in the small of her back. It felt so good. Just being touched felt so wonderfully good.

After a while he asked, "What are you going to do after you leave Lyonhouse?"

"University of Chicago," she replied, her head pillowed against her folded arms. "Masters degree in psychology, specializing in therapy for young children."

"You'll do great. It's obvious you have a gift."

"Sure." But there was a lump in her throat. Six weeks gone, six weeks to go at Lyonhouse. She would have liked for her leaving to be her choice. "If I wanted to, would you let me stay on at Lyonhouse?"

"No." The word was final, oppressive, in direct contrast to the luxury of his hand against her sun-warmed skin.

She turned on her side to face him, so that his fingers fell to rest upon her waist. "Why not, Reid? Surely I've proved myself to your satisfaction."

"You've proved that you're wasted at Lyonhouse. You have gifts that far surpass what you're doing there."

His words surprised her, and she blinked. But he had no right to make her decisions for her. "There is no greater gift," she said, "than to touch the life of a child. And my leaving should be my choice, Reid. Not yours."

He distracted her by yet another question. "What about you, Diana? Would you like to have a child of your own?"

His hand was still on her waist, and his head was propped up on a bent arm, so that he could see the expressions flitting across her face. "Yes," she said, "That's what I want. I want to be a mother." Then she added, very softly, "I want to have a husband. I want to be a family. I want to believe that the future is full of promise."

"I, too, know what I want," Reid said.

"What?"

"To kiss you again, Diana. I'm not Harry Reichenbach, content to be your brother."

He leaned over to reach for her face, turning it more completely toward him. His lips lowered to hers. Then he kissed her.

And she was finished with resisting. Her lips opened beneath his, welcoming the hunger and passion that flared between them like a sweet summer storm. She wrapped her arms around him and held him close, even as his hands buried themselves in her hair, and his body moved with power against hers.

For a time nothing else mattered. They had wanted each other for so long, had hurt each other so deeply, that the touch of their hands against each other spoke comfort, and the message of their mouths was reassurance, and the heat of their hearts said desire.

But they were lying on a blanket on the lawn, and a sleeping boy was only a few feet away, so some time later Reid pulled his body from hers. He moved his hand lightly across Diana's face before he laid his head against her breast. She put her arm around him, holding him to her, and tried to slow her breathing in an attempt to regain a semblance of control.

"We could have an exclusive relationship," he said, wanting her more at that moment than he ever had before. "You could pursue your education, and I could commute to Chicago from New York and Lansing. Or I could fly you to me."

His hand covered hers upon his chest. "And, perhaps in time, a couple of years, we could get married." In his eagerness to convince her, he did not notice how her arm had moved slightly, nor how her head had reared up.

For a long time Diana did not answer. When she did, her voice was devoid of any emotion. "That is all you can offer me? Still?"

He retorted without thinking. "Some women would think I had offered you a lot.... I want you, Diana." He stroked her arm as it lay across his bare chest. "I'm quite obsessed. I'm totally fascinated. You're beautiful. You're intelligent. You're compassionate. But I need time. Time to get over the irrational jealousy that plagues me. Time to convince myself that what I see is not an illusion, time to know that we will last longer than—"

"In other words, I would be on trial. If I work out, you might consider marrying me."

When he said nothing, she said in a cold, harsh voice, "And what of Jamie? He would have no part in such an arrangement, would he? I would have no part of his life because he would be too devastated if I were to disappear, wouldn't he? What was between us would have nothing at all to do with him." She made no effort to hide the sudden tears in her voice.

He rolled away from her and rose to his feet. Without looking at Diana, he stalked back to the water, and stood gazing at the empty horizon. Unable to help herself, she joined him. They stood without touching, not even looking at each other.

At last Reid spoke, his voice low and furious. "You need to get one thing straight, Diana—*Jamie is not mine.* He was Cynthia's mistake, that's all. I made a promise to do my best by the child, and I *will* do my best. But what is between you and me, Diana, has nothing to do with Jamie, and never did. He was not even born when I first saw you." He turned on her fiercely. "The night I rescued Lucy from your party Jamie was only three months old, and I had never once held him in my arms. What I feel for you has nothing to do with Jamie."

"Tell me how you felt when he was born," she said, not even knowing where the question came from.

"I felt nothing, Diana. Absolutely nothing." But he could not hide his anger, and his face was dark and shadowed, so that she knew he was lying. And she knew at last what she had to say.

"Well, I think you're wrong," she began. "I think that little boy has everything to do with us. You can't go on forever putting your life into tidy little compartments—this one for Jamie, this one for Diana. Jamie is an orphan, and you are his protector. It is your obligation to love that child. Your *duty*. He is no more mine than yours, but I could love him easily enough. Because I'm not afraid, Reid. It is your fear that's keeping you separate from him, and your rage." Then she threw her head up, and the slight breeze lifted her hair off her neck. "As for me, I don't want what you have to offer. If other women would find such a gift wonderful, then offer it to them. I have no desire to be on trial, until you can decide you can trust enough to make a vow. You once offered me your heart, but I don't think you could find it to give to me. I think you've forgotten what a heart is. What you suggested today is a poor substitute for the real thing, and I will not accept it."

She strode out into the water, and soon buried herself in it. The lake was cool, and she was quickly submerged, hidden from the man who stood watching her on the shore. But it was not long before he joined her, his body keeping time with hers, his strong arms capturing her, his lips wet and warm once again against her own.

She fought him, there in the water, until her strength was gone, and his hands were touching her intimately, and he was showering her face with kisses. "I don't want any other women," he said roughly. "I want you, Diana. I am tired of you telling me no."

More aware than ever of the body held beneath his hands, and of his barely controlled fury and raging need, he thought how easy it would be to force her, to have her now, at last. He remembered his thoughts of the past several days. How he had been determined to have Diana Rowe, on his terms, on his time. So he held her, and something of his thoughts must have shown in his eyes, because Diana's tears stopped, and her body stretched in the water, and she faced him with the cool defiance he remembered. "All right then," she said. "Do it now. Take what you want now. But I will never be yours again, and you will remember forever how you had to steal what you most desired. All your life you will remember." Her glorious eyes were drenched with grief and power, her hair was plastered around her head, her body barely hidden beneath her black suit. And he knew that he had spoken the truth: he could never want any woman except the one who stood before him. He stared at her, thinking that he could never forget how she looked, this day in July, wet and beautiful and defiantly unattainable.

He held her still. When he could speak, his voice was deep with fury and frustration. "Why didn't you let me go this morning? I can't give you what you want, and you will not give me what I want. We are making each other miserable."

She answered him quickly, her words rushed and passionate. "Because even as you want me, I want you. But I will have all of you, or none of you." Then she said, "Let me go now."

As soon as he did so, she was gone, swimming with sure, strong strokes to the shore. He shouted her name, but her head was mostly underwater, and she didn't hear him. He watched her rise from the lake and walk toward the still sleeping Jamie, her body lithe and supple and altogether too perfect. He knew he should leave now, this instant, but he was too obsessed to think clearly, and she was unmanning him, twisting him in knots. But even as the thoughts came to him, he knew he would not leave. She had been a hunger in his blood for too long. And she was so close. He would not walk away now.

That night, Reid stumbled through the story of *Hansel and Gretel,* and Jamie watched him while he told it. Reid finished the story with some relief, anxious to leave the child, but Jamie caught at Reid's arm, and touched Reid's lips, so that Reid knew he wanted to hear the story yet one more time. With a sigh, he sat again by the boy's bed, and told the tale again, this time a little more smoothly, a little more sadly, for it was, after all, sad to be lost and alone and left to die in a confusing wilderness, even though the children won in the end, of course. And when the story was done there were tears in Jamie's eyes. Clumsily, Reid smoothed the blankets around Jamie's face, and touched his brow. "Good night," he whispered. Then he went to find Diana.

He found her standing on the porch. Across the lake was a small town. Fireworks were being shot from there, and Diana was watching them. He slipped an arm around her waist and drew her close.

"It's a funny thing," he said. "You keep putting me in my place, yet every time I see you I want to touch you."

She leaned into him. "I like it when you touch me."

She made him angry. The signals she was sending him were so damned mixed up.

A particularly colorful display of lights lit the sky. The separating water muffled the accompanying explosion until it sounded like a mere popgun. The blaring of horns could be heard—people in their cars showing their approval.

Then another firework went off, and another.

Diana Rowe stood still in the circle of his arms, smiling gently, watching the lights.

She was all that was soft and womanly and desirable. She drew him, filled him with need so strong he hardly knew himself.

And she told him no. Again and again and again.

He thought it was very possible he hated her.

"Damn you," he said. He turned from her and stalked back into the house, back to the room that was his alone, back to the bed that was cold and empty and full of loneliness. He would leave tomorrow. He would.

It was not quite dawn when he awoke. He lay still for a moment, wondering what had roused him, when he heard the slight sound of small feet on the floor outside his door.

Jamie.

He wondered if the boy was merely heading toward the bathroom, when he heard the front door of the cabin open. Jamie was going outside.

He supposed he should go and see what the child was doing.

He swung his legs off the bed, and pulled on his swim trunks from where they had been spread on the back of a chair. Then he walked through the quiet house to the front door, which Jamie had left open. He stepped out on the porch, scanning the surrounding area for the little boy.

Jamie was on the beach, still in his pajamas, acting in a most peculiar manner. It took Reid a moment to discover what the boy was about.

He was on tiptoes, his skinny little body stretched as far as he could make it, his arms reaching up to the sky. The sun was not yet up, though its light was everywhere, and there was a glorious cloud cover, filled with the colors of dawn. Jamie was a silhouette against the horizon, and he was reaching with his fingers, reaching for the sky. Then the boy began to move his legs.

Reid remembered the letter he had received from Diana, and he knew Jamie was dancing with the clouds.

Reid leaned against a porch pillar and watched the child. There was an exuberance in Jamie's movements that he had never seen before. Jamie seemed totally spontaneous, completely uninhibited. He was taking little running leaps at the edge of the water, each time throwing his arms upward.

Then, vaguely at first, but with steadily growing strength, Reid remembered his own childhood. He was at Cape Cod. It was summer. His mother was in the ocean, swimming. His father was lying on the beach, reading a book. And Reid had been playing with Bruiser, the family Airedale, in the sand. He remembered laughing unrestrainedly as the big dog knocked him down time and time again.

Then the memory faded, as he realized what he was hearing now.

Jamie was laughing.

It was a strange kind of laughter, a ha! ha! ha! that sounded forced and awkward, but it was laughter just the same.

He left the porch and walked toward the boy. As he got closer, Jamie's laughter stopped, and was replaced by a guttural type of humming noise, as if he were trying to sing. Only when Reid got closer, he realized Jamie *was* singing. The words were soft, but they were clearly distinguishable. "The clouds dance fast, the clouds dance slow, but I am so small and low, it's hard to reach the clouds, you know."

A rage so powerful he shook with it coursed through Reid. Jamie was singing. Jamie was singing *words*. Jamie could talk. All this time, *Jamie could talk*.

Then Jamie turned so that he was facing Reid. Instead of the mischief he thought to catch in the boy's expression, Reid saw instead a face that was covered with tears, and eyes that were filled with misery.

Then Jamie saw Reid, and froze. The little arms were held high, in rigid stillness. The small legs paused in their forward movement. A look of horror crossed the child's features.

"You can talk," Reid said flatly. "You can talk perfectly well."

Jamie began to back away from him, toward the water. "Please," the boy said, his voice high-pitched with fear. "Please . . ."

"Please my foot. You and I are going to have a discussion, young man."

"Please, please." As Reid drew closer he saw that Jamie's teeth were chattering with terror, that his hands were held outstretched in front of him as if warding off a physical blow. "Please."

"Reid, stop." Diana's voice came from right behind him, and he turned to see her standing there. She had obviously come out in a hurry—she was still wearing her pajamas, but without the covering robe the rose material revealed as much as it concealed. "Let me talk to him, Reid."

She walked forward quickly, touching his arm as she passed him. Reaching Jamie, she knelt with unconscious grace. "Jamie, it's all right," she said. She reached for the boy, who was at the water's edge, and lifted him in her arms. "Please," Jamie said again, through chattering teeth.

She moved a few steps back from the water, then sat abruptly on the beach. "What is it, darling? Why are you so frightened? What are you trying to tell us?"

Reid had to take a step closer in order to hear.

The boy was sobbing against Diana's breast. "I'm sorry," he said. "I'm sorry. I won't talk again. I promise. Only please don't throw me away," he said. "Please, please, please. Please don't throw me away!"

Diana was rocking Jamie back and forth soothingly. "Of course we're not going to throw you away. Of course we're not. Who told you that we would, Jamie? Who told you this thing?"

"Mama." His hands clutched against her neck; she could feel his fingernails piercing her skin.

Diana's eyes flew upward to meet Reid's, who stood watching her inscrutably. "What did Mama say, darling? What did she say?"

"Daddy hates me and wants to throw me away. But she wouldn't let him. But I have to be very quiet, I mustn't talk so much, I must be a good boy. Then Mama won't let Daddy throw me away."

"Where was he going to throw you, Jamie?"

"He was...he was going to throw me in the woods." The boy's sobs were quieter now, as if revealing his burden was already comforting his fears.

"When did your Mama tell you this terrible thing, Jamie?"

He hiccuped against her breast. "In the car. She told me to be quiet in the car. She told me if I said a word Daddy would throw me away, and I would be alone in the woods, and a monster would come and eat me...."

"Dear God," Reid said quietly.

"The time she was in the accident," Diana commented. "It's probably the last thing he remembers before the accident."

Jamie turned in her arms and looked at the man he knew as his father. "Are you?" he asked. "Are you going to throw me away, Daddy?"

Reid stared at the boy, his hands clenched at his side. "Of course not, Jamie. Of course I would never throw you away, just because you talked. Of course I would never do a thing like that."

Shame, black and dark and deep, washed over him. He remembered a silent little boy, sitting still and alone in his bedroom in New York. He remembered all the time he had spent away, escaping from this child's presence.

In a frenzy of movement Jamie wrenched himself from Diana and ran to Reid, his arms outstretched. Automatically Reid put out his own arms, and lifted the boy to his chest. Jamie put his hands around Reid's neck, and hugged him tight. "Can I talk? Can I talk all the time? Is it really all right?"

"Of course." There was a lump in Reid's throat the size of a boulder.

"Can I do the cloud song?"

"Go ahead."

"Will you dance with me?"

Reid glanced at Diana. *Do it,* she mouthed. *Do it now.*

"All right," he said.

And Jamie began to chant, in a clear, beautiful child's voice, "The clouds dance fast, the clouds dance slow..."

It had been a long time since Reid had been a child. Yet the memory that had surfaced just a few minutes ago threatened to do him in. He remembered a time when life had been simple, when every hurt had been kissed away, when he had been surrounded by a parental love so profound just the memory of it made him feel like crying—him, Reid Hudson, who could not remember the last time he had cried about anything. What has happened? he asked himself. What has happened to the child that I was?

Jamie's eyes were shining, luminous. Almost shyly Reid began to move his feet, feeling the sand under his toes, feeling the morning air against his skin. The sun had just broken free of the horizon; its light warmed him. It felt good. This felt *good.* Reid laughed aloud. "Dance, Jamie," he said. "Dance!" But Jamie didn't have to be told. In a burst of spontaneous action, the boy was jumping, leaping, turning, running. Reid found himself laughing and singing and shouting, "Touch the clouds, Jamie! Touch the clouds!" And his own arms were raised high, and his own heart was beating fast, and the light from his eyes was pure joy.

For the first time in a long time, Reid Hudson remembered what it was to be young.

He played with Jamie in the sand by the lake quite a while, until he heard the sound of an engine starting, and turned around to see Diana driving her car out of the driveway. In the house he found a note:

I am going back to Lansing. Use what time is left to learn to know your son. When you know that you love him, come and see me at Lyonhouse. Diana. Then, hastily written at the bottom, *I will wait for you, Reid.*

He crumpled the piece of paper in his hand, and looked at the redheaded child at his side. Cynthia's bastard. Jamie.

And he felt his joy leaking out of him, as if he had been a vessel that was full, but now a weak spot had been found, and a hole made, so that his happiness was leaving him, drop by drop.

He must have looked incredibly stupid out there.

He had a ridiculous voice—he had never been able to hold a tune. And he had been singing. Some silly child's song.

How embarrassing.

Well, at least Jamie was talking. That was something.

But Diana should have been here, waiting for him. She should have known he would need reassurance. She should have realized that he could not handle this thing with Jamie alone. She should have known that he would want to touch her, rest his head against her breast as he had yesterday afternoon.

He needed her, dammit. And she had left him.

One wild romp in the sand did not mean he loved the child.

What she asked was impossible. Everything Diana Rowe asked was impossible. Loving a little boy. Making promises to Diana. Those things had been impossible yesterday, and were impossible still.

So he told himself, but he uncrumpled the note, refolded it with exquisite care, and put it in his pocket.

Maybe he would try, just the same.

Chapter Thirteen

Tuesday morning after the long holiday weekend found Diana back at Lyonhouse, following her usual routine of greeting children and parents as they came in the front doors. She was aware of feeling an unusual nervousness, and she knew the feeling stemmed from the way she had left Reid at the Sevilla cottage. She had been sure she was doing the right thing, but she had plenty of time over the next couple of days to regret her impetuosity.

She looked up and saw Reid walking with Jamie toward the door. Feeling suddenly shy, she moved back slightly, as Nancy Cook walked down the hallway.

Jamie came in the door first, and smiled broadly at Nancy. "Good morning," he said with precocious precision. "I can talk now."

Nancy's eyes widened, her mouth dropped slightly, before a big grin split her face. "Well now, that has got to be the most beautiful thing I've heard in a year!" she exclaimed. She reached down and lifted Jamie into her arms, and swung him around and around. "I'm so happy!" she said. "So darned happy!"

Reid stood with a quiet smile on his face, watching as others—adults and children—gathered around to hear the news. Jamie could talk! Jamie was talking!

Diana leaned against the wall, waiting for Reid to see her. Her nervousness had vanished in the newly rediscovered miracle of Jamie's speech.

"I can sing, too," he was saying proudly.

Reid looked over the bent heads and saw Diana. His smile faded, and his eyes grew serious. He neither nodded nor spoke, but turned quietly away. Jamie was the center of attention—the child hardly noticed when his father left.

Diana noticed, though. She was left numb and disbelieving. Why hadn't he at least nodded? Why had he refused to acknowledge her at all?

The week passed, and during the entire time Reid never tried to call her at home, or speak to her at work. Not even when she smiled at him encouragingly when he dropped Jamie off in the mornings or picked him up in the afternoons. If she did happen to catch his eye, he just looked at her gravely, spoke quietly to Jamie and left.

And so the seventh week of her time at Lyonhouse was passed.

By the end of the eighth week she knew that Reid was not going to make any attempt to see her, or speak to her alone. She told herself she understood. Her note had been clear, and Reid had not been able to meet her conditions.

At the beginning of the ninth week, Diana found herself in a tearing rage. She had fought as hard for Reid as she knew how, but she doubted that he even comprehended the battle. She wrote him a four-page letter, filled with anger and pain, but she never sent it. Instead the letter ended in a hundred tiny pieces in her wastebasket.

By Friday of the ninth week, Diana was in mourning. She had finally accepted that Reid was finished with her, and therefore she had to be finished with him. But the memory of his kisses would come upon her unexpectedly, and she would be suddenly trembling. And she would wake in the night, troubled and grieving, and find her pillow wet with tears. She began to reexperience her old insecurity, and fought it fiercely.

In her moments of weakness, she wished she had given Reid everything he wanted. She was sorry she had made demands of her own. She could have had him for a little while, at least. For a time she could have lived on the illusion that she was loved.

Her hope still lay in Jamie. The boy was so transformed that it was difficult to recall the quiet, withdrawn child he had been just weeks before. And the change in him changed the people around him, also.

Sandy Buxted told Diana that Jamie helped her face the impending death of her cancer-ridden father. "He lifts my spirits," she said. "I listen to his chatter, and feel...oh, it's so hard to explain...*joyful.* I never before realized how circular life really is. My father's life is ending, and Jamie's is just so...new. Somehow it helps, you know? Makes death less terrifying."

Sally Nussbaum, struggling with the needs of a young family and an irresponsible husband, was walking down the hallway with Diana when they heard a burst of Jamie Hudson's laughter. Sally started to cry. "Great odds *can* be overcome," she said, her voice raw with determination. "If Jamie can learn to talk again, I can handle my life. I can, Diana."

Nancy Cook, mature and wise, experienced in the ways of children, listened to Jamie shout with excitement on the playground swing, and turned to Diana with a smile of pleasure. "I'm so glad I chose to work with children," she commented. "I'm so glad I've known Jamie Hudson. He gives my life meaning. He gives all of us such happiness."

Jamie changed them all, infused everyone with new purpose, with quiet delight. And because he gave everyone so much, he became the pet of Lyonhouse, and everyone's favorite playmate.

Even Diana, buried as she was in her grief and bitter loss, watched Jamie, and was comforted. If she had loved Jamie when he was silent and only half-alive, her heart opened to the child who found such pleasure in rediscovering communication. She still rocked him every day, not because Jamie needed the touching, but because she did. And every day she told Jamie she loved him, just to hear him say *I love you* back. It was all worth it, she told herself. Everything she had gone through was worth it to see Jamie live again.

One Tuesday morning the public relations people from Heritage House came to see Diana. "We want to move up your first big media presentation," Tim Novak told Diana. "The first quarter after the merger will end August first, and we want you to have your presentation at the same time."

So Diana told her staff, and preparations were accelerated for the important day.

Shortly before August first Lucy Hudson called. "Diana? Is this Diana Rowe?"

"Yes."

"It's Lucy, Diana."

They talked for a few minutes, then set the time and place of their meeting. Diana knew her life was going forward. Decisions were being made, changes accomplished. She gave herself up to the passage of time.

Then, just three days before the open house, Reid came to Lyonhouse and stayed. "I'm taking the day off," he told

Nancy Cook. "I thought I would stay here with Jamie, and see what he does all day."

He was as good as his word. With apparently endless patience, he stayed by Jamie's side, playing four-year-old games, hearing four-year-old stories, admiring four-year-old pictures. On the playground he was captain of the boat that was half-buried in the ground; he built highways in the sandbox; he pushed a dozen children on the swing set.

Reid stayed the entire day. In the afternoon, while Jamie slept, he went through the Lyonhouse records, noting the seemingly endless red tape that followed every procedure. Then he asked Diana for a private meeting in her office.

He took a chair across from her desk, and for a moment they studied each other unsmilingly. Finally he said, softly, "Hello, Diana."

She inclined her head. "Reid."

"How have you been?"

"Well," she lied.

"I've been wondering about the little girl. Sarah Davidson. Have you ever seen her again?"

"I haven't seen her, but I did testify. She's been placed away from her parents."

"That will be better for her, I suppose."

"I don't know. It's hard to know what's right or wrong, sometimes."

"And Archie? Has he kept away?"

"Yes. Although his wife came to see me last week. She actually thanked me. She said she had been living in fear, she hadn't known what to do. But now that things have happened as they have, she has some hope. She's thinking of leaving her husband."

Reid shifted slightly, crossed one leg over the other. "Did you encourage her to do that?"

"I encouraged her to get counseling. Too often women leave a man like that only to quickly join in a similar union with someone else. Different name, different face, same problem. So I would not advise her one way or the other." She paused, then added, "But I would never live with a violent man."

"No," Reid said. "I don't suppose you would. You know your own worth too well."

His words took her by surprise. She searched his expression for some sign of mockery, but there was none. Instead a light appeared in his eyes, briefly, fleetingly. He stood, and she said with swift intensity, "Can't I stay longer than the three months, Reid? Can't I now?"

But he shook his head. "No," he replied tonelessly. "Our original agreement stands, Diana. And you have other things to do with your life."

She knew then that he was trying not to be cruel, but he wanted her gone from his life entirely.

Later, after Reid and Jamie had left, she sat in her office and thought about the day just passed. Reid had come to Lyonhouse, and played with Jamie. All day long. Surely that meant he was trying to be a real father. Surely it meant he was learning some affection for the boy.

And still he wanted nothing to do with her.

Again, Diana came to the bitter realization that it was only she who was being deliberately excluded from his life. Reid was changing, but none of his changes included her. Best for her to accept the finality of that understanding.

She had been in limbo too long. As Reid had said, she needed to get on with her life. It was time she put him out of her mind, as completely as he seemed to have forgotten her. She was young. She was resilient. And she would endure.

That night Diana and Lucy Hudson met at a quiet restaurant that overlooked a peaceful park. At first they were awkward with each other, making small talk that meant nothing. Finally Diana said, "I want to tell you what happened, four years ago."

"Yes," Lucy replied evenly. "I would like to know."

"Reid forbade me to see you anymore, but I could have done it anyway. I had been defying authority for far too long to let a little thing like an ultimatum from your big brother stop me."

"I see."

"Maybe. Anyway, two days later I had a flaming row with my father, and we parted angry. I have not seen him since."

"Not once in four years?"

Diana shrugged. "He called me for the first time, this summer, after he saw me on television representing Lyonhouse."

"What about your mother?"

"I really think she forgets I exist most of the time. We have never been close."

Lucy absorbed that information, then said, "But you haven't told me what happened, not really."

So Diana explained more fully the events of the days that followed the party. She also told Lucy, as dispassionately as she could, some of the details of her life before Phillip died, and how she had lived afterward. Hiding nothing, she continued with the life she had led up to the time she had met sixteen-year-old Lucy.

Then she said, "I think the real reason I never tried to contact you, and why I didn't leave a trail so that you could follow me, was that Reid was right. I was not fit company for a girl like you. You had someone at home who loved you, and you were still so trusting and innocent. I had none of those things. You looked at me with such worship, Lucy, but I knew who I really was. I didn't deserve your friendship, and in the end, I couldn't bear the responsibility of having you turn out just like me."

Lucy had been looking at the table, her fingernail making little marks in the napkin as she listened. When she met Diana's eyes, her own were full of tears. "You thought that much of me?"

"I thought more of you than I did of myself, Lucy."

As she said the words, Diana understood for the first time the importance of what she had done four years ago. Instead of abandoning Lucy, she had moved to protect the girl. At the time, leaving Lucy had been the only truly selfless act she had committed since Phillip's death.

Lucy was smiling. "Can we try again, Diana? Will you be my friend?"

"I would like that. I would like that very much."

Then it was Lucy's turn. She told about returning home, that long-ago April night, to a sister-in-law who was in a screaming rage, furious that Reid had left her to search for his sister. She reported how Reid had shepherded her to her room, and how she had lain awake, to hear Cynthia's shrill voice go on for what seemed like hours.

But after that, Cynthia had left her alone. No longer was Lucy subjected to the little barbs that Cynthia had constantly sent her way, nor to the larger insults that Cynthia would utter when Reid was away. And Reid had stayed closer to home, until Lucy had left for college.

As Lucy had grown older, she gained a greater understanding of her brother's vast loneliness, of the great burden he was shouldering every day. It had come as a shock to her that the family business had almost failed, yet Reid had told her nothing. She learned to love her big brother again, and discovered that she was one of the few people who could make him laugh.

"Tell me more about Cynthia," Diana requested.

"She was a first-class bitch. Excuse me, but I know no other term to describe her. She was terribly unfaithful to Reid. I wasn't supposed to know, of course, but it was something that couldn't be hidden, and after a while Reid quit trying. And she hated me. I think she hated me because Reid loved me, if that makes any sense. She couldn't stand for Reid to be happy. Even toward the end, when she was fighting for a reconciliation, she really didn't want Reid to be happy."

"She wanted a reconciliation?"

"Uh-huh. She wanted Reid's status. She wanted to stay a Hudson. After all, on the East Coast the Hudson name still opens a lot of doors."

Diana found she didn't want to hear any more about Reid's dead wife. "Tell me about growing up," she said.

"There's really not much to tell. Mom and Dad died, and Reid changed overnight from a fun-loving, protective big brother into someone frightening. He was so intense about doing the right thing. I don't think he ever realized what a task he set for himself, taking over the family business as he did. To this day I don't think he knows how heroic he really was."

After that their conversation passed on to other things, and they talked on, sharing easily matters of the heart. Until Diana looked up and saw they were the last patrons in the restaurant, that their waitress was the only one still there, that the cashier was eyeing them with frustration. "Lucy," she said. "We're holding everyone up. We'd better go."

They walked together out the door, embraced each other and left each other once again. But this time there were promises of friendship between them, and there was comfort in their parting.

"Call me," Lucy said.

"I will."

"Don't wait four years!"

"I won't wait four weeks!"

"I do love you, Diana. You're the sister I always wanted."

A pause. A glowing within. Joy. "I love you, too, Lucy."

And then, a single wave, and Diana got into her car and headed home.

The media open house was to be held on Friday. Thursday afternoon Diana called the staff of Lyonhouse together.

Except for the few workers who had been left to watch the children, everyone gathered in the multipurpose room. Diana looked at them: approximately twenty-five women were there. In the ten weeks she had been at Lyonhouse, she had gotten to know them all, some better than others. She knew that Sandy's father was dying, that Sally's husband was a problem to her. She knew that Wanda wanted desperately to get married, but her boyfriend was not yet ready. She knew that Marla Cummings was raising an illegitimate child on her own, without any support from its father. She knew that Barbara had lost a teenage daughter, two years ago, in a drunk driving accident, and that SueEllen had a son hooked on drugs. And she knew that Martha's oldest boy had won a scholarship to Harvard last spring, and was getting ready to go.

She knew these people. They had become like family to her and she was going to be sorry to leave.

Everyone was waiting for Diana to speak. She took a deep breath. "I want you to know that I am leaving Lyonhouse in two weeks. In fact, I knew when I accepted this position that I would only be here three months. I am going on to the University of Chicago in September, to obtain a masters in psychology, with an emphasis on therapy for young children.

"Some people think I was merely dabbling here at Lyonhouse. After all, my name is Diana Rowe, and you have all learned what that means. But I want you to know I had wanted to stay here, for years. It was only after I learned that I would not be allowed any longer than three months that I made other plans. And I want you to know that Lyonhouse is and will be worthy of all our best efforts, now and in the future. I have come to appreciate all of you, and I am deeply sorry to be going."

For a moment there was silence, then someone asked, "Who will be taking your place?"

Diana smiled. "Someone you all know and love—Nancy Cook."

There was applause then, because Nancy was surely one of the most popular people at Lyonhouse.

Sandy Buxted stood. "Nancy is an excellent choice," she said, "but I think Diana should know what it has meant to all of us to work with her here at Lyonhouse. The last months have been some of the most pleasant in my life, and I know others feel the same."

"Here, here."

"That's right."

Then, as if all had the same idea at once, everyone stood and clapped their hands. And Diana was pleased, and told everyone thank you, and smiled gratefully. For even though things were moving on, it was nice to know that she had been appreciated for a while. It made the thought of leaving just a little easier.

That evening Diana stayed late at Lyonhouse. Everything was in a state of preparation for the next day. The rooms were clean and beautifully decorated, the hallways had special greetings from the children to the reporters and other important people that would be here. Two national television networks were going to be represented, along with numerous local and statewide news agencies of various kinds. Tilly Martel and Tom Lyon would be present, as would the heads of several children's agencies. There was a chance the governor himself would put in an appearance.

And of course there would be representatives from Heritage House and Knotingsly.

It was going to be a big event.

Diana knew that part of the interest came from her participation in Lyonhouse. While the publicity regarding "Princess Di of Day Care" had died down in the past weeks, she was still a celebrity. Her name alone could draw a small crowd.

She heard a timid knock on her office door. Surprised, she looked at her clock; it was almost eight. She had been sure she was alone in the building.

The knock came again. Diana rose from her chair and opened her door.

Jamie Hudson stood there, grinning from ear to ear. He was carrying a bouquet of fresh flowers. Reid was standing at his side.

Diana's heart began pounding very hard and very fast. "What have we here?" she asked.

"We wanted to wish you good luck, tomorrow," Reid said.

"I brought you flowers!" Jamie exclaimed.

"Well. Come in, then. Let's see where we can put them."

"I know where," Jamie said. "We'll put them on your table. Right in the middle."

Diana laughed lightly. "All right." She was looking at Jamie, at the flowers, at her desk. Anywhere but at Reid. "Thank you."

"The flowers were entirely Jamie's idea," Reid said.

Of course. The time was past when Reid would bring her flowers. "I think they're beautiful."

Jamie beamed. "Daddy helped," he said. "He picked the colors. Yellow for... yellow for... what is yellow for, Daddy?"

"Yellow for courage, red for an understanding heart, blue for loyalty, and white for..."

"I know what white stands for," she said flatly. She turned from him, blinking hard.

"Diana."

She ignored him.

"Diana, I'm going to New York tomorrow night. I probably won't be back for another three weeks."

She would be gone from Lyonhouse in three weeks. He was saying goodbye. She forced herself to turn, to meet his eyes. "And Jamie?"

"Jamie is going with me. But this trip will be different from the last."

"That's good."

He reached out to touch her face, but withdrew before any contact was made. "I wanted to tell you I was sorry," he said. "I cannot be what you wanted me to be. I tried, but I could not do it. But I wish you the best of luck, with everything."

"Thank you."

"You changed me, you know."

She was silent.

She thought he was going to say something else, but he shook his head slightly, and said merely, "Goodbye, Diana Rowe."

Then Jamie's hand was in his, and they were walking out the door. Her whispered goodbye came far too late for Reid to hear. She managed to control herself until she knew they were in their car, until she heard the roar of the engine and knew they were pulling away.

She walked around the building, making sure all the doors were locked, all the windows closed. She doubted if she would ever see Jamie or Reid again. Just like that, they were out of her life forever. She looked at the pictures on the walls, the toys on the shelves. Just like Lyonhouse, Reid and Jamie would become a memory, no more than a fading picture that would dim in time. She went back to her office, saw again the flowers on her table. *Yellow is for courage, red is for an understanding heart, blue is for loyalty, and white is for...* Diana laid her head upon her desk and cried.

Facing Diana Rowe like that was one of the hardest things Reid had ever done. But she had deserved at least that much.

Still, he hadn't told her everything. He hadn't explained that he had really tried to do what she had asked. He had attacked the challenge of loving Jamie as he attacked any other problem in his life—systematically, logically, relentlessly. He had spent time with the boy, talked with him, even spent that day at Lyonhouse with him. He had discovered that he *liked* Jamie rather well.

But he had failed to *love* Jamie. Quite miserably. He finally decided that such an affection was not his to give. And if he couldn't give it to Jamie, he certainly couldn't give it to Diana. Yet even to himself he would not admit what bleak loneliness that conclusion caused him.

There *were* times, however, that he almost forgot Jamie was not his. Like the time at the zoo, when an elderly woman had commented on what a nice boy his son was. His chest had actually swelled with pride, before the light had bounced off Jamie's red hair, and Reid remembered no one in his family had hair the color of the sun.

So he was leaving Diana. He tried to tell himself that he was no longer obsessed with her. Even though he had wanted to kiss her tonight, one last time. When she had taken the flowers, he had breathed in her special fragrance and had been filled with want. Which was why he had not allowed himself even to touch her.

She deserved better than him. Somewhere she would find a man who could give her what she wanted. Marriage. Children. That elusive thing she called love.

The thought was like a knife in his stomach, and he shoved it away. Maybe the next man wouldn't know about her past, he thought bitterly. Maybe another man would be more forgiving. Maybe another man . . .

He would kill any other man. The thought brought him up short, and he laughed mirthlessly. He was obsessed all right. He still wanted Diana Rowe.

When he packed that night, he found the note Diana had left for him at the cabin. It was smudged now, and wrinkled from having been folded and unfolded so many times. He threw the piece of paper in the garbage.

But later, when he was done packing, and Jamie was asleep, he dug the note out again. *I'll be waiting for you, Reid,* she had written. And even though he knew that promise was no longer true, he folded the paper one more time, and tucked it into his wallet.

Lyonhouse was packed with strange people and even stranger equipment. At least thirty reporters, a dozen or so politicians, and of course, one hundred plus children all made for an interesting afternoon. But so far, everything was going remarkably well.

Diana had dressed carefully. She was wearing a royal-blue suit, with a white blouse, and a red silk tie. She led everyone through the rooms, then out to the playground. The children were all curious, and crowded as close as they were allowed. Several children were interviewed. Diana was amazed; the normally noisy children grew tongue-tied, yet the quiet ones showed little fear.

Finally, with the help of Nancy Cook and others, Diana gathered all the guests into the multipurpose room. The temporary stage had been set up, and Diana stood upon it in order to answer questions. First there were the practical queries: how much did the Center cost? What was its yearly budget? Could she describe the licensing challenges? Could a Center take the place of a family? And so forth.

Then, inevitably, the questions became more personal. Had Diana Rowe talked with her father? Did he approve of what she was doing? Someone had said she was soon leaving Lyonhouse. What was she going to do? Did she have a boyfriend? And then the title Princess slipped out.

Diana stood silent, waiting until she had everyone's attention. Someone flashed a camera in her face, and she smiled graciously. Finally she raised her right hand, signaling for silence.

"When Lyonhouse first opened, someone called me Princess Di of Day Care. It was a sarcastic title then, and remains so until this day. Somewhere in that nickname is the assumption that I am a frivolous person, and Lyonhouse nothing more than a frivolous activity. Because of who I am, my ability to actually participate in a truly worthwhile project was doubted, and my intentions questioned.

"I guess it should come as no surprise, then, that the appellation hurt. All of us at Lyonhouse wanted this center to be a work of substance, of value, not overshadowed by personalities and names and other things that blow in the wind.

"But it wasn't long before I realized something.

"If I were a princess, a *real* princess, then this building was my kingdom, and these children my people. I have tried to put words of love and safety into their hearts. I, and all of us here at Lyonhouse, have tried to teach that the world is a thing of beauty, that friends are to be trusted. And I learned something else—each boy and girl, each infant in arms, each person working here, is someone of inestimable value. All were princes and princesses, kings and queens. All were royalty.

"But we are day care workers, providers of care while parents work. We are limited in what we can do. You asked me if centers like this would ever replace the family. I trust with all my heart that they will not. There are more important titles than king and queen, prince and princess. Those are the titles of Mother and Father. So I take this opportunity to say to parents everywhere, love your children. Know that your children are worth any sacrifice, that the greatest gift you can give them is the sure knowledge that they are loved, that they are valuable and important. For the world's best hope will always be its children.

"One more thing you asked—did the people here know what a privilege it was to have Diana Rowe here at Lyonhouse? But you should know that I was the privileged one. It has been my pleasure to work among these little ones. I will miss them all."

Her voice had been low, almost expressionless, but there was a rare music singing through her words, so that all the men and women in that room stood silent, listening.

Diana did not understand the silence, and wondered if she had reached anyone here. She wondered if she ultimately made a difference to anyone at all.

Then, from a corner of the room, a child—Sheila Phillips—walked forward, bearing a single flower. Shyly, walking wide-eyed past the reporters and politicians and the professional equipment, the little girl walked up on the temporary platform. She handed Diana the flower.

"Thank you, Diana," Sheila said, very carefully, "for bringing us a dream of what it is to be children, to be safe, and to be loved."

Suddenly, both rear doors of the room opened, and all the children in Lyonhouse entered, and all the workers, too. Standing in a rough, obviously unrehearsed group, the voices began:

"The clouds dance fast,
the clouds dance slow,

and I am so small and low
It's hard to reach the clouds...

And all the children were singing, and dancing, and all the workers had their arms stretched upward, reaching for a sky beyond the ceiling, beyond the clouds.

Pictures were taken, films shot. Then the song ended, and Nancy Cook came forward. Facing the group of reporters with obvious nervousness, Nancy began, "I don't have Diana's confidence in speaking, but I have something important to say, so I hope you will bear with me.

"Diana Rowe came to Lyonhouse as an unknown. None of us knew who she was when we were hired, and we were all surprised when the truth was out. Yet never did Diana act the prima donna, nor was she less than kind in any way. She worked long hours, yet she was never too busy to give a helping hand wherever it was needed, nor was she too busy to listen to the words of a child. Lyonhouse is Diana's creation, and in the process of that creation, all of us have learned something from Diana Rowe.

"Over a hundred years ago a poet wrote that we come here 'trailing clouds of glory.' But it was not until I saw Diana teach a silent little boy how to dance with the clouds, and thus reach the sky, that I understood what the poet meant. So, because I have learned...we all have learned...from Diana, we want to offer her this crown..."

There was a stirring among the children, and Jamie Hudson came forward, bearing a glittering, handmade golden paper crown.

"...which bears the name of each child at Lyonhouse, and each worker. We sincerely hope, Diana, that you will accept this gift in the spirit in which it was intended. Every time you look at this crown, we want you to remember that there was a group of people in Lansing who loved you, not because of the famous name you bore, but because of who you were to us. You *are* our princess, Diana. We—all of us—love you, and we thank you.''

Bulbs were flashing, reporters were talking, and Diana stood in front of them all, wearing her crown of stiff paper, jeweled with love and friendship and memories, and fought to hold back the tears.

Standing in the back of the room, Reid Hudson watched it all. He was leaning against the back wall, one hand in a pants pocket, his face expressionless. Tilly Martel appeared at his side.

''She's quite a person,'' she said softly. ''It will take a special man to be worthy of her.''

''Yes.''

All this time, he had been worried about Diana's past. All this time, he had condemned her. Yet he was the unworthy one. He was the one who could not learn from his mistakes. He was the one who had no courage to really change. He was the one who was afraid to trust.

She was standing up there, tall and straight and true, his silver girl, and a group of women and children were hugging her. There was more love in this room than he had experienced in his entire adult life. And he thought, she *is* an aristocrat, she *is* a princess.

He thought of Diana as a young girl, raised to feel like nothing. Taught by her mother that her body was her most important asset. Taught by her father that she was worthless next to her brother. And still she had risen about it all, and made someone of herself, someone incredibly rare, someone that deserved to be treasured and loved.

He had told her *he* could not bear her past. He, who never fought her battles, had judged and judged and judged again. All the while she was healing him, healing Jamie, and fighting for her own right to be.

And he had talked to her of lust, offered her his body and his pleasure and waited for her to melt in gratitude.

What a fool he had been. More than a fool. And tonight he was taking Jamie and flying to New York. He had told Diana so, just last night. He was leaving. He had said goodbye, had ended things between them calmly, honorably.

He was not calm now. He felt shattered, terribly lost, and quite, quite stupid.

He looked across the room one more time. Jamie was making his way toward him. He watched as the little red-haired boy approached, so obviously filled with pride at the part he had played in the little ceremony just past. Jamie reached his side and lifted a hand, confident that Reid would take it.

"Did you see me, Daddy? Did you see me give Diana her crown?"

Reid nodded. "Yes," he said. "I saw you."

Jamie beamed. Then, with the wonderful irrelevance of youth, he said, "I love you, Daddy."

I love you, Daddy.

Reid's throat felt unbearably tight. Inside his chest a strange and unfamiliar glow began to spread, seeping into his heart and lungs, down his legs and into his toes, through the sinews of his arms to his fingertips.

Without stopping to think, he reached down and swept Jamie into his arms, and strode hastily out of Lyonhouse into the warm sunshine of the playground.

Reid was having trouble seeing—something hot and wet kept getting in the way.

"Daddy?" Jamie asked, uncertain now, his arms around Reid's neck.

"It's all right, son," Reid whispered, his voice barely working around the lump in his throat. "Everything is just fine."

Then Reid lowered his head so that the darkness of his hair blended with the red-gold streaks of Jamie's. There, standing in the middle of the Lyonhouse playground, Reid found it in his heart to love the son who was not his son.

And there, for the first time that he could remember since earliest childhood, with his arms wrapped around a four-year-old boy, Reid wept.

Chapter Fourteen

That night Diana fell asleep early, and slept the sleep of the deeply exhausted. When her buzzer first rang, the harsh, insistent summons seemed part of a scene far removed from reality, so that at first she simply ignored it.

Then she remembered another time her buzzer had awakened her from an early sleep. She sat up, disoriented, past and future flowing into one confused present, as she reminded herself that Reid and Jamie had left for New York early this evening. Still, when she made her stumbling way to her intercom, her heart was beating abnormally fast.

"Yes?" she said into the little metal mouthpiece.

There was silence on the other end, and she felt her sudden hope die its own foolish death. Then, "It's me, Diana. Reid." Another pause. "I've brought you flowers."

She leaned against her wall, her hand to her heart. As on that other night, she was wearing nothing except her short nightgown. "I'll...I'll make myself decent," she said breathlessly. "Then I'll buzz you up."

She was still heavy with sleep, and she walked as if in a dream to her closet, pulling out casual jeans and a yellow blouse. Without bothering with shoes or slippers, and using only her fingers for a comb, she was back at the intercom in less than five minutes. She buzzed the downstairs door open. Reid was at her apartment door so quickly, she thought with an almost hysterical wildness that he must have flown up her three flights of stairs.

He thrust what seemed like a hundred roses into her arms; later she realized they were only three dozen. Burying her head in their sweet fragrance, she studied him with insatiable, if surreptitious, curiosity. He was dressed casually, in dark pants and green shirt. His hair was combed back away from his face, lending additional prominence to his gypsy-like cheekbones and flashing dark eyes. His eyes, she noticed, were eating her alive.

She turned from him, using the excuse of finding a vase to escape his blazing hunger. "I thought you were going to New York," she said, pleased and surprised to find her voice low and steady. She ran water into the crystal vase she had found for the roses, and placed them there. When there was no longer anything for her to do, no reason for her to keep her back turned to him, she found she was suffering from a sudden paralyzing shyness. Without looking at him she walked to her window and stared out upon the street.

She did not hear him cross the room to her. The first inkling she had of his nearness was his hands upon her shoulders. "I missed my plane," he said, with some wry, quiet humor she could not quite understand. His hands slid down her arms, then moved to encircle her waist. She bent her head, hoping desperately that he could not feel the wild beating of her heart. But his right hand stopped between her breasts, and she knew he felt the pounding there. He pulled her against his muscular frame. "I missed you," he said simply.

She was suddenly perilously close to tears. What cruel game was being played out now? Out of the corner of her eye she saw the golden, glittering cardboard crown she had been given just this afternoon, from where it rested upon her bookshelves. She had seen Reid there, at Lyonhouse, standing in the back, watching the whole proceeding with an impenetrable, brooding silence. She had felt an almost painful relief when he had gone, knowing that he was returning to New York, knowing that her heart would have time to rest, at last.

Then, later this evening, when she had returned to her apartment, she had felt so utterly drained, so strangely empty, that she had sat without thinking for hours, before readying herself for bed.

She had been blessedly numb, totally devoid of feeling. Now Reid's hand high upon her rib cage mocked her strange objectivity, her almost deliberate indifference. And she found conflicting emotions washing through her with fierce strength—relief mixed with fear, a soaring happiness tempered with a terrible anger.

Anger, she decided, was safest.

"Why are you here?" she asked coldly.

His hands stilled against her skin. She felt him sigh, his breath fluttering against her temple as he did so. "Diana," he said, his voice low and filled with a nameless longing. "Don't make me beg."

She stiffened against him. "I don't believe you know how," she said, carelessly cruel.

For a moment he said nothing. Then, "You were beautiful today," he said.

She was silent.

He gave a husky laugh. "There was more love in that room than I have felt in a very long time."

She felt her anger weakening, her resolve melting away. He turned her in his arms, and stared down at her face. Whatever he saw there must have reassured him. He lifted his left hand and brushed her hair away from her eyes, before he leaned over slightly to kiss her gently on her forehead.

She began to tremble. He smiled slightly in acknowledgement. "Come sit down," he said. "Right here, where we sat once before, and you told me so much. No," he continued, when she made a halfhearted effort to pull away. "I see that you've decided I'm not worth risking your heart for." He put his fingers against her lips when she would have spoken. "No. Listen. It's my turn to talk. Will you please listen for a little while? I'm not used to baring my soul, and if you interrupt I might lose my nerve entirely. Will you just sit quietly, here with my arm around you, and listen?"

"All right," she whispered, carried away by the strangeness of his mood. She found herself seated on her sofa, her head tucked against his shoulder, his arm around hers. The feel of him was an all-too-familiar sweetness, his manly smell a slight intoxication to her senses. Unknowingly she breathed deeply, then sighed.

"Where to begin?" Reid asked quietly. "You know about my marriage, about Jamie. You probably know more than you realize what my life has been like these past years. No, I don't have to tell you those things."

He was silent for a minute. Then he continued, his voice a low and husky sound in her quiet room. "Today. I'll start there, I guess. I watched you speak to all those people, and wondered how I had dared to..." His voice faded away.

"Jamie," he said, his thoughts jumping in a seemingly random pattern. "Jamie came to me, after you were all done, and he must have been feeling some of what I had sensed, because you know what he said? He tucked his little hand in mine, and he said, 'I love you, Daddy.' And do you know what? For a moment I was absolutely startled. And I looked down at that little...that little red-headed boy, and I tried to tell him...I knew I loved him, too." Diana felt Reid's chest shudder slightly. The joy she had denied ear-

lier was swelling again. She felt a smile creep across her face.
But Reid wasn't done. "It was so easy. All this time it
seemed as if I had some impossible mountain to climb, some
incredible hurdle to leap over, and all he had to do was put
his hand in mine, and..." Again Reid paused.

"Do you know," he asked, with seeming irrelevance,
"that in all my life I have never missed a plane?"

She turned in his arms. Her joy was full-blown now—she
was filled with the power of it. "Why did you?" she asked
softly. "Why are you here, Reid?"

His head was turned away from her. His sculpted gypsy
face was tight with some inner tension. She reached up and
traced his lips with her fingertips. "I came to beg your pardon, Diana. And to tell you that I love you. And to ask you
to be my wife."

His voice was flat, almost hard. His cheek, now beneath
her hand, was cold. Gone was his enormous self-assurance,
his confident power of persuasion. Reid Hudson—this man
of power and wealth, of prodigious drive and vast intelligence—was plain and simply terrified. And Diana knew a
surge of tenderness for the man on the inside.

"Yes," she said.

It took him a moment to comprehend what she had said.
"Diana?" His voice was shaken, uncertain.

"Yes."

His hand clutched her shoulder spasmodically. He started
to speak, could not, tried again. She looked up at him, but
he still would not meet her eyes.

She melted against him. She remembered another time
they had sat together on this couch, of words he had said to
her. "Reid," she said with some urgency, reaching up with
both hands to cup his face. "I'm going to kiss you now. Kiss
me back."

He looked at her then, and his eyes were burning fires of
love and fierce possession. She saw his uncertainty fade as
joy and a different kind of hunger grew in the flames she

saw there. "Diana," he said again, but this time her name was no question.

"Kiss me," she demanded again.

And, laying her down upon that long piece of furniture, and easing his own body next to hers, he did.

They shared their wedding with Harry Reichenbach and Jenny Sevilla. Tilly was there, and Thomas Lyon, and Lucy. "Now we'll be real sisters, forever," Lucy said.

There were others: Bill Tyrell from New York, David Stone, all the workers from Lyonhouse. Tilly's wedding present to Diana was a piece of iron rod. Reid raised his brows questioningly. "It was a bit of advice Tilly gave me once," Diana explained. "Something about holding fast to what I knew to be true."

Reid had given her his own presents: a silver brooch in the shape of a crown, "for my princess," he said; a golden heart on a single chain, "I give you my heart," he said; and a piece of paper, barely readable, which held the promise: *I will wait for you, Reid.*

Gregory and Alicia Rowe sent a fine silver tea set, but regretted they could not make it to the wedding.

Harry and Jenny headed to the Caribbean for a honeymoon trip.

Diana and Reid settled quietly in a house in Lansing, from which Reid would commute, when necessary, to New York.

They kept with them the child, Jamie.

Their well-loved son.

* * * * *

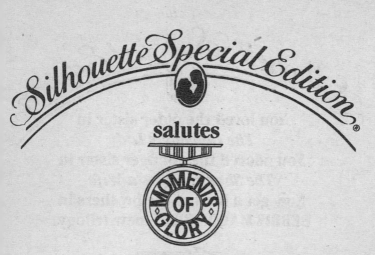

Silhouette Special Edition

salutes

MOMENTS OF GLORY

from Lindsay McKenna

In a country torn with conflict, in a time of bitter passions, these brave men and women wage a war against all odds . . . and a timeless battle for honor, for fleeting moments of glory, for the promise of enduring love.

February: RIDE THE TIGER (#721) Survivor Dany Villard is wise to the love-'em-and-leave-'em ways of war, but wounded hero Gib Ramsey swears she's captured his heart . . . forever.

March: ONE MAN'S WAR (#727) The war raging inside brash and bold Captain Pete Mallory threatens to destroy him, until Tess Ramsey's tender love guides him toward peace.

April: OFF LIMITS (#733) Soft-spoken Marine Jim McKenzie saved Alexandra Vance's life in Vietnam; now he needs her love to save his honor. . . .

SEMG-1

Take 4 bestselling love stories FREE
Plus get a FREE surprise gift!

NORA ROBERTS

Love has a language all its own, and for centuries, flowers have symbolized love's finest expression. Discover the language of flowers—and love—in this romantic collection of 48 favorite books by bestselling author Nora Roberts.

Starting in February 1992, two titles will be available each month at your favorite retail outlet.

In February, look for:

Irish Thoroughbred, Volume #1
The Law Is A Lady, Volume #2

Collect all 48 titles and become fluent in the Language of Love.

LOL192

THE LANGUAGE of LOVE